KERRY BARRETT was a bookworm from a very early age and did a degree in English Literature, then trained as a journalist, writing about everything from pub grub to EastEnders. Her first novel, *Bewitched, Bothered and Bewildered*, took six years to finish and was mostly written in longhand on her commute to work, giving her a very good reason to buy beautiful notebooks. Kerry lives in London with her husband and two sons, and Noel Streatfeild's Ballet Shoes is still her favourite novel.

Also by Kerry Barrett

The Could It Be Magic? Series
Bewitched, Bothered and Bewildered
I Put a Spell on You
Baby, It's Cold Outside
I'll Be There for You
A Spoonful of Sugar: A Novella

A Step in Time
The Girl in the Picture
The Hidden Women
The Secret Letter

Readers Love Kerry Barrett

'A thoroughly enjoyable read!'

'Fantastic book, really loved reading it'

'Loved it! The best yet!'

'Gripped from start to finish'

'It's definitely worth a read'

'I devoured the story it's a real page turner with a great twist'

The Forgotten Girl

KERRY BARRETT

HQ
An imprint of HarperCollins*Publishers* Ltd
1 London Bridge Street
London SE1 9GF

This paperback edition 2020

First published in Great Britain by
HQ, an imprint of HarperCollins*Publishers* Ltd 2020

ISBN: 9780008389222

MIX
Paper from
responsible sources
FSC
www.fsc.org   FSC® C007454

This book is produced from independently certified FSC™ paper
to ensure responsible forest management.

For more information visit: www.harpercollins.co.uk/green

Printed and bound by CPI Group (UK) Ltd, Croydon CR0 4YY

Chapter 1

2016

I was nervous. Not just a little bit wobbly. I was properly, squeaky-voiced, sweaty-palms, absolutely bloody terrified. And that was very unlike me.

The office was just up ahead – I could see it from where I stood, lurking behind my sunglasses in case anyone I knew spotted me and tried to speak to me. I wasn't ready for conversation yet. The building had a glass front, with huge blown-up magazine covers in its windows. In pride of place, right next to the revolving door, was the cover from the most recent issue of Mode.

I swallowed.

'It's fine,' I muttered to myself. 'They wouldn't have given you the job if they didn't think you were up to it. It's fine. You're fine. Better than fine. You're brilliant.'

I took a deep breath, straightened my back, threw back my shoulders and headed to the Starbucks opposite me.

I ordered an espresso and a soya latte, then I sat down to compose myself for a minute.

Today was my first day as editor of Mode. It was the job I'd wanted since I was a teenager. It had been my dream for so long,

I could barely believe it was happening, and I was determined to make a success of it.

Except here I was, ready to get started, and I'd been floored by these nerves.

Shaking slightly, I downed my espresso in one like it was a shot of tequila and checked the time on my phone. I was early, but that was no bad thing. I had lots of good luck messages – mostly from people hoping I'll give them a job, I thought wryly. I couldn't help noticing, as I scrolled through and deleted them, that there was nothing from my best friend, Jen. She was obviously still upset about the way I'd behaved when I'd got the job. And if I was honest, she had every right to be upset, but I didn't have time to worry about that now. I was sure she'd come round.

I stood up and straightened my clothes. I'd played it safe this morning with black skinny trousers, a fitted black shirt and funky leopard-print pumps. My naturally curly blonde hair was straightened and pulled into a sleek ponytail and I wore a slash of red lipstick. I looked good. I just hoped it was good enough for the editor of Mode.

A surge of excitement bubbled up inside me. I was the editor of Mode. Me. Fearne Summers. I picked up my latte and looped my arm through my Marc Jacobs tote.

'Right, Fearne,' I said out loud. 'Let's do this.'

I wasn't expecting a welcoming committee or a cheerleading squad waiting for me in reception (well, I was a bit) but I did think that the bored woman behind the desk could have at least cracked a smile. Or she could have tried to look a tiny bit impressed that I was the new editor of Mode. Mind you, if this office was anything like my old place – and I was pretty sure all magazine companies were the same – there would be a never-ending stream of celebrities, models, and strange PR stunts (last Christmas we'd had mince pies delivered by a llama wearing a Santa hat, and that was one of the more normal visitors). Perhaps a new editor was terribly run of the mill.

'Here's your pass,' she said, throwing it across the desk at me. 'The office is on the third floor, but you're to go up to fifth first of all to meet Lizzie.'

I was surprised. Lizzie was the chief-exec of Glam Media, the company that owned Mode along with lots of other magazines. I knew I'd have to catch up with her at some point today but I thought she'd give me time to meet my team, and find my office first.

Lizzie was waiting for me when I got out of the lift. The bored receptionist must have told her I was on my way.

She was in her early fifties, petite and stylishly dressed, with a cloud of dark hair. She was friendly and approachable, but she had a reputation of being ruthless in pursuit of profit for the company. She scared the bejeesus out of me if I was honest, but she'd been very nice when I met her at one of the many interviews I'd done to get the job. Now she smiled at me and shook my hand.

'Great to have you on board, Fearne' she said. 'This is a time of big change for Mode.'

'I've got loads of ideas,' I said, following her down the corridor to a meeting room. 'I can't wait to get started.'

She gave me a brief smile over her shoulder.

'Great,' she said again.

Except she didn't really mean great, I quickly discovered. She meant, *yeah good luck with that, Fearne.*

It turned out that Glam Media was worried about Mode. Really worried. I'd looked at the sales, of course, and seen they weren't as good as they could be but I hadn't really grasped just how much trouble the magazine was in.

'The problem is the competition has really raised its game,' Lizzie explained as I stared out of the big window in her office and tried to take in everything she was saying.

'Grace?' I said. It had been a fairly boring, unadventurous magazine called Home & Hearth until it was bought by a new company and had loads of money pumped into it. Now it had

3

a new name, it was exciting and fun, and it was stealing lots of Mode's readers.

'So the finance department have redone your budgets for this year,' said Lizzie. 'To reflect Mode's sales.'

She slid a piece of paper across her desk and I stared at the figures she'd put in front of me in horror.

'I can't run a glossy mag on this budget,' I said. 'How am I supposed to pay for fashion shoots? Or commission writers?'

Lizzie shrugged.

'Times are tough,' she said. 'That's all that's in the pot.'

'Can't I have some of the website budget?' I asked.

She shook her head.

'Digital budget is separate,' she said. 'The website's going very well. Advertising and readership are both up. It's the magazine that's in trouble.'

I looked at her, suddenly realising where this was going, and why my predecessor had been so keen to leave her job.

'Are you going to close Mode?' I asked.

She stared back at me.

'Nothing's decided yet.'

'But it's possible?'

Lizzie looked at a point somewhere past my ear.

'Print isn't working,' she said.

'But Mode is an iconic brand,' I said desperately. 'It's been going since the sixties. It was the first ever young women's glossy. You can't close it.'

Lizzie still didn't look me in the eye, but she did at least assume a slightly sympathetic expression.

'We'd still have the website,' she said. 'It's not ending, it's just changing. Mode will still exist – just in a different form.'

'A glossy mag is a treat,' I said. 'People will pay for that.'

She shrugged.

'Would people lose their jobs?' I asked, suddenly realising this didn't just affect me.

4

'That's also possible,' she said.

I put my head in my hands. This was a nightmare. My dream job was collapsing around my ears.

Lizzie took a breath.

'Fearne, we took you on for a reason,' she said. 'You're a great editor with a good reputation.'

I forced myself to raise my head and smile at her. That was nice to hear.

'But you're also known for being cut-throat,' she carried on. 'We all know you're single-minded and determined. That you don't let anything get in the way of success,'

I nodded slowly. I wasn't sure I'd use the word 'cut-throat' but I was definitely single-minded.

'We know you won't let emotions or sentiment get in the way of doing your job.'

Oh.

'You brought me here to close the magazine?' I said, as I worked it all out.

Lizzie had the grace to look slightly shame-faced.

'Well,' she said. 'Close it or make it work. Take back some of the sales we've lost to Grace.'

I looked at the budget again. With the figures she'd given me it was obvious which option she wanted. I could barely cover the staffing costs with this amount of money – and I had no chance of booking top photographers or paying for big-name writers. It was an impossible task.

'How long have I got?' I said. 'How long do I have to make Mode pay?'

Lizzie looked a bit confused. She'd clearly not considered this. 'Six months?'

I swallowed.

'Give me a year,' I said, wondering how on earth I managed to keep my voice steady when I was so terrified by the task that lay ahead. 'I need a year to have a proper go at this.'

Lizzie looked at something on the papers in front of her. She rubbed the bridge of her nose and sighed.

'Nine months?' she said.

I shrugged.

'Is that the best you can offer?' I said. She nodded.

'So if I can increase sales enough in that time, you'll let the magazine carry on?' I said.

Lizzie nodded again.

'If you can make it work on the new budget, then we'll reconsider,' she said, sounding incredulous that I was even thinking about it.

'Great,' I said, faking excitement when all I felt was despair. 'Nine months is more than enough.'

I gathered up my things and stood up, hoping she couldn't see my legs trembling. 'If you'll excuse me, I'm going to meet my team now.'

Chapter 2

That may have been a fairly terrible way to start my new job, but as it turned out, Lizzie was a pussycat compared to the rest of the Mode team.

There weren't many of them – lots of staff had left recently and a few people had gone with the former editor, Sophie, to her new role on a supermarket magazine. The features desk was down two writers, I had no deputy, and the art editor was working out her notice. The words rats and sinking ships crossed my mind, but I dismissed that. I had to make this work. I'd sacrificed a lot for this job.

My office was bare, with a clean desk and a shiny computer. There was no good luck card, or welcoming cup of coffee. In fact, there weren't even many smiles. I stared round at the stony faces in our planning meeting that morning and wondered if I hadn't just made a massive mistake.

'So,' I said, uber-brightly. 'What have we got for the next issue?'

I looked at my new features director, whose name I couldn't quite remember. She was tall and angular with pale skin and fine blonde hair pulled back into a bun – like a ballerina with a bad attitude.

She looked back at me, unsmiling.

'Veronica?' I said.

'Vanessa.'

Shit.

'Sorry,' I sang. 'Vanessa, who's on the cover this month?'

She named a soap star, Dawn Robin, who was well into her forties and though stylish, nothing like the celebs our readers were interested in.

'Oh,' I said, so surprised that manners deserted me. 'That's an interesting choice.'

'It was Sophie's choice,' Vanessa said.

I chuckled.

'You got that right.'

No response. Clearly humour didn't work.

'Is the interview done?' I asked. Perhaps Dawn had said something amazing that we could spin.

'It's done, and her PR has approved it,' Vanessa said. She stared at me as if challenging me to tell her to start again.

For a moment I considered pulling rank, spiking the whole thing and getting a new cover star. But it was early days and I needed the team behind me if I was going to make this happen.

Instead I smiled.

'Great,' I said. 'It's good to have it in the bag. What about next issue?'

Vanessa made a show of flicking through the pages in her notebook and I forced myself to stay smiling.

'I'm talking to Sarah Sanderson's agent,' she said. I groaned inwardly. Sarah Sanderson was a breakfast news presenter who'd been around for donkey's years. Maybe it was time to get tough.

'She's not the right cover star for us,' I said. 'Scratch that. Give the interview to one of the other mags if you like. We need someone younger, sassier, more exciting.'

Vanessa pointedly scored out something on her notebook and gave me a steely glare.

'Like who?'

I looked round at the tiny team.

'Let's have a brainstorming session tomorrow,' I said. 'We can line up some really exciting interviews. Anything goes – don't just stick to actresses and musicians. Think about politicians, sports stars, writers, bloggers – anyone doing anything or saying anything interesting.'

Vanessa scribbled something in her pad without meeting my eyes.

'Oh and Vanessa,' I said. 'I don't want publicists approving interviews.'

She rolled her eyes.

'Tricky,' she said.

'I know,' I admitted. 'Let them sit in on the chat if they have to, but remember we're Mode magazine – they need us just as much as we need them. In the future, let's be a bit sassier.'

Vanessa made a face.

'Do we have one?'

'I'm sorry?'

'A future. Does Mode magazine have a future?'

My stomach lurched. I'd been hoping to give the team a boost before I started talking about closures and redundancies. But judging by the grim faces that surrounded me, I had to tackle this now.

I was sitting behind my desk, but now I got up and came to perch on the front instead.

'Honestly?' I said.

Vanessa nodded, her pale lips a tight line.

'I hope so,' I said.

I took a breath.

'I have always wanted to work on Mode,' I said. 'This is my dream job and I was so excited about it.'

'But?' Vanessa said.

'But things are trickier than I thought,' I admitted. 'Our circulation is lower than it's ever been.'

'Because of Grace?' said the art editor – a tiny redhead called Milly.

'Because of Grace,' I agreed. 'They've really raised their game, and of course print's a tricky place to be anyway because of digital. But Grace's success is proving there's still a place for glossy mags – we just need to remind people we're here and we're the best.'

There was a murmur of voices, but Vanessa wasn't giving up yet.

'I heard they want to close us,' she said, raising her voice so I could hear her over the chitchat.

Everyone fell silent and stared at me.

'Is that true?' Milly asked. 'Are they closing us?'

I thought about lying, but they were all seasoned magazine journalists. I knew I couldn't fool them.

'No,' I said firmly. 'It's not true. But it's a possibility.'

The chitchat became a hubbub of voices. I let them all talk for a moment, then I held my hands up.

'Hold on,' I said. 'Listen …'

Eventually everyone stopped talking.

'Okay,' I said. I closed my eyes briefly and sent up a silent prayer to the magazine gods that I was doing the right thing and that my already depleted team wouldn't all hand in their notices immediately and leave me trying to save Mode on my own.

'They've given us nine months to turn things round,' I said. 'To improve sales, to get our brand out there, to get people talking about Mode again.'

I paused.

'We've got a lot of work to do.'

I spent the next hour fielding questions about exactly what Lizzie wanted ('I don't know,' I said), about what redundancy packages might be on offer ('I don't know,' I said), about how they would measure our success and whether it would just be sales or if it would be profits too ('I don't know,' I said) and how I was planning to make this all happen.

'I don't know,' I said, yet again. 'But I do know this is a brilliant magazine with a long history.'

I looked round at the team once more.

'And I know you're all great writers and editors and designers,' I said. Vanessa made a face but Milly smiled. 'I want this to work and I can't do it by myself, so I need you all on board.'

I thought for a moment.

'Let's spend tomorrow afternoon coming up with some ideas,' I said. 'Not just cover stars, but let's think about what we can do to get a buzz round Mode magazine again. Anything and everything you can think of – I don't care how off the wall the ideas are, but I want everyone here to come up with something.'

I wrapped up the meeting and the team all filed out of my office and back to their desks, muttering to each other – no doubt saying all sorts of rude things about me – and I was alone once more.

'Bloody hell,' I said out loud, feeling shell-shocked by my morning. But, I had to admit, being honest with the team had been the right thing to do, even if Vanessa had forced my hand a bit.

Hopefully we could come up with some exciting ideas tomorrow, I thought, leaning back in my chair. I already had lists of cover stars, features ideas and campaigns that I wanted us to try, but I knew that I needed this to be a team effort. I needed everyone with me if this was going to work.

Not for the first time that day, I wished I was still working with Jen. She was such a brilliant sounding board for ideas – and always came up with different approaches and creative ways of doing something.

But I was on my own with this, and I had to do my best.

I spun round in my chair and stared out of the window at the bustling Soho streets below me.

'I can do this,' I said out loud. 'I can bloody well do this.'

'You can do anything you want,' a voice said. A very familiar

Australian accent that I'd not heard for more than five years. 'You always have.'

I froze. Then slowly, I turned my chair round so I was facing into my office again.

'Damo,' I said. 'What on earth are you doing here?'

The huge figure of my ex-boyfriend filled the doorway. His hair was longer than I'd ever seen it, and he was wearing a grey beanie hat on his head. He looked absolutely knackered, very scruffy, and really, really hot. My heart started to beat a little bit faster.

'What kind of a welcome is that?' he said, laughter in his eyes. 'I just came to wish you luck.'

'All the way from Sydney?'

'All the way from over there,' he said, tipping his head in the direction of the team that produced the men's mag Homme, and who shared our office.

What. The …

He laughed properly at my startled face.

'Don't read Homme much, huh?' he said. 'I've been working here for ages.'

'Not full-time?' I said. My voice was wobbly.

'Nah,' Damo said. 'Bit of this, bit of that. You know how it is.'

I did. His lack of focus was one of the things that we'd clashed about when we were together. But now I was grateful that despite the bad luck that had brought him here on the biggest day of my life, his unwillingness to commit to anything was still intact. If he was only freelance, our paths wouldn't have to cross.

'But,' Damo said. 'I'm actually covering for the art editor for a while. She's gone on maternity leave.'

Ah.

'Got to run. Features meeting,' he said, rolling his eyes and making me wonder how he'd cope with the day-to-day business of life on a magazine. 'Catch up later?'

I nodded, dumbly, staring at the door as he shut it, then I put

12

my head in my hands. What should have been the best day ever was turning into the worst. The magazine was in trouble, my new team were hostile – at least some of them were – and my ex-boyfriend (and not just any ex-boyfriend, THE ex-boyfriend) had turned up. What on earth was I going to do?

my bed in my hands. When she did have breakfast cooked, the
vomiting hit the voices. The problem was in trouble the new
and went back to ... at what ... one of them went ... and the
exhausted, and not just any ex-boyfriend. The ex-boyfriend I
had turned my ... on earth was I going to do.

Chapter 3

1966

'Bye, Dad,' I called as I shut the front door. There was no reply
but I wasn't surprised. I'd put a cup of tea next to his bed before
I left and he'd barely stirred. Sleeping off last night's whisky, I
assumed. I guessed his assistant, Trev, would've already gone to
the shop to open up. No doubt Dad would drag himself along
when he finally fell out of bed.

I checked my watch. I was going to have to hurry to catch my
train and I didn't want to be late for work. Deftly, I picked up
the hold-all I kept stowed in the bin shelter in our front garden
and set off.

I made it to the station with seconds to spare – thank goodness
– and immediately shut myself in the tiny toilet on board the
train. My journey from Beckenham – the sleepy suburb of south-
east London where I lived – to the centre of town where I worked,
took exactly half an hour. Which gave me more than enough time
to transform myself from the accounts assistant in an insurance
company based just off Oxford Street that I pretended to be, into
the junior writer on a magazine in Soho that I really was.

Things at home were … difficult. We'd been a happy family,

once. At least, Mum worked hard to make sure me and my brother Dennis were happy. Dad just worked hard. He was a stickler for appearances and making sure we were all respectable. But he had a temper that he didn't always keep under control.

And then Mum died. I was only thirteen when she got ill. Dennis was seventeen and doing his A-levels, and he went off to university not long after. So it was just Dad and me.

It was hard, without Mum. I missed her with a quiet intensity that never really went away. In the early days I'd unthinkingly set four places at the table and then have to put one set of cutlery back in the drawer, or shout hello when I came home from school, only to have my voice echo round the empty hall. I learned to cook and to clean and to sew because Dad was traditional. And he fell apart when Mum died, spending some days in silent grief and others in a furious rage, lashing out at the world – and me.

When the girls at school said their mums wouldn't allow them to do something, I pretended my dad was strict too. Actually he didn't really care what I did, as long as things looked okay on the surface. As the years without Mum went by, his periods of silence got worse, so did his drinking, and so did his temper. I learned to keep out of his way when he'd had a drink, never to talk back to him or disagree, and to have his dinner on the table when he wanted it. The one thing I'd dug my heels in about had been my job. He'd not been keen on me taking a job in town instead of working in the family newsagents, so I'd lied that working in accounts would be valuable experience that could help us expand the business and he'd eventually agreed.

'Just until you and Bill are married,' Dad had said, his lip curling with disdain. 'London is no place for a married woman.'

I'd smiled and agreed, confident I'd never be foolish enough to marry anyone, let alone my devoted but dull boyfriend, Billy.

So I left home every day dressed neatly and wearing sensible shoes, with my hair pulled back into a ponytail. I arrived home looking the same.

But in between, I had a very different life.

Shut in the tiny loo, I unzipped my bag and took out a burgundy knitted dress, tights and boots. Wriggling in the small space, I pulled off the beige suit and blouse I was wearing and swapped it for the mini dress. I slipped on the tights and shoes, folded up my boring clothes and tucked them into my bag for later.

I pulled out my ponytail and brushed my straight dark hair and heavy fringe so it fell flat to my shoulders. If I got a slower train I sometimes backcombed it, but there was no time for that today.

I powdered my face quickly, then painted on a swoosh of liquid eyeliner. A slick of frosted-pink lipstick and I was finished. As the train pulled into Charing Cross, I slipped off my engagement ring and dropped it into my make-up bag. Done.

I breathed out in satisfaction. It wasn't easy living my double life, but there was no doubt I was getting better at it. It made it even worse that I couldn't see any way of it continuing much longer.

'Morning Nancy,' our receptionist, Gayle, shouted as I walked into the building. 'Love the shoes.'

I grinned. Gayle and I were the only young women in the whole office. The rest of our team – the team that put together Home & Hearth magazine every month – were older women. They were all well turned-out and interested in fashion, but none of them were what I considered cutting edge. I hung up my coat and stowed my hold-all under my desk.

I was normally one of the first people in work, which I liked. I made myself a cup of coffee in the tiny kitchen and settled at my desk. Junior writer sounded thrilling, but there was a lot of filing and typing. I didn't mind, though. I was learning so much that sometimes I felt like my head could explode.

Today I had a pile of recipes to type up. It was normally a dull, mindless task, but today's were all based on locations our readers might have gone to on holiday so they were full of odd ingredients that I'd never tasted which meant I had to concentrate. I'd never been abroad. When we were kids, Mum took Dennis and me to stay with her parents in Eastbourne for two weeks every August. Dad never left the shop. Those two weeks every year – when it was just me, Dennis and Mum, were some of the happiest times we ever had.

I finished the last recipe for something called moussaka, and added it to the pile on my desk.

'Nancy?' My editor, Rosemary, had a sixth sense when it came to knowing when I was about to relax.

She stood in the door of her office looking chic in her camel-coloured twinset and tweed skirt. Her blonde hair was twisted up at the back and high on her crown. I had no idea how old she was. Late forties? Perhaps fifty? She was very glamorous and I hoped I would be like her one day.

'Can you pick up some prints from Frank?' she asked.

'Course,' I said. Frank was the photographer we used most often. His studio was just down Carnaby Street so I never minded going for a walk down there. It felt like the place where everything was happening, and I loved just watching what was going on. 'Can I just make a quick phone call?'

Rosemary nodded.

'Take him an issue,' she said, gesturing towards the teetering pile of magazines next to my desk, and disappeared back into her office.

I checked my watch, then I picked up the phone on my desk and dialled Dennis's number. He answered almost straight away.

'Landsdowne Grammar School.'

'Den, it's me,' I said. 'Can you talk?'

'I can spare five minutes,' my brother said. 'If the headmaster comes back, I'll pretend you're trying to sell me exercise books.'

I giggled.

'So come on then. How was the big engagement do?'

17

I groaned.

'It was a lovely party,' I said mechanically.

'Really?'

'Really,' I said more firmly.

It had been a nice party, if you liked that sort of thing. Which I definitely didn't. I wasn't even sure I liked Billy very much and I still wasn't completely sure how I'd ended up engaged to him, other than I hadn't really liked to say no when he asked me and I'd had a vague idea that getting married could have been an escape of sorts. Except it seemed to have ended up trapping me.

'Did Dad behave?' Dennis asked.

'He was on good form,' I said. Dad was always gregarious and generous in company. 'He charmed Billy's nan, he bought everyone a drink … you know what he's like.'

Dennis snorted.

'Do you need any money?' he said.

'No, I'm okay,' I said. He always looked out for me, my big brother. 'I'm saving up to get my own place.'

'In London?'

'Of course in London.'

'Come to Leeds,' he said

'I can't, Den,' I said for the millionth time. 'My job's here.'

He wasn't offended.

'The offer's there,' he said. 'I have to go, I'm teaching this afternoon and the head's going to observe, check I'm doing it right.'

'Good luck,' I said. 'You'll be great.'

'You too,' he said. 'Stay out of Dad's way, okay?'

'I will,' I promised.

I said goodbye and I dropped the receiver back onto the cradle. I picked up my coat and bag, and grabbed a copy of the magazine to give to Frank, thinking about the stupid mess I'd got myself tangled up in and envying Dennis for his simple life in Leeds, far, far away from Dad …

'Oooph!'

I walked out of the building and straight into a girl who was coming the other way. She shrieked in horror and dived onto the pavement.

'Sorry,' I said, starting to walk round her.

'Sorry?' she said. 'Sorry? Look what you've done.'

She stood up and thrust some dripping wet papers at me. I backed away.

'This is the best story I've ever written and you made me drop it in a puddle,' she wailed. 'It's ruined, look.'

She unfolded the wet pages and held them up to my face. Some of the ink had run and the words were difficult to read. I felt a glimmer of sympathy for her. Losing work was never nice.

The girl looked at me properly for the first time, and I looked back at her. She was a similar height and age to me, but her dark hair was very short and she was wearing a dress without a coat over the top, despite the rain. Her thick black mascara was running down her cheeks.

'Are you a writer?' she said. 'Do you work for Home & Hearth?'

I smiled in what I hoped was a writerly fashion.

'I do,' I said.

She gripped my arm so tightly it made me gasp.

'You have to help me,' she said. 'You have to help me get a job.'

Chapter 4

I stared at her hand, which was digging into my arm through my mac. Her fingernails were bitten down, and there was a smear of mascara and eyeliner across the back of her hand. I tried not to recoil from the dirt.

'Sorry,' I said. 'I don't think I can help you.'

The girl let go, much to my relief.

'Really?' she said. She ran her fingers through her short hair and made it stick up at the front. 'I'm just so desperate for a job, you see. I wrote this article and I think it's really good – at least I thought it was really good. No one will be able to read it now.'

I shrugged.

'Don't you have a copy?'

'No,' the girl wailed.

I subtly glanced at my watch. Rosemary would be expecting those proofs and I really wanted time to have a chat with Frank's assistant, George. I needed to get rid of this girl.

'Look,' I said. 'I'm the lowest of the low at Home & Hearth. I don't get to decide who works there. But if you write another feature and send it to me, I'll make sure Rosemary, the editor, sees it.'

The girl grabbed my arm again, this time in excitement.

'Would you?' she said. 'Would you really do that?'

'Sure,' I said. I noticed for the first time how thin she was, and how she was shivering violently because she wasn't wearing a coat. Again I felt a flash of sympathy for this funny-looking urchin girl.

'Have you got any money?' I asked.

The girl raised her chin and looked at me through defiant eyes.

'Why do you ask?'

I was too embarrassed to say I felt sorry for her.

'Thought you might have rushed out in a hurry, and forgotten your purse,' I lied, nodding towards her. 'No coat.'

'Oh,' she said. She let go of my arm – thank goodness – and smoothed down her damp dress. 'Yes, I didn't realise it was raining.'

I opened my black patent bag – my pride and joy – and dug about for my purse. I found a ten-shilling note and thrust it at her.

'I'm really sorry about your article,' I said. 'But I've got to go and run an errand for my editor. There's a cafe there …' I pointed across the road to a narrow shopfront, nestled in between two offices. '… go and get yourself a coffee and warm up.'

She looked doubtful, but she took the note anyway.

'I'll pay you back,' she said.

I nodded, even though I was fairly sure that would never happen.

'Tell Bruno that you're my friend and he might throw in a free slice of cake,' I said.

She grinned at me.

'What's your name?' she said.

'Nancy Harrison.'

'I'm Suze,' she said. 'Suzanne Williams.'

I smiled back.

'Hi Suze,' I said. 'Sorry, I have to go.'

I patted her briefly on her soggy arm and headed towards Carnaby Street.

'It was nice to meet you,' Suze called, over her shoulder as she crossed the Soho cobbles to Bruno's. 'See you soon.'

'Not likely,' I muttered.

I dashed down the road towards Frank's studio, pleased to have got away from the girl. I would miss the ten shillings but I couldn't help thinking I'd got off likely as I climbed the many stairs to Frank's attic and rapped on the door.

George answered and my stomach did the usual flutter it did every time I saw him. He had longish dark hair that curled over his collar at the back – Dad would call him a hippy even though he wasn't – and a cheeky smile that he rewarded me with now.

'Hoped Rosemary would send you,' he said. 'Frank's in the darkroom, just sorting the prints out. Tea?'

I followed him inside, shrugging off my damp mac and hanging it on a hook behind the door. I spent so much time in Frank's studio, I felt very at home there.

George made me a cup of tea and we sat on the battered sofa together, waiting for Frank to finish.

'I just met someone who thought I could get her a job on Home & Hearth,' I said.

George raised an eyebrow.

'She thought you were Rosemary?' he said. 'I can see why someone would mix you two up ...'

I gave him a friendly shove and he laughed.

'She was hanging about outside the office,' I said. 'She'd brought an article to show us, but I knocked her and she dropped it in a puddle.'

'Unlucky.'

I made a face.

'I felt a bit bad, so I bought her a coffee,' I said.

George laughed.

'You're such a sucker,' he said. 'You're way too nice.'

I laughed too.

'She might be an editor one day,' I pointed out. 'She might remember I was nice to her, and give me a job.'

George shook his head.

'You'll be the editor,' he said. 'You're going places, Nancy Harrison.'

'You're right,' I said, only half joking. 'I'm going to be a big name in the magazine world. I'll run my own mag, and maybe – just maybe – I'll need a good photographer.'

George nodded mock-gravely.

'I'll think to myself, who do I know in the photography business,' I said. 'And I'll remember George. And I'll think, I know – I'll ask George ...'

I paused.

'I'll ask George, if he knows any good photographers.'

George threw his head back and laughed. I was pleased. I got a real thrill from making him laugh and he obviously felt the same about me. We were sitting closer together now, I noticed. His long thigh was touching my leg. I knew I should move away – I was engaged after all, even if George didn't know that – but somehow I couldn't bring myself to shift along.

We looked at each other for a moment – a long moment.

Then Frank threw open the door to the darkroom.

'Prints,' he announced. 'Hi, kid.'

'Hi Frank,' I said, annoyed and relieved in equal measures that he'd interrupted me and George.

'Fashion,' he said, giving me a large envelope. 'I'm pleased with them. Get Rosemary to call and tell me what she thinks.'

I nodded.

'Did you bring me an issue?'

'Oh yes,' I said, I'd thrown it on a side table when I came in, so I fetched it now. Frank – who was in his forties with a bushy beard that he claimed he'd cultivated to make him look like a grown-up – held the issue at arm's length and looked at the cover.

It was a photograph of a pie, taken from above, on a dark-brown background.

'Fucking dreadful,' he said.

I grinned. I agreed entirely.

'Why don't you put people on the cover?'

I shrugged.

'Not up to me,' I said.

'One day it will be up to you,' George said.

'One day,' I laughed. I pulled on my mac again and picked up the envelope of prints.

'I'll get Rosemary to ring you,' I said. 'Bye George.'

George blew me a kiss and I floated on air all the way back to the office.

As I was walking past Bruno's though, a shout made me look round.

'Nancy,' Bruno called from the door of the café. 'Nancy! I need you.'

Oh god, had that Suze stolen something or caused a commotion? Heart sinking, I crossed the road.

'Your friend,' Bruno said, his Italian accent heavier than usual. 'She is sick. You have to help her.'

24

Chapter 5

I can't lie, for a moment I thought about telling Bruno I barely knew Suze, and going back to work. But then I remembered the slump of her shoulders when she picked up her wet article, and I knew I couldn't abandon her. What had George called me? A sucker. Sounded about right.

'Nancy!' Bruno sounded panicky. 'She's at the back.'

I went into the long narrow café, enjoying the warmth after being outside in the rain. The windows were fogged up and there was a buzz of chatter fighting with the hiss of Bruno's fancy coffee machine that he'd brought with him from Italy.

The left side of the room was lined with booths with maroon, PVC benches. It was close to lunchtime now, so the café was busy and I glanced at the customers as I walked past, appraising their hairstyles, their clothes and their shoes. The counter was on the right, and at the back of the café, past the serving hatch, there were another two booths. That's where Suze was – right at the back – curled up on one of the PVC benches.

'She came in, all bouncy,' Bruno said. 'She said she was your friend, ordered a coffee and then she fainted. We put her here and gave her some water.'

'Is she asleep?' I said, looking at the top of Suze's dark head, which was all I could see.

'No,' she said, her voice muffled. 'I'm awake. I just feel woozy when I sit up.'

'Sit up, and put your head between your legs,' I said, remembering my friend Delia from school, who fainted all the time. 'It gets blood to your brain, or something.'

Suze didn't reply, but she slowly sat up, giving me a glimpse of her very pale face, then spun her legs round so they were outside the booth, and lowered her head in between her bony knees.

'Suze,' I said, studying her shoulder blades, which stuck up like chicken wings. 'Did you have breakfast?'

She moved slightly – a brief shake of her head.

'Bruno, can you get her some orange juice and a sandwich?' I said, wondering if Suze still had that ten-shilling note – junior writer wasn't a very well paid job. 'I think she needs to eat something.'

Bruno looked relieved that I was taking charge. He slunk off behind the counter, poured an orange juice, which he handed to me, and busied himself making a sandwich.

I sat down opposite Suze. From the look of her, it wasn't just breakfast she'd skipped. I wondered if she'd eaten anything all week.

'Suze,' I said. She raised her head and I was pleased to see some colour coming back into her cheeks. I pushed the glass of orange juice towards her and she drank it all in one go. 'Suze, is there anyone I should phone for you?'

She shook her head.

'A friend?' I said. 'Boyfriend? Parents?'

She smiled at me, weakly.

'No,' she said. 'I'm sort of a loner.'

Bruno put the sandwich in front of her and she tore into it. She ate like a child, holding her sandwich two-handed, not

26

worried about how she looked. If my mum had been here to see her, she'd have been horrified at her lack of table manners.

'It's fine,' she said. 'I only live round the corner. I'll just go home and sleep. I was up late finishing my article.'

I looked at my watch. It was lunchtime now, so Rosemary would assume I'd taken my break after going to Frank's.

'Round the corner?' I said.

'Peter Street,' she said, through a mouthful of bread.

That really was just round the corner. I was surprised and impressed that she actually lived in Soho and I wondered if she was one of those society kids who'd dropped out of their rich world but were still supported by their parents.

'Finish your sandwich and I'll walk you home,' I said, partly out of concern for her and partly because I was curious to see where she lived. 'Make sure you're okay.'

Suze's eyes widened in horror.

'No,' she said. 'Honestly, I'm fine now. You go back to work and I'll pay Bruno and get home.'

'I'll walk you home,' I said firmly.

Suze had finished her sandwich. She looked at me, her head tilted to one side, like she was sizing me up. Then she nodded.

'Okay,' she said. 'I'll just pay Bruno.'

She eased the 10/- note out of her pocket and I grabbed her hand.

'Keep it,' I said. Like I said, sucker. 'I'll pay.'

I settled the bill and with Suze hanging on to my arm like an old lady, we left the café and headed for Berwick Street.

Suze knew everyone. The market traders all called out to her as we passed, and she had quick responses to their questions and jokes.

'Had one too many?' the guy on the fruit stall shouted. He had tattoos all over his arms and one crawling up the back of his neck, but his smile as he looked at Suze was kind. I'd probably walked past him every day for a year, but I'd never seen him before.

'Ha ha,' Suze said. 'Just feeling a bit off.'

He threw her a bag and she caught it deftly.

'Can't sell these, they're all bashed,' he said, winking.

Suze grinned.

'Thanks.'

She put her mouth close to my ear.

'Nothing wrong with them,' she said. 'He's such a softie, though you'd never know to look at him.'

I glanced at the greengrocer over my shoulder. She was right about that.

Peter Street ran along the bottom of Berwick Street. One end led to Wardour Street, and the other was a dead-end. Suze led me that way, to a barber's shop, tucked right in the corner. There was a boarded-up door in between the entrance to the barber and the shop next to it and that was where she headed. She stuck her hand down the neck of her dress and pulled out a tiny key.

'I keep it in my bra,' she said, smiling. 'I'd lose it otherwise.'

Then she unlocked the padlock that was keeping the plywood door firmly shut and pushed me inside, shutting the door behind us and moving the padlock from the outside to the inside.

'It's best to keep it locked,' she said, in a tone that told me she hadn't always done that.

She led the way up the narrow stairs in front of us. They were covered in threadbare carpet, and the only light came from a dirty, skinny window on the landing.

At the top was a bed-sitting room. It had fabric draped at the two large windows and the day was gloomy so it was hard to see properly. I looked at Suze and she gasped.

'Oh I'm not being a very good host, am I?' she said. 'Come in, come in, sit down.'

She scurried over to the corner of the room and switched on a tall lamp. I was surprised she had electricity in what was clearly a squat, but I didn't say anything.

Suze, though, read my mind.

'One of the guys on the market sorted it for me,' she said. 'I think he's connected it to a streetlight.'

I wasn't sure what to say. Instead, I looked round at the room. Suze, who was still looking a bit wobbly, threw her arms out. '*Mia casa*,' she said. 'What do you think?'

It was a fairly large, square room with two big windows that looked out over Peter Street and a bit of the market. I could hear the buzz of chatter and music from the barber shop below, and the shouts of stallholders and shoppers at the market. The windows were covered in offcuts of material – as was the single bed in the corner to my right – I guessed Suze had begged, borrowed or stolen them from the many fabric shops nearby. Piled up near the bed were rows of battered paperbacks. Off to one side was a tiny toilet with a small sink and straight ahead of me was a tiny, two-ring electric hob with one pan, a couple of plates and two mugs neatly stacked next to it.

Beneath one window was a big table with a typewriter on top.

'My pride and joy,' Suze said, seeing me looking.

I grinned.

'I've got the same one at home.'

Mine was covered in stickers, though, and my desk at work wasn't nearly as tidy as Suze's. She had a stack of blank paper next to the typewriter and two thick cardboard folders on the table, along with a notepad and a pot of pens and pencils.

'What do you think?' Suze said. 'I've never had a guest before.'

I smiled at her.

'It's lovely,' I said honestly. 'It's perfect.'

Chapter 6

2016

I felt funny when I got home that evening. A bit low, a bit lost, and – I had to admit – a bit lonely.

I wanted to eat a nice dinner, drink some wine and tell someone about my day. But what I actually did was change into my pyjamas, make tea and eat chocolate. By myself. I lived alone in a once shabby flat, in a once shabby corner of south-east London. Every time I got off the train to go home, I noticed a new juice bar or artisan bakery and thanked my lucky stars I'd got in when I did. I'd never be able to afford my flat now – shabby or otherwise.

I had two bedrooms – one was tiny but I used it as a walk-in wardrobe – a cosy lounge and a very small kitchen, and normally I loved living alone. Today, though, I felt like the flat was just too big.

'Maybe I should get a cat,' I wondered out loud. Then I thought about the many, many houseplants I'd killed over the years and decided that was a very bad idea.

I flopped on the sofa in my jimjams and scrolled through endless Netflix options, without choosing anything to watch.

I thought about ringing my mum to tell her I'd started my new job.

'Darling, well done!' I imagined her saying. 'I'm so proud of you and I know how hard you've worked.'

What were the chances of her saying that? Slim to nil. She'd listen in silence, making sure I was well aware that she wasn't remotely interested in what she considered the frivolous and superficial world of women's magazines. Then she'd tell me about some lecture she'd been asked to give somewhere prestigious – she was an economics don at a college at Oxford University and was always jetting off round the world to be a guest speaker at various conferences. She'd probably throw in some fawning about my future sister-in-law, Isabelle, who was one of Mum's former PhD students – she'd met my brother Rick at a department summer party that I'd not been invited to. Isabelle was going some way to making up for the terrible disappointment my career choices had brought my mother and she talked about her a lot. She might even do the thing where she'd tell me about a friend's son or daughter who'd just been made partner at a law firm, or published some ground-breaking scientific research, or started their own charity. She'd fill me in on all the details, then with self-pity dripping from every word, she'd say: 'I always thought you'd end up doing something like that, but you went a different way …'

No. Mum was not the person I needed to speak to right now. And ringing Jen wasn't a good idea either. She was ignoring my calls for a reason and I wanted to give her time to calm down.

Maybe I couldn't settle because I needed to get down some ideas for the magazine? I turned on my laptop and opened a new document, but after staring at the blank screen for half an hour, I admitted defeat. Instead, I padded through to the kitchen, made another cup of tea, and grabbed the rest of my family-sized bar of chocolate out of the fridge. Then, even though it was only eight p.m., I went to bed and snuggled up under the duvet. I spent the rest of the evening looking at old photos of my time in Australia – my time with Damian – on my laptop.

What can I say? Every girl needs a hobby.

I'd always regretted the way Damo and I had split up – it had been pretty brutal – but I'd never regretted moving on because I knew I'd had good reasons at the time. But now I'd seen him I was struggling to remember what those reasons were.

I scrolled through the pictures until my eyes were burning. Damo and me climbing Sydney Harbour Bridge, trekking in the bush, messing around at the pool on the roof of our apartment block … It was like watching a montage from a rubbish romcom.

I woke up at five a.m., with a crick in my neck and my head resting on my laptop. I'd dribbled on the screen, which was frozen on a photo of Damo sitting on the edge of a bright blue pool, wearing nothing but denim shorts and a smile. I shut the laptop with a snap and, groaning, I dragged myself out of bed.

'Back to work,' I told myself firmly as I pulled on my gym gear. 'No distractions. No complications, just work.'

One spin class, one shower and two flat whites later and I was raring to go. I gathered the team in my office, ready to start brainstorming ideas to transform Mode and send its sales soaring.

At least, I was ready. The rest of the team looked at their feet and didn't speak.

'So we're looking for someone to put on the next cover,' I said. 'I know Vanessa mentioned Sarah Sanderson but I'm really after someone zingy and exciting and a bit younger than Dawn Robin – lovely though she is.'

I'd read Vanessa's interview with the soap star yesterday and it was fine. Great, in fact. It just wasn't very Mode. Passionate as Dawn was about home baking, I couldn't see sassy, twenty-something professionals queuing up to find out what she used to make her scones rise.

I beamed at Vanessa.

'It was a great chat,' I said through gritted teeth. 'Any ideas about who we should do next?'

Vanessa leafed through her notebook painfully slowly. It was obvious to me she'd not prepared for the meeting at all.

'I met that MP, last month, at a book launch,' she said finally.

'MP?' I tried very hard not to roll my eyes.

'That young one,' she said, still turning pages. 'The one who no one expected to win, except she did and now she's an MP even though she's only just graduated.'

'Oh, yes,' I said, feeling a bit excited. 'Joanna Fuller?'

'That's it,' Vanessa said. 'What about her?'

'Perfect,' I said. 'We'd need to shoot her though – make her look more Mode. And MPs are a nightmare to get time with. We might need to do the shoot and the interview whenever we can and sit on it.'

Vanessa nodded.

'So what about next issue,' I said. 'Any ideas? We need to be quick, because we're late planning this one.'

Not content with taking half the team with her to her new job, Sophie had apparently stopped planning future issues as soon as she'd handed in her notice, leaving me with barely anything in the bag and very tight deadlines.

No one seemed to share my sense of urgency.

Vanessa shrugged. She really was infuriating. I looked at my own notes.

'What about Amy Lavender?' I said. 'She's everywhere right now and her agent owes me a favour, which is lucky because our budgets are very small. If we can shoot her and interview her on the same day, we'll have time to use it next issue. I'll sort it out.'

'Great idea,' said Milly. 'I love her. She's hilarious.'

Vanessa looked furious.

'Fine,' she said, even though it was clearly anything but. 'What else?'

'We've got the Jurassic diet plan,' Vanessa said. 'It's the new paleo. Basically you only eat kale and chia seeds, mushed together in a kind of primordial ooze.'

I brightened up. This was more like it.

'Get someone to do it,' I said. 'And write a diary. And find a nutritionist to sing about how fabulous it is, and another one who'll trash it completely.'

Vanessa sighed, but she didn't complain. She wrote something on her pad that seemed to be a lot more detailed than what I'd just said. I wondered if she was writing rude things about me. I used to do that when I was an intern and editors were dismissive of me – though I really thought someone of Vanessa's age and experience should have been past that by now.

I moved on.

'Fashion?' I said.

The fashion editor was a woman called Riley who I had worked with briefly years ago. I'd been so grateful to see a familiar face when I'd realised who she was yesterday, that I'd almost hugged her. Thankfully I'd stopped myself just in time.

Now she leaned back in her chair, stretching out her long brown legs – which were bare even though it was January – and smiled at me.

'I've got a dresses shoot that's in the bag,' she said. 'But if we're doing Amy Lavender, we could hang on to the dresses for next issue and perhaps we could get her to do something instead?'

'Yes,' I said, ridiculously pleased that finally someone was using their initiative.

'She wears lots of vintage stuff, right?' Riley went on thoughtfully. 'How about I take her for a trawl round some of the shops near here. We can do a feature on how to wear vintage clothes, ask Amy for her tips, and get her to model what we find.'

I loved that idea. I told her so.

'We could do a whole vintage issue,' said Milly, looking excited. 'Theme the whole magazine.'

'We could use Vanessa's feature on Dawn Robin,' I said wryly. Everyone laughed – except Vanessa. Oops.

'Seriously, though,' I said. 'Theming the issues is a great idea. We could definitely do that. It might give us a bit of an edge – make us different.'

And help us survive, I thought.

A tiny voice spoke from the corner of my office.

I looked round. Our work experience girl, a quiet student whose name I had absolutely no chance of remembering, was there, hunched over a notebook and blushing furiously.

'Pardon?' I said.

She blushed even more and cleared her throat.

'I was just saying, it's Mode's fiftieth anniversary,' she said. 'In September. So if you wanted to do a vintage theme, that would be a good time to do it.'

I stared at her. She looked down at her notebook.

'What's your name?' I asked.

'Emily,' she said.

'Emily, you are a genius.'

She beamed at me.

'Let's do it,' I said. 'Let's theme every issue. This one could be ...'

I thought for a moment. Everyone looked at me expectantly.

'... back to basics,' I said. 'Inspired by Vanessa's Jurassic diet.'

A ghost of a smile crossed Vanessa's face. Just a ghost, mind you.

'I'll do black and white fashion with Amy, then,' Riley said. 'Maybe some denim? And do the vintage stuff too, and hang on to it for a couple of months.'

I nodded.

Slowly, painfully, but finally, everyone started to come up with ideas of themes, of features, of fashion shoots, cover stars – the works. The beauty editor, who was aptly named Pritti, wowed me with her knowledge of different make-up looks that could fit

35

with every theme someone shouted out. Vanessa didn't offer many ideas, but even she didn't seem quite as hostile as she had done.

Eventually we had a plan for the back-to-basics issue, and the beginning of a plan for future issues, too. I knew this was going to be hard work. Harder than hard work. But maybe, just maybe, we were going to pull it off.

Chapter 7

I can't lie, those first few days on Mode were a slog. I started work early and stayed late, going over page proofs, rewriting features to make them fit within our back-to-basics theme, making endless lists – and avoiding Lizzie.

I'd expected to see Damo around but actually I'd not crossed paths with him since that first day. Once, I'd been staring out of my office window and seen him crossing the road outside, and I'd heard his laugh a few times echoing down the open-plan office from Homme, but I'd not actually spoken to him. I couldn't decide if I was pleased or disappointed about that.

Desperate to get everyone involved in the process of revitalising Mode, I got a big white board put up in the office and urged everyone to write ideas on it.

'Anything goes,' I trilled, putting some pens on the shelf next to it. 'The crazier, the better. Features ideas, cover ideas, events, sponsorship plans – absolutely anything.'

But now, a whole week after it had been put up, the board was still mostly bare. Riley had written up some ideas for future fashion shoots, but I wasn't sure 'SOMETHING FUNNY' was really what Mode readers were after. I did, however, love the idea for a monthly 'unlikely style crush'. How to recreate outfits worn by cartoon characters, people from books, old ladies ... Riley had scrawled on the board.

I picked up a pen and wrote 'I love this!' next to her idea, then I stared at the rest of the bare board in despair.

'Come on,' I said, under my breath, even though it was barely eight a.m. and I was alone in the office. 'I can't do this by myself.'

I'd come in early to wrestle with the budgets for the next few issues, which wasn't a fun way to start the day. The rest of the office filled up gradually, and by ten a.m. everyone was there. I left my office door open all the time but no one popped their heads round to say hello. I was still very much an outsider.

I sent my budget outline to Lizzie, hoping she'd agree with how I'd moved the money around, and then I sat quietly for a minute, trying to pluck up the courage to go and speak to my team. I didn't want to – how ridiculous was that?

I picked up my phone to call Jen, then put it down again. She probably wouldn't answer anyway, and – I thought with uncharacteristic insecurity – I couldn't say I blamed her.

A knock on my office doorframe made me look up. It was Emily, the intern, wobbling under the weight of a pile of magazines.

'I've been using these for my uni research project,' she said. 'Thought they might be useful.'

She lurched over to my desk and dropped the pile in front of me.

'They're the first issues of Mode,' she said. 'They're amazing.'

I looked at the issue on the top. It was from the late 1960s and had Twiggy on the cover. I felt a shiver of excitement.

'Where did you get these?' I asked Emily.

She grinned at me.

'There's a guy called Kevin, works in the library in the basement,' she said.

'There's a library?' I was impressed with her knowledge.

'It's not massive, but it's brilliant,' she said. 'Anyway, Kevin's got a daughter about my age, I gave him some advice about something, and bob's your uncle – he bent the rules and let me take the magazines away.'

I was impressed. I studied Emily carefully. She had strawberry blonde hair that was twisted back and up on her head, Adele-style, and she was wearing capri pants and a fitted fifties-look blouse. She looked great and absolutely nothing like the interns I was used to, who were like one great identical mass of oversized tote bags and false eyelashes.

She looked back at me for a moment then lowered her eyes shyly.

'Just thought they might be helpful,' she said.

'They're not just helpful,' I said, picking up the Twiggy issue. 'They're life-saving.'

She grinned again.

'How long are you here for, Emily?' I asked.

'One more month,' she said.

I made a note on my to-do list to speak to HR about taking her on full-time, and to re-do the budget I'd just sent to Lizzie to pay for her, then smiled at her.

'There are some photos in there,' she said, gesturing to the magazines. 'I found them inside one of the issues.'

She leafed through the pile and pulled out an A4-size black and white glossy print.

'It's the team who worked on the very first issue,' she said.

I looked at the photo. There were about ten people in the shot, their arms linked. At the centre, holding a magazine, was an older woman – about fifty-ish – stylish in a boxy Chanel suit. It was mostly women and they all looked incredible. I breathed out.

'Those clothes,' I said.

'I know,' Emily said. She came round my desk and leaned over my shoulder.

'That's the first editor,' she said, pointing to the older woman. I nodded.

'Margi Matthews,' I said. I'd read about her, of course. She'd come from the States and had been a real trailblazer.

'And that is Suze Williams,' Emily pointed to a young woman at one end of the picture. She had dark hair in a crop just like Twiggy's, and she was wearing a very short, black pinafore dress over a white long-sleeved t-shirt and white tights.

'No way,' I said. Margi was the founding editor of the magazine, but it was Suze who'd made it what it was now. She'd been editor in the late seventies and had taken Mode from its cautious beginnings as a fashion mag, to one of the most controversial and sassy women's mags in the business.

'She started out as editorial assistant,' Emily said. 'She worked on the very first issue, and eventually took over.'

'I didn't know that,' I said, staring at the pic. 'Can you take some of these, go through them and make some notes about features that catch your eye?' I said, a germ of an idea taking root in my mind. 'I'll take the other half.'

'Of course,' Emily said, looking like I'd given her a present. 'I'd love to.'

She took a bundle of mags from the top of the pile and headed out of my office.

I sat back in my chair, pleased with her initiative, and started leafing through the issues. They made me really sad. It was such a brilliant magazine and if Lizzie had her way it would be the end. I loved digital and how you could react to things happening immediately online, but in my opinion there was nothing better than treating yourself to a glossy magazine and curling up on the sofa to read it. Grace was a great magazine, I liked it a lot, but it didn't have the history that Mode had. It had changed its image so many times over the years that its early days as Home & Hearth were completely forgotten now – except to magazine geeks like me.

I read for well over an hour, jotting down ideas. Magazines had really changed, that was for sure, but what surprised me about those early editions was just how blunt and honest they were. There was loads of sex in them, hard-hitting features on things like abortion and racism, there was humour, advice, and a real feeling of being in this together. We could learn a lot from these issues, I thought.

I picked up the photograph of the first Mode team again and stared at it. There were only about ten people in the picture. They all had their arms linked and they were laughing. Margi Matthews, in the middle, was holding a round glass of champagne and the man to her left, who was wearing Mad Men style glasses, was gripping the bottle. There was so much energy and enthusiasm oozing out of the photo I could almost feel it.

I tapped the photo against my chin, thinking. The difference between the team in this picture and the team I was looking at – the nervous, quiet, worried team I had – was astonishing. Somehow I had to get that enthusiasm into my team if we were going to have any chance of beating Grace's brilliant sales. I couldn't rely on Vanessa to come up with exciting ideas, that was clear. I needed a right-hand woman. Someone I could work with. Someone who knew me inside out. In short, I needed Jen.

She and I had worked together on and off for years. We'd met when we were both interns on magazines in the same company. Our careers had followed similar paths and we'd ended up as deputy editor – me – and features director – her – on Happy magazine. We'd loved working so closely together. I was in awe of Jen's creativity and her knack of knowing exactly what the magazine needed each issue, while I knew I was better at managing a team and getting the job done.

We'd worked so well together in fact that we'd hatched a plan. We'd started plotting to launch our own online magazine, which we'd planned to call The Hive. We'd approached writers, spoken to designers, I'd even had some tentative meetings about getting finance in place. The feedback was enthusiastic, there was a real buzz about it and things were moving. And then Lizzie had called me to chat about this job. I'd not mentioned it to Jen at first, thinking it would come to nothing. But somehow I'd gone for one interview, then another, then presented to the board … and suddenly I was the new editor of Mode. I had to tell Jen – and more importantly we had to put all our plans for The Hive on hold.

Not surprisingly, Jen was furious. She'd put a lot of work into The Hive.

'Carry on,' I'd said, as we sat in our favourite bar the day I told her. 'Carry on without me.'

She'd shaken her head, her bleached blonde hair brushing her shoulders.

'You know that wouldn't work,' she'd said. 'It's called The Hive for a reason. It's not a solo venture.'

'I'll help,' I said desperately. 'At evenings and weekends. I'll do whatever you need me to do.'

Jen stared into her glass.

'You won't,' she said. She didn't sound angry, she just sounded disappointed and really tired. 'You'll do whatever you want to do. That's what you always do.'

She fished a ten-pound note out of her purse and shoved it at me.

'For the drink,' she muttered. Then she picked up her bag and left.

I'd not seen her since then. I was put on gardening leave as soon as I handed in my notice, so I'd not gone back to Happy. Jen hadn't replied to my emails and she cancelled all my calls. I knew she was acting as editor while the bosses at Happy found someone new to fill my role and I hoped she was doing well. She'd make a great editor and I knew she'd been bored to tears before – it was one of the reasons she'd been so keen to launch The Hive.

Although, I thought now, tapping my nails on the front cover of the first ever Mode, it might be good if she was bored.

Without stopping to think, I scrolled through my phone to her number and hit call. It rang a couple of times, then went straight to voicemail as I'd thought it would.

'Jen, it's me,' I said. 'Sweetheart, I'm sorry about everything. I've got lots to say to you but for now, let me just say this ...'

I paused.

'Do you want a job?'

I ended the call and sat back. As I'd hoped, my phone rang almost straight away.

'What sort of job?' Jen said.

Chapter 8

'I'm not staying,' Jen said, sliding into the seat opposite me. She looked tired and her hair was scraped back into a tiny bun.

I nodded. I knew this wasn't going to be easy.

'Drink?'

Jen shook her head.

'I'm not staying,' she said again. I poured myself a glass of wine, took a huge mouthful and grimaced at the acidic taste. We were in an old-fashioned pub down a side street near my office – I'd wanted to be sure no one from work would see me meeting Jen and as the only other customer was an older man in a creased grey suit with beer stains on the sleeves, I was fairly sure no one would.

'Just say what you've got to say,' Jen said. She fixed me with her unflinching gaze and I wilted a bit.

'Firstly,' I said, taking another swig of horrible wine. 'I want to apologise. I should have told you about the offer from Mode as soon as they rang me. I was stupid and inconsiderate.'

'And selfish,' Jen said.

'That too.'

There was a pause. Jen carried on staring at me.

'I still want to launch The Hive,' I said. 'And I think this job

44

is going to help with contacts and giving us an edge when we approach writers and financial backers.'

Jen shrugged.

'Perhaps,' she said.

I took a breath.

'Being editor of Mode is my dream job,' I said. 'When I was a teenager, it was what I dreamed of. I couldn't turn it down, Jen. I couldn't.'

Jen looked at me for a moment longer.

'I know,' she said. 'I know. I get it. I was just so hurt.'

'I'm sorry.'

'It's what you do, Fearne,' Jen said, a bitter edge to her voice. 'It's what you do. You pretend you need people, that you're there for people, but when push comes to shove, all you really care about is your career.'

'That's not true,' I said, even though it was a bit. 'I care about you. I do. We're a team, Jen, in work and out.'

A tiny, humourless smile worked its way onto Jen's lips.

'You're never not working,' she said.

'I'm sorry,' I said again. 'I'm sorry I ran out on you and our plans.'

Jen sighed.

'All that work we'd put in …'

'It still counts,' I said. 'We can still do it. In a year or so, maybe.'

I gulped the wine again. It was beginning to taste a bit nicer.

'But for now I want to save Mode,' I said. 'And I want you to help me.'

Jen blinked at me.

'Save it?'

I nodded.

'You know I said it was my dream job?'

Jen picked up the wine bottle and poured some into her empty glass. I was pleased. Maybe she was staying after all.

'Yes.'

'Well it's actually more of a nightmare.'

45

Jen had been perched on her chair, looking as though she might flee at any moment. Now she shrugged off her jacket and sat back. I almost wept with relief.

'Spill,' she said.

So I told her all about Mode and how it was haemorrhaging sales to Grace. How I had barely any staff, a shoestring budget and a defiant features editor. How I was trying to theme the issues and give ourselves an edge.

'So we're kind of forcing this issue into Back to Basics,' I explained. 'Next we're doing body confidence, and then I'm thinking about feminism or something like that.'

'Sounds pretty meh,' Jen said. 'It's hardly groundbreaking.'

I stared at her.

'That's exactly my worry,' I said with relief – she was already beginning to engage with the project. I pulled my notes out of my bag and thrust them at her. 'Look, this is what I'm planning. It's all okay but I'm not sure it's going to be enough.'

She smiled for the first time since she'd sat down.

'You need something big,' she said. She picked up the notes and leafed through them – I could almost see her brain working, churning out ideas as she read, and my stomach squirmed in excitement.

'Jen,' I said. 'Come and work with me.'

She looked at me over the top of my scribbles.

'What?'

'I need a deputy. And I need someone who'll tell me the truth, tell me when my ideas are hopeless and when they're working. I need you.'

Jen lowered the notes slowly.

'Thought you had no budget,' she said.

'All my staff have left,' I said. 'I'll move some stuff around.'

She bit her lip and I sensed she was weakening.

'Unless you want to stay at Happy,' I said. 'Must be nice being the boss at last …'

'I hate it there,' Jen said. 'I'm slogging my guts out as editor, and no one's said thank you, or told me I'm doing a good job. And they're still recruiting to replace me.'

She paused.

'And, I suppose I miss you.'

I grinned.

'So are you in?'

'This doesn't mean I've forgiven you.'

'Of course not.'

Jen waved the notes at me.

'This has got something already and I can make it better,' she said. 'But you need to promise me you'll listen to my ideas, and not shout me down or pull rank?'

'I promise,' I said, so grateful she was listening to me that I'd have promised anything at all.

'Then I'm in.'

I squealed in delight and reached across the table to hug her. She drew back and gave me a fierce look.

'No hugging,' she said. 'We're not at the hugging stage yet.'

'Sorry,' I said.

'Who else do you have?' Jen said. She found a notebook and pen in her bag and started making notes. 'Who's your team? You've got Riley Dean, right?'

'Right,' I said.

'And Milly Thompson?'

I shook my head.

'Gone,' I said. 'I've basically got Riley, an intern called Emily who's enthusiastic and potentially brilliant but very green, a good beauty editor called Pritti, and a sulky features ed called Vanessa.'

Jen made a face.

'Vanessa Bennett?' she said. 'I remember her from years ago. She's not really an ideas person.'

I chuckled.

'That's a nice way of putting it,' I said. 'I'd have said boring and uninspired.'

'Ouch,' said Jen. She made a note in her book. 'Who's on your art desk?'

I shrugged.

'Designers work across a few mags, so that's fine,' I said. 'But Milly was my art editor and she's left now so I need a replacement. A really good one.'

'Any ideas?' Jen said, frowning as she thought. 'What about Danielle Watson?'

'She's gone to Hot,' I said. 'She'd never come to us now.'

I paused.

'I did have one idea,' I said. 'But it might be crazy.'

Jen looked at me.

'Who?'

'Damian Anderson,' I said quickly. 'I thought I might ask him.'

Jen looked at me, not understanding.

'Damian ...?' she said, frowning slightly as she tried to work out how she knew the name. Then realisation dawned.

'Damo?' she said in astonishment. 'You want to ask Damo to be your art editor?'

I stared into the bottom of my wine glass.

'He's really good,' I muttered.

'I know he's good,' she said. 'But he's not good for you. And anyway, isn't he in Sydney?'

'He's working on Homme,' I said. 'He's in my office.'

'Shiiiiiit.'

I nodded.

'And you've seen him?'

I nodded again.

'And you didn't ring me?'

I gave her a fierce look.

'You wouldn't have answered,' I said.

She shrugged.

'Fair point,' she said, with a grin. 'Seriously, though, Fearne – is this a good idea?

I shook my head.

'Probably not,' I said. 'But I'm desperate, Jennifer. The magazine's dying, my team is uninspired and uninspiring, and I really want to make this work.'

She looked at me for a moment, then she drained her glass.

'So ask him,' she said. 'But keep it professional.'

Chapter 9

1966

'You think my flat is perfect?' Suze sounded surprised. 'It's not perfect at all.'

'It's all yours,' I said. 'It's just me and my dad at home, but he's … well, we stay out of each other's way most of the time.'

'Fair enough,' Suze said, with a nod that suggested she knew what I was talking about. She sat down on the floor next to the bed.

Not wanting to discuss my father, I changed the subject.

'So, I'm guessing you're not supposed to live here,' I said, sitting down next to Suze. The carpet was rough under my thighs, so I lifted them up and rested my arms on my knees.

Suze opened the tiny bag she wore and pulled out a packet of cigarettes. She offered one to me and I shook my head.

'I knew some guys who lived here,' she said with the cig clasped in her lips as she hunted in her bag for matches.

'What sort of guys?' I asked, though I knew what kind of men lived in squats in Soho. 'Druggie guys?'

Suze lit her cigarette and smiled a vague smile at me.

'Just guys,' she said. 'They moved on and I stayed. I got a friend to put the lock on the door.'

'In case they came back?'

She shook her head.

'I'm not like them any more,' she said. 'I just want to write.'

She took a huge drag on her cigarette and threw her head back so she could blow the smoke up at the ceiling.

'What about you?' she said.

'What about me?'

'What do you want to do?'

'Write,' I said.

'And?'

I shrugged. Where to begin? It was easier to say what I didn't want. I didn't want to marry Billy and work in my dad's shop.

'I want to live on my own, in a flat, with a massive wardrobe full of gorgeous clothes, and a tiny kitchen,' I said. 'And I want a handsome boyfriend. George Harrison, perhaps.'

Suze fake shuddered.

'Oh no,' she said. 'Mick Jagger.'

'Fine,' I said, giggling. 'We wouldn't want to share.'

'What else?'

'I want to edit a magazine for young women like us,' I said.

'Oh wouldn't that be peachy,' said Suze. She knelt up to stub out her cigarette and smiled at me.

'We could invent our own magazine,' she said. 'All about the things that interest us and girls like us.'

'Fashion,' I said. 'And music.'

'And careers,' Suze said. 'And books.'

'Travel,' I said, imagining getting on a plane to anywhere far, far away.

'Men,' said Suze. 'Sex.'

I giggled again, quite shocked despite myself. Billy and I had only ever kissed – though he'd been eager to take things further. I'd told him I didn't want to do it until we were married, but the truth was, I felt nothing when he kissed me and I really couldn't see what all the fuss was about.

'Do you write about sex for Home & Hearth?' Suze asked, a cheeky glint in her eye.

'Oh shit,' I said, suddenly remembering Home & Hearth. 'I have to go back to work.'

I looked at my watch. I was only a little bit late – hopefully Rosemary wouldn't realise how long I'd been gone.

'Do you want to meet up tomorrow?' Suze said. She looked at me from under her eyelashes and I thought she was much less worldly-wise than she wanted me to believe.

Yes, all right,' I said, surprised to realise I had enjoyed spending time with her. 'Lunchtime?'

'I'll meet you outside the office,' she said. 'Thanks for today.'

I grinned at her as I stood up and brushed fluff from the carpet off my tights.

'Pleasure,' I said.

I thought about Suze a lot that afternoon. She wasn't like anyone I'd met before. Some of my friends from school had a wild side, and even though I didn't really like to drink too much – my dad had put me off booze for life – I enjoyed watching their show-offy, smoking-behind-the-bike-sheds antics. But they all came from nice families. Families with a mum and a dad and siblings, and tea on the table at six o'clock, and church at Christmas. Somehow I sensed that Suze came from a very different place.

The truth was, my own family was anything but nice. And when Mum died, things got worse. On the surface, we may have looked perfect – respectable, community-minded mum and dad, working hard running their own business and making it a success, clever older brother, quiet younger sister. But I knew the reality was very different.

Like I said, Dad had always liked a drink, and he'd always had a temper, but he really loved my mum. And when she got ill and then died, he struggled to hold it together. He put so much energy into seeming fine, that it was like there was none left for me.

Mum's friends queued up to bring us food, and to cover shifts in the shop, and everyone talked admiringly about how well Dad was coping. Dennis went off to university less than a year after Mum passed away, and I missed him like a lost limb. When it was just me and Dad at home, he mostly ignored me and spent his evenings drinking. Occasionally, he'd snap and shout at me. Increasingly – if I caught him at the wrong time or I'd done something he thought was wrong – he'd lash out. I'd become pretty good at hiding bruises with make-up and I had a routine now where I made sure the house was clean and Dad's dinner was on a plate keeping warm in the oven when he got home. I'd say hello, then disappear to my room.

I planned to follow Dennis to university but Dad wouldn't let me go. That was about the time Billy asked me to marry him – or at least when he started talking about when we'd get married as though it was a done deal – and I thought it might be the only way I could escape. And I'd also stepped up my efforts to get a job – and eventually had landed an interview at Home & Hearth.

I lied about where I worked, and I lied about my actual job, and I lied about how much I was paid. I cut my actual salary by a fair amount when I told Dad what I'd be bringing in, and offered to hand over nearly all of it each month as payment for my room and board. And the rest – the money Dad didn't know about – I saved. I'd been at the magazine for a year now, and my savings account was beginning to look pretty good. I told myself I was saving for when Billy and I got married, but I knew that wasn't true. It was my running away money. My independence money. It was my safety net.

So when it came to families, I knew how bad things could be. How frightening it was to know that when push came to shove, you had no one you could rely on. And I had stayed. I'd stayed with grieving, grumpy, volatile, violent Dad because it was better than going. I had no idea just how bad things had to have been for Suze to make her go. Because living with 'some guys' in a squat in Soho, stealing electricity and eating sympathy fruit from the market wasn't easy. And for that to be better than the alternative, the alternative had to be really, really bad.

But despite all that, I knew the reason I was looking forward to seeing her again tomorrow wasn't that I felt sorry for her. It was because I liked her.

Chapter 10

My journey home was the reverse of my journey to work. As soon as I got on the train, I headed into the small toilet and pulled off my knitted mini dress and boots. I stuffed them into my bag and put on the beige suit and blouse I'd left the house in.

I brushed my hair over and over until all the lacquer was gone and it was back to hanging limply round my face. Then I pulled it into a sensible ponytail and grimaced at my reflection in the mottled mirror.

Finally, I scrubbed the make-up off my face and watched as the water swirled away down the plug – a murky mixture of pan stick, black eyeliner and rouge. Then I powdered my nose, put on the tiniest slick of mascara, pushed my engagement ring back onto my finger, and emerged from the loo with time to spare. I slumped in a seat, breathing slightly heavily. It was exhausting leading this double life and I envied Suze for the ease of her solo life.

As the train pulled into my station, I spotted Billy waiting for me on the platform. I groaned. I was planning to drop my dress into the launderette on the way home, and now it would have to wait. But as I got off the train with a bundle of other commuters,

I couldn't help smiling. Billy looked so pleased to see me and his grin was infectious.

'Thought I'd walk you home,' he said, taking my bag.

I looped my arm through his and he hoisted my bag on to his shoulder.

'Blimey, what have you got in here, Nance?' he said.

I waved my hand in the air vaguely.

'Oh just work stuff,' I said, hoping he wouldn't want to look. 'And wedding stuff.'

'Wedding stuff,' Billy said, kissing my cheek. 'I'd better not peek, then.'

Oh bless him. He was so predictable. And traditional, I thought, with a trace of venom. Boring.

But he was nice; that was the trouble. I liked Billy. He made me laugh. He looked after me. He listened when I talked – far, far more than I listened when he talked. I could see myself marrying him. That was what scared me. I'd marry Billy, we'd buy a house round the corner from his parents' place and I'd probably be pregnant within a year. Then I'd have to leave work and that would be it. The closest I'd ever get to Home & Hearth magazine would be leafing through it for Sunday lunch ideas and remembering that one day, I'd typed those recipes and dreamed of something more.

Billy squeezed my arm.

'Are you okay, Nance?' he said. 'You're miles away.'

'Tired,' I said. 'It's been a long day, and we were up late last night, weren't we?'

'It was a good party, wasn't it?' Billy said.

I nodded. It was a good party – we had a lot of friends and family who were delighted that we'd got engaged. We had piles of cards and presents to open. It was all lovely. And I hated even thinking about it.

I sighed. Other girls would be thrilled to be in my position. To be engaged to a lovely bloke like Billy who was handsome and funny and had a good job and great prospects. And there was ungrateful me, wishing I was living in a smelly squat like a girl I'd only just met, who was possibly on drugs and definitely starving.

Billy laughed.

'Early night for you, Nancy,' he said, as he opened my garden gate. 'You're all over the place.'

'We were going to open our presents,' I said.

'They'll keep,' Billy said. 'I'll come round tomorrow and we can tackle them together. See what delights my Auntie Marge has given us.'

I rolled my eyes.

'You'd better write her thank you letter,' I said, smiling despite myself. 'Not sure I can be convincing if she's given us that coffee pot your mum gave her for Christmas.'

Auntie Marge was famous in Billy's family for passing on unwanted gifts. It had become a bit of a joke and I suspected some of his relatives chose Marge's presents intending them to be given to someone else one day.

I liked Billy's family, too. They were nice. Normal. His dad liked a drink, but he knew when to stop, and his mum was funny and warm. He had two younger sisters who thought I was the bee's knees, and his granny – who lived with them – was sharp-tongued and an absolute hoot.

It wouldn't be so bad to be part of that family, I thought to myself sternly. Maybe I just needed to get over myself and start appreciating what I had.

Billy and I walked up the path together and he put my bag on the doorstep. Then he gently tilted my chin up and kissed me.

'Night Nancy,' he said. 'See you tomorrow.'

I watched him head off down the road, hands in pockets. Everything was perfect in his world. He had a good job, working with his uncle in his garage with an eye to taking it over one day. He was looking forward to getting married and liked nothing more than talking about the children we'd have one day. I knew he wanted us to have our own family and be just like his parents and I couldn't see anything wrong with that. I just knew it wasn't what I wanted. At least, not yet. I was twenty-one years old and I lived just ten miles from central London. I wanted to be part of it. But as far as my dad, and Billy, were concerned, it was a whole world away.

Billy reached the corner, looked back to see me watching and waved. I waved back.

'I'm going to break your heart,' I said out loud. Then I pulled out my key and went inside.

I stuck some chops under the grill for dinner, chopped some carrots and peeled potatoes for mash. Then I sat at the kitchen table and wolfed my portion down as fast as I could so I'd be finished before my father came home. I'd wait to hear him come in, give him his meal and later, as Dad settled down in front of whatever sitcom he was watching that week, I'd go up to my room to read or listen to music.

That night, I had some sorting out to do.

I kept most of my clothes at work – my good clothes. Our fashion editor, who'd been sympathetic when I lied that my dad didn't really like the latest trends, had cleared a rail in her cupboard for me and I used it as my wardrobe. But I still had to make sure I had an outfit at home every day and keep them laundered. Like a lot of girls my age, I made most of my own clothes. I even often whipped up an outfit during the day on a Saturday to wear out with Billy in the evening. I wasn't a brilliant seamstress, but I could make the shift dresses that everyone was wearing.

Now I pulled everything out of my bag and checked what I had. The dress I'd worn today was fine, I'd take that back to the office tomorrow and hang it up. But I had a couple of mini-skirts that needed washing, and two polo neck sweaters that could do with a clean, too. I shoved them under my bed – I'd take them to the launderette at the weekend.

For tomorrow I had a denim pinafore dress with buttons right up the front. It was one of my favourite outfits. I wore it with a bright, rainbow striped t-shirt underneath, and some white boots – which were also in my bag.

I put everything for the next day in my hold-all, neatly packed in plastic bags in case it rained. Checked my make-up was all fine – it was – and felt in the side pocket to make sure my Post Office book was still in there. I had two Post Office accounts – one was a joint account with Billy. We were saving for the wedding and a house and our life together. The other was my escape fund.

'Just going to post a letter,' I called as I went downstairs. I could hear my dad laughing at something on the TV.

I went outside into the cold night air, stashed my hold-all in the shed where I could get it tomorrow, walked round the block and then went back home and went to bed. Billy was right, I was exhausted. But it was more the strain of my double life that was taking it out of me, not the engagement party.

As I snuggled down in bed, I looked over at the piles of unopened engagement cards and presents stacked on my chest of drawers. But the last thing I thought of before I fell asleep, was Suze.

Chapter 11

2016

'Professional?' Damo said, shovelling a forkful of rice into his mouth. 'What does that mean?'

I snapped a poppadom in half, put both pieces back on my plate and sighed.

'It means,' I said. 'That we put whatever happened between us to one side, and we move on like grown-ups.'

Damo grinned at me.

'Move on?'

'Stop repeating everything I say,' I said, remembering how infuriating he could be.

'I need a good art editor, you need a job and you're a good art editor. We can help each other.'

Damo didn't look very convinced.

'I've got a job,' he said. 'So why would I come and work for you?'

'You've got some freelance shifts,' I pointed out, offering him my broken poppadom. I wasn't very hungry and I definitely didn't fancy curry at lunchtime – I'd only agreed to come to Damo's favourite restaurant as part of my campaign to butter him up.

'Yeah, but I like being flexible,' he said. 'And you're really bossy.'

I glowered at him.

'I'm not bossy, I'm the boss,' I said. I was beginning to recall why we'd split up. Damo was so laid back he was virtually horizontal. He wouldn't commit to anything, he had the itchiest feet of anyone I'd ever met, and he really didn't like being tied down. When we'd first met – when I moved to Sydney to work for a year on a mag out there – his spontaneity had thrilled me. He'd moved into my tiny apartment within about three weeks of us getting together and we'd spent weekends exploring the city and our holidays travelling all over Australia. Then, when he'd decided it was time to move on, I'd agreed. Except, I was putting down roots in Sydney. I had a lot of misgivings and doubts about his plans – and I'd never quite got round to telling him about those doubts.

As Damo gave away the few possessions he'd accumulated during his time in Sydney, and planned a route round South East Asia, he'd tell me stories about amazing things we'd see in Thailand and Laos and Cambodia.

But I had my eye on another prize – the next step on the career ladder. The deputy editor on the magazine I worked for had told me she was leaving and I wanted her job. I wanted it so badly it was like a physical pain. I knew I could do it, and do it really well. I knew I'd work brilliantly with the editor and I knew she wanted me to apply. It was perfect – but I'd not mentioned to Damo that I wanted to stay in Australia.

'Tell him,' Jen emailed me. 'Tell him that you're not going.'

'I can't,' I typed back. 'There's never a good time.'

'Better now than at the airport,' she'd written.

But in the end, I'd chosen the worst possible time. We'd gone out one Saturday, into the city centre. Damo was fidgety with excitement because he'd hit his savings target, he'd shed his belongings and he'd decided today was the day we were going to buy our tickets to Bangkok.

'And after the full moon party, we'll head over to some of the smaller islands ...' Damo was saying.

I stopped walking.

'Fearne?' Damo said. 'What's up?'

I looked at him, standing in the clean Sydney street, his shaggy hair blowing in the wind and his brown eyes scrunched up against the sun, and I couldn't believe what I was going to say.

'Fearne?' he said again.

'I'm not going,' I said.

Damo looked confused.

'I thought you said you were free all morning,' he said. 'We can go to the travel agent later, if you've got something else on ...'

I shook my head.

'I'm not going to Asia,' I said. 'I'm staying here.'

Damian got it straight away.

'Patti's job?' he said.

I nodded, biting my lip.

'I really want it, Damo,' I said. 'I need that job.'

'There will be other jobs.'

I shook my head.

'Maybe,' I said. 'Maybe not.'

Damo took my hand.

'You can spend your whole life trying to make your parents proud of you,' he said. 'And who knows, maybe one day it'll work.'

I looked at my feet, tanned in my flip flops – thongs they called them here, though I'd never get used to that. I couldn't meet Damo's eyes.

'But maybe,' Damo carried on. 'Maybe nothing you do will ever be good enough, and maybe you should live a little. There are more important things than work, you know.'

I gave a small smile.

'Like what?' I said.

'Like me.'

For a moment we stared at each other, both of us knowing it was one of those Sliding Doors moments. And then, slowly, I shook my head.

'I'm sorry,' I said. 'I'm not going.'

Damo let go of my hand.

'I'll see you around,' he said.

And then he walked away. He'd taken all his stuff out of my apartment by the time I got home that evening and he booked his flight to Asia for a few days later. I was heartbroken, of course. Despite everything, I'd fallen really hard for him, and he'd hit a nerve when he'd talked about my parents. But, true to form, I dusted myself off, threw myself into making Patti's job my own, and returned to London a year later to carry on climbing that career ladder.

I missed Damo of course. I thought about him a lot during my time in Sydney and even when I returned to London. But I didn't see him again until he showed up in my office.

Now, sitting opposite him, I was amazed he didn't hold more ill will towards me.

'Damo,' I said. 'I'm sorry about what happened. With us, I mean.'

He shrugged.

'Long time ago,' he said.

'I know.'

My mouth was dry. I hated apologising.

'I handled it all really badly,' I said. 'And I still think about you a lot. I'm sorry if I hurt you.'

Damian looked up at me. He had odd greeny-brown eyes, which looked bright in his brown face – he was still tanned, even though the London weather had made him paler than I'd ever seen him before.

'I've not been moping for five years,' he said, bluntly. 'We had a great thing, but it ended and we moved on. We're over it. I'm over it. Aren't you?'

63

I swallowed.

'Of course,' I said in a squeaky voice. I couldn't look at his face so I focused on his arms instead. His buff, brown arms … Nope. His face was better. I was over it. At least, I had been, until he turned up in my office.

I took a deep breath.

'Give me six months,' I said. 'I've got some brilliant ideas to turn the magazine around, but I need you to help make it work. Six months is all I need.'

Nine months would be better, but somehow that sounded much longer.

'Six months,' Damo said. He wiped his plate with a piece of naan.

'That's it,' I said, hoping to appeal to his flighty nature. 'Six months.'

'Is Jen in?'

'She's in.'

'All right,' Damo said. 'I'll do it.'

I swallowed the squeal of delight that rose up in my throat and instead I gave him what I hoped was a professional smile.

'Great,' I said. 'I'll let HR know.'

64

Chapter 12

Getting Jen and Damo on board was the easy bit, I knew that. But I hadn't quite expected the rest of it to be so hard.

We'd finished the Back to Basics issue, and moved on to Body Confidence. I was very aware that I'd already been at Mode for a month and basically done nothing. My deadline was getting closer and things hadn't changed. I hardly did anything but work and sleep, although I had to confess that was nothing new. And despite all that, I couldn't help thinking my ideas were dated and tired. I spent ages poring over back issues of Mode and Grace, trying to find out where we'd gone wrong but I hadn't yet hit on the magic formula that would make our readers come back.

It was Monday, the Back to Basics issue had been on sale for a week, and I was getting a bit antsy about getting some early sales figures which I was expecting that day.

And I knew I had to have a catch-up meeting with Vanessa too, which I was dreading. She'd gone from being obstructive and rude, to being outright hostile – I wanted to get to the bottom of it.

She slid into my office a little while later and sat opposite me in such a sulky fashion that I almost expected her to stick her tongue out.

'Hi,' I said, cheerfully, gathering together my pile of old issues of Grace and Mode and dumping them on top of the vintage issues Emily had given me.

Vanessa gave me a tight smile and I suddenly felt angry. I had worked with all sorts of people over the years, some nice, some not – and she was just one more. If she didn't like me, fine, but we had to work together.

I took a breath.

'Vanessa,' I said. 'Do we have a problem?'

She flushed.

'What kind of problem?'

'You tell me,' I said. 'You're sullen, unhelpful and you obviously don't like me. But we have to work together and unless you can lose the attitude, you can't stay.'

Vanessa looked horrified and for a moment she stared at me in defiance. Then her angular shoulders dropped and she nodded.

'That's the problem,' she said.

I raised an eyebrow and she sighed.

'I wasn't supposed to stay,' she said. 'I was supposed to be going with Sophie to her new magazine – as her deputy. But they had someone in place, and Sophie ditched me rather than miss her chance.'

She looked up at me.

'I guess I'm still a bit annoyed.'

Well, that was an understatement. But I felt a slight flush of shame – what Sophie had done to Vanessa wasn't a million miles away from what I'd done to Jen.

'Look,' I said. 'I don't know exactly what went on between you and Sophie, and you don't need to tell me, but let me lay my cards on the table. Unless we all pull our fingers out, Mode is going to close. They're desperate to shut us down, and unless we all start coming up with some ideas, we're toast.'

Vanessa winced.

'I'm not very good at ideas,' she said.

Another understatement. I started to speak but she hadn't finished.

'But I did have one idea,' she continued. 'About where we sell the mag.'

I nodded.

'I love magazines,' she said. 'I work in the magazine business. And I can't remember the last time I went into a newsagent. Probably at the airport last summer.'

I nodded again, not sure where she was going with this.

'So I look online – because my phone is always where I am and magazines aren't.'

'You're not making me feel any better,' I said.

Vanessa smiled.

'We need to sell the magazine where the readers are,' she said. 'Gyms, cinemas, coffee shops, Topshop ...'

I was staring at her, open-mouthed.

'It was just an idea,' she muttered.

I reached across the desk and gripped her hand. She looked alarmed.

'It's an absolutely brilliant idea,' I said. 'Brilliant.'

Vanessa pulled her hand away but she gave me a proper smile this time.

'Really?'

I smiled back.

'Really.'

Thinking on my feet, I realised this could be the thing that I needed to get Vanessa out of my way – and make her a bit happier.

'I've recruited a deputy,' I said in a rush.

'Oh,' Vanessa looked a bit put out.

'It means, I could free up some of your time,' I carried on quickly. 'If you'd like to work on distribution ideas? This is such a great plan, but it might take some time to persuade the people who need to be persuaded. Do you want to take it on?'

Vanessa thought for a minute, and I hoped she wasn't going to say no. Then she smiled.

'Yes please,' she said. 'If you're sure you don't need me on features?'

'We'll miss you, of course,' I lied. 'But Jen can cover it.'

'Can I start now?' Vanessa said. 'I've got a friend from uni who works in PR for Topshop – I'll give her a call and get things moving.'

'Go for it,' I said. She gave me a quick grin, uncurled her long body from the chair and headed out of my office. I watched her go, breathing a big sigh of relief. I'd dodged a bullet there, no mistake. And her ideas about changing our distribution really were brilliant. I'd never have thought of that so if she pulled it off, I'd definitely owe her one.

Now I just had to make the magazine brilliant too.

I picked up my pile of magazines and started laying them out on the floor to see if looking at them all together would give me inspiration about why early Mode was such a hit, why Grace was selling so well, and why modern Mode's sales were falling off a cliff.

Carefully I laid out the magazines, immediately seeing how much energy old Mode had. I put the Grace issues in a row, and the most recent Modes, and then I paused. In among the old issues of Mode was an issue of Home & Hearth from 1966 – the magazine that had undergone change after change before eventually turning into Grace. Interested, I picked up the issue from 1966, which seemed a world away both from modern older women's magazines and how I imagined the sixties. It had one of the worst covers I'd ever seen – it was brown and the picture was a pie, shot from above. It looked tasty but it definitely didn't make me want to read the mag.

Despite the unappealing cover, I sat down at my desk to have a look. I loved all magazines and I'd learned over the years that ideas could come from anywhere.

To my surprise, it was a good read and I was quickly engrossed. It had a lot of fiction – something hardly any magazines featured any more – some horrible fashion spreads and very little beauty, but it had an interesting travel feature about Israel, and quite a hard-hitting report on giving up babies for adoption. There was much more to it than I'd first thought. And what it had in common with early Mode and modern Grace was the energy, enthusiasm and excitement that made it a magazine worth reading.

I sighed and tapped my keyboard to wake up my computer, thinking I'd make some notes about Home & Hearth while it was fresh in my mind, but I grimaced as I saw an email from Lizzie with the subject line: sales figures.

Urgh. The early sales from the Back to Basics issue. Bracing myself I opened the email and looked in horror at the numbers, which were lower than I'd feared. Much, much lower. Mode was in big trouble and I wasn't sure all the good ideas we'd had were enough to save it.

Chapter 13

1966

'Waiting for me?' George crept up behind me and made me jump.

I turned and grinned at him, pulling my hair away from my face as the wind whipped it across my lips.

'No actually,' I said. 'I'm meeting a friend.'

It was lunchtime and I was waiting for Suze outside my office. It was raining again and I was huddled under an umbrella.

'What friend?' said George, ducking under as the rain suddenly got heavier. 'Anyone I know?'

'The girl I met yesterday,' I said. 'Her name's Suze Williams. She wants to be a writer.'

George was a lot taller than me, his lanky frame folded up under my brolly. Now he frowned down at me.

'Sucker,' he said.

I shoved him.

'She's nice,' I said. 'Interesting.'

'Pretty?'

I felt a flush of jealousy and unfairly I shrugged.

'Guess so,' I said.

'Not as pretty as you, though,' said George and my stomach flipped over.

He was very close to me as we sheltered from the rain, which was getting heavier by the minute. I felt the warmth of his body through my mac and I wondered what he would do if I stood on my tiptoes and kissed him. I was fairly sure – positive, in fact – that he'd kiss me back. But I wasn't quite ready to open that can of worms yet.

'Nancy,' Suze squeezed in between me and George. I'd been so engrossed in my thoughts that I'd not even noticed her approaching. 'I've had the most wonderful idea.'

'This is Suze,' I said to George, tilting my head to peek round her. Suze's hair was wet but it was so short, it didn't look bad. She was still coat-less, even though the rain was now torrential.

'Hi Suze,' George said. 'I'm George.'

Suze shot him a quick dismissive smile over her shoulder then gripped my arms.

'I've had an idea,' she said again.

George reached round Suze and squeezed my fingers.

'I'm going to take my chances with the rain,' he said. 'See you later.'

He ducked out from under the umbrella, pulled his jacket over his head and dashed off in the direction of Carnaby Street.

I watched him go. Suze watched me.

'Who's he?' she said.

'Friend,' I said. 'Photographer.'

I flexed my fingers where George had squeezed them.

'Do you like him?'

'He's nice,' I said, deliberately misunderstanding.

Suze shoved me. Her energy was amazing. She was never still. Even now she was bouncing on the balls of her feet like an excited child.

'You like him,' she said. 'Why don't you tell him?'

'It's complicated,' I said.

71

Suze reached into the top of her jumper and pulled a ten-shilling note from her bra.

'I'll buy you a coffee,' she said. 'And you can tell me all about it.'

I didn't want to ask where she'd got the money from, but I let her buy me a coffee and we settled into the same booth at the back of the café where we'd sat yesterday.

'So what's with George,' she said, blowing across the top of her cup to cool it down. Her skinny fingers were chapped with chilblains.

'What's your idea?' I said.

She giggled.

'I'll tell you if you tell me,' she said.

I shrugged.

'I'm not that bothered,' I said, suspecting she'd not be able to resist telling me, whatever I said.

She lasted about a minute before she sighed in a dramatic way.

'Okay, then,' she said. 'Look I don't want to sound like an oddball, but yesterday I thought we got on really well.'

I nodded slowly, reluctant to commit to whatever she was obviously going to ask me.

'Don't look so scared,' she said. 'I just thought we could be friends, that's all. And you did me a good turn yesterday so now it's my turn.'

'Go on,' I said, interested despite myself.

'Let's work together,' she said. 'You said you don't get any time to write at home. Bring your typewriter to mine and we can work on some stuff together.'

'Work together?' I repeated, turning the idea over in my mind. 'Write together?'

Suze made a face.

'Probably not actually writing together,' she said. 'But tossing around ideas, that sort of thing. It was fun yesterday when we were joking about running our own magazine.'

'It was,' I agreed. 'So we could write some articles, and see if we can get them published in Home & Hearth, or other magazines?'

'Exactly,' said Suze, clapping her hands together. 'I think we'll be good for each other.'

She reached over the checked tablecloth and gripped my fingers.

'I know I'm a bit out there,' she said, giving me a sheepish grin. 'Sometimes my ideas are a bit out there too. But I'm a good writer, Nancy. Really good. And I bet you are too.'

I made what I thought was a modest face.

'I keep thinking we'd make a good team,' Suze went on. 'Two heads are better than one.'

I thought about how I had to keep all my writing hidden away at home. How I never had anyone to read my stuff. How I loved my job but how I was bored to tears typing up recipes and replying to readers' letters, and how much I longed to write proper features for magazines.

I grinned at Suze.

'Okay, then,' I said. 'Let's do it. I'll probably have to tell my dad that I'm doing an evening class or something, not that I expect he'd care very much, and I couldn't do every night because I need to see …'

I trailed off.

'Who do you need to see?' Suze said, raising her eyebrow. 'George?'

'No,' I said, miserably, thinking of Billy's swagger as he walked down the road. A man without a care in the world – for now. 'I need to see Billy. He's my fiancé.'

Suze shrieked.

'You're engaged!' she said. 'Let me see the ring.'

She grabbed my bare left hand and looked first at my finger, then up at my face, confused.

'No ring?'

'I've got a ring,' I said, snatching my hand away. 'But I don't wear it.'

'Why not?'

'Because,' I hissed. 'I don't want anyone to know I'm engaged.'

'You don't want George to know,' Suze said.

'Not just George,' I said. 'Anyone. No one at work knows about Billy. And no one at home knows about …'

Suze looked at me.

'About?'

'About work,' I admitted. 'About the magazine, about what I do – none of it.'

Suze looked bewildered.

'But your job is brilliant,' she said. 'Why don't you want to talk about it?'

I made a face.

'Things at home are … tricky,' I said. 'My mum died when I was little and Dad's, well, he really only pays attention to me when I annoy him.'

Suze nodded.

'Go on.'

'I've not told him about my job because it's just not worth the grief he'd give me.'

'Handy with his fists, is he?'

I felt a flush of embarrassment.

'Once or twice,' I admitted. 'Well, bit more than that really. More when he's drunk. Or angry at the world.'

I'd never told anyone what Dad was really like. I forced my gaze upwards to meet Suze's and was relieved to see no pity in her eyes, just understanding.

'So where does he think you go every day?' she asked, raising a narrow eyebrow.

'He thinks I work in insurance and he thinks I'm only doing it until I get married – or until I go and work for him in his shop.'

74

'Shit,' said Suze. 'That's a tangled web.'

'Isn't it,' I said, wryly.

'So when's the wedding?'

I winced.

'We've not set a date yet,' I said. 'But I'm thinking … never.'

'Ouch,' said Suze. 'What are you going to do?'

I looked up at the ceiling.

'No idea,' I said. 'Marry Billy, leave work and have some babies?'

Suze shuddered.

'No,' she said.

'Break Billy's heart, make my dad furious and end up on the streets?'

'Sometimes,' said Suze, her elfin face serious, 'the streets are better than the alternative. You just have to be brave and take a risk.'

We looked at each other for a minute. I felt a sort of connection to her, even though we'd really only just met.

I nodded.

'You're right,' I said, wondering what had happened to her. 'I have to take a risk.'

I smiled weakly.

'Let's do it. I'll bring my typewriter to yours and we can get busy. Who knows, if we sell enough articles we'll be able to afford to rent a flat.'

Suze bounced up and down in her seat.

'Oh I'd love that,' she said. 'Imagine the fun we'll have.'

And the funny thing was, I could imagine it. I really could.

Chapter 14

So we put our plan into action. I sowed the seeds at home that evening.

'There's a course I'm hoping to do,' I said to Dad as I sliced carrots for dinner. 'It's book-keeping and it's aimed at small businesses. It's perfect for the shop.'

Dad was reading the Standard at the kitchen table, cup of tea at his elbow. I was pleased he'd not started drinking as soon as he came home, like he sometimes did. It would help me if he could follow the conversation without flying off the handle.

'I do the books,' he said, not looking up.

'Oh I know,' I said, sweeping the carrots into the mince. 'But one day you might want me to take over. Or I can help Billy at the garage. It's a useful skill to have.'

Dad looked a bit distant for a moment and rubbed his temples. He swigged his tea and made a face, but I didn't offer to get him a beer from the fridge. Not yet.

'I suppose,' he said, eventually. 'Where's the course?'

'Oh it's at work,' I said. 'All paid for. The only trouble is it's an evening class. Twice a week, after work.'

'All paid for?' Dad said.

'Yes,' I said. I turned away from him and stirred the meat so he couldn't see my face. I was getting pretty good at lying but that didn't mean I enjoyed it.

'All right,' he said.

'All right?' I repeated. But he didn't reply.

Assuming that meant he had engaged as much as he was going to, I turned the heat down under the meat.

'Dinner will be half an hour,' I said.

Dad snorted.

'I need to go into work on Saturday to register for this course then,' I carried on casually. 'And afterwards I'm meeting a friend to go to the pictures. Girl from work,' I added. 'Suze.'

I'd learned long ago that the best lies had an element of truth.

'She's doing the course too.'

Dad nodded and I thought that was it. But later when we were eating, he looked at me and said, 'What does Billy say?'

'About what?'

'This course of yours.'

Hoping to distract him, I got up and went to the fridge. I pulled out a can of beer, opened it and handed it to Dad with a glass.

'He thinks it will be useful for when he's running the garage.'

Dad nodded, then turned his attention back to his dinner. And it was done.

Billy had actually been chuffed to bits, making me feel waves of guilt that I was actually going to be spending my evenings writing articles, furthering my own career and not his.

'Get a grip,' Suze said in disgust when I told her how I was feeling as we walked to her squat that Saturday. 'You've got to stop worrying about what everyone else thinks and start looking after yourself.'

'You think?' I said. I shifted my heavy typewriter case to the other hand. I'd told Dad that it had a fault that needed mending and I would drop it into the shop on my way to the station. 'I can't help wondering if it's not worrying about what everyone else thinks that's got me into this mess.'

Suze waved away my concerns with a flick of her wrist.

'Rubbish,' she said. 'If there's one thing I've learned, it's that you can't rely on anyone but yourself.'

She grinned at me.

'You've got to look out for number one.'

She opened the door of the squat and I followed her inside, glad to put my heavy typewriter down.

'Suze,' I said. 'What happened to you?'

'I cleared half the desk,' she said, ignoring my question. 'And Bert off the fruit stall found me another chair.'

She showed me her desk, which she'd pulled out from the wall. She'd put the two chairs on opposite sides, diagonally across from each other. Her typewriter was on one side and she picked up mine and put it on the other.

'There's loads of space,' she said. 'We can chat if we want, or zone out if we need to concentrate.'

I felt weirdly close to tears.

'This is amazing,' I said. 'Thank you.'

Suze gave me a funny, wonky sort of smile.

'Someone once told me that when things aren't going well for you, you should do something to help someone else,' she said. 'I thought this would be good for both of us.'

I nodded, not wanting to speak in case I cried.

'So what do you think?' she said.

I swallowed.

'I think,' I said, unclipping my typewriter case. 'That we should get to work.'

We typed together in companionable silence all afternoon. I was working on a piece that had been swirling round in my head for weeks – a personal take on why I didn't want to get married. It was a bit too out there for Home & Hearth but I thought I might show Rosemary once it was finished and see if she had any suggestions about which magazine might print it. Suze was writing an article about which pop stars she thought would be best in bed. It was cheeky, slightly shocking (at least to my suburban mindset) and really, really funny. She occasionally read bits out to me and I would giggle at her clever turn of phrase. I was relieved to discover she was indeed a good writer – I had been a bit concerned she'd turn out to be lacking, which would have been embarrassing and awkward.

Finally, as it was growing dark outside, I stood up and pulled my final version of my article out of my typewriter.

'I need to go,' I said. 'It's getting late.'

Suze was hunched over her piece of paper, reading it through.

'Stay,' she said. 'There's a party tonight. Stay and let's go to the party.'

'Really?' I said, doubtfully. 'I'll have to tell Dad.'

Suze shrugged.

'So tell him,' she said. 'What can he do? You're an adult.'

So I did. I phoned Dad, told him I was going to a party and Suze said I could stay at hers. I lied a little bit and said Suze had a landlady who'd said it was fine. Just to make it all sound more respectable than it really was.

Dad grunted. He hated talking on the phone.

'I'll be back early enough to help with the papers,' I said. Sundays were a busy day at the shop.

'Make sure you are,' he said.

Pleased to have got away with it so easily, I came out of the phone box and grinned at Suze.

'Done,' I said. 'I'm all yours.'

Then, arm in arm, we walked down Wardour Street.

'Let's go for a drink first,' said Suze, steering me into a pub on the corner. 'The party won't get going for hours.'

I wasn't used to going to pubs. Billy sometimes took me for a drink, but I had never been into a pub without him.

Suze winked at the barmaid and she grinned.

'All right love,' she said. 'Vodka and lime?'

Suze nodded.

'Two,' I said. 'Is there anyone you don't know?'

Suze laughed. She picked up both our drinks and went off to find a table, leaving me to pay.

Annoyed with her, I handed over the money, took my change, then weaved through the customers to find her. I sat down on a velour stool and took a slurp of my vodka.

'Why do you live in a squat?' I said abruptly. 'What happened to you that makes living in a squat better than where you came from?'

Suze made a face.

'I don't want to talk about it,' she said.

'I thought we were friends,' I said. I knew I was being a bit prickly because I felt uncomfortably like I was in her territory, where she knew everyone and let me pick up the tab. 'I told you my secret.'

Suze looked at me over the top of her vodka glass, her kohled eyes blinking. Then she sighed.

'Not much to tell,' she said in a matter-of-face tone. 'Mum always liked men more than she liked me. She had loads of different men round all the time. Some of them were nice. Some not so nice. Sometimes I went to live in foster homes for a bit when she went off with a bloke. I always liked that, and I hated when Mum came to get me again. When I was thirteen she moved in a bloke called Gordon. When I was fourteen, he felt me up.'

'Urgh,' I shuddered. 'What did you do?'

Suze drained her drink.

'I ran away,' she said.

'To the squat?'

She shook her head.

'Not then. I went to my teacher. She was nice, Miss Broxburn. She was the one who said I was good at writing. She was an older

80

lady, lived on her own. She said I could stay with her while I did my O levels.'

'So did you?'

Suze pinched her lips together.

'No,' she said flatly. 'Mum came and got me. She said I was a slut for making a move on Gordon and that I had to come home and make it up to her.'

I felt sick.

'She blamed you?' I said. 'That's awful.'

Suze carried on, like I'd not spoken.

'Gordon had gone by then,' she said. 'Mum was angry with me. She hated being on her own. So I knew it wouldn't be long until she found herself another fella and probably it would all start again.'

'One morning, I pretended I was going to school but instead I stole Mum's purse, then I got on a train and came to London.'

'And you were fourteen?' I was amazed by her courage and determination.

'Yes,' she said. 'I wanted to get a job, but it was hard without an address. And then I met this guy – Walter – and he said he had a place where I could crash. But his friends were, well, not nice …'

'Did you take drugs?' I said.

Suze shrugged.

'Drugs,' she said. 'Booze. Whatever. It helped me forget stuff.'

'How did you pay for them, Suze?' I said, not really wanting to know. 'How did you pay for the drugs?'

'I'm not proud of it,' she said fiercely, staring into her glass. 'I didn't choose it. I was just surviving …'

She paused for a moment, then she looked up at me. I half-expected her to be crying but her eyes were dry.

'Then Walter got nicked for something. Nothing major, but it was enough to lock him up for a bit. I saw my chance and took over the squat. I don't reckon he'll come back,' she said with what

I assumed was false bravado. 'He's pissed off too many people round here.'

The big padlock on the door made more sense now.

'I reckon you're right,' I said. I reached out and squeezed her hand. 'Sorry for dragging it all up again.'

'It's fine,' she said. 'I'm fine.'

Chapter 15

2016

Since I'd handled the whole Damo situation back in Oz so very badly, I'd forced myself to change from a stick-your-head-in-the-sand type of person to someone who faced my problems head-on. I'd learned that scary situations never got more scary if you dealt with them, and generally they got less frightening once you took them on. If I'd spoken to Damian about my change of heart maybe we could have sorted things out but instead I was left with the memory of him walking away from me on that sunny afternoon in Sydney.

As I stared at the dreadful sales figures for my first issue of Mode, though, I went back to my old default position of hiding away from problems. I knew I should go and speak to Lizzie about them but I just couldn't face it. I was worried she'd force me to tell her what I was going to do to shake things up and I wasn't ready yet. If I presented my ideas too soon – and she didn't like them – I'd probably have to abandon them and come up with something else and I didn't want to do that.

Instead, I replied to her email like a coward.

'Disappointing,' I typed. 'But not entirely surprising. Next issue should be different.'

I pressed send before I could add the apology I was itching to write, and sighed. These sales figures meant I had to be seen to be acting quickly and dramatically. I picked up my phone and called Jen.

'Busy?' I said.

'Reading page proofs,' she said, sounding like she'd rather be anywhere else.

'Spare me an hour?' I said. Jen's office wasn't far away and it was almost lunchtime.

I heard the relief in her voice.

'Your office?' she said. 'I'll be there in half an hour.'

Grinning to myself, I ended the call and pulled out the first issue of Mode again, and the issue of Home & Hearth. These magazines had a lot of stuff in them to read, I thought. They were more like Sunday supplements nowadays in that they covered fashion and style and newsy issues … and they had given me an idea. We had to give our readers more – and it wasn't free gifts they needed.

'What free gifts?' Damian was lurking in my office doorway again and I realised I'd been muttering out loud again.

'Would you stop doing that?' I said, smiling in spite of myself. 'I keep spilling my coffee.'

Damo crossed my office in one long stride and folded himself into the chair opposite me.

'Sorry,' he said, with an unapologetic grin. 'Thought you might want to know – I'm all yours.'

'You are?' I said, my heart beating a little bit faster with a mixture of relief and dread. 'When can you start?'

Damo shrugged.

'Now?' he said.

I raised an eyebrow.

'Don't you have Homme stuff to do?'

'Nah, it's all good,' he said. 'Might have to pop over and check some pages now and then but I'm out of there.'

'Can you stay now?' I said. 'Jen's on her way and I've got an idea to run past you.'

'Sure,' said Damo. 'I'll grab us some coffee and come back up in half an hour?'

'Great,' I said, trying my best to sound professional, even though my heart was racing. 'Get a latte for Jen too. See you in a bit.'

I bent my head to look at the old issues again. I could sense Damo watching me for a moment but I didn't look up until he was gone.

I greeted Jen like a returning hero when she arrived ten minutes later.

'Oh thank god you're here,' I said as she hurried into my office and shut the door behind her.

'What the bloody hell is that?' she said, gesturing outside. My office was like a glass box and through the large windows I could see the editorial team staring in with blatant hostility. Apart from sweet Emily who was typing madly with her headphones on.

'They're not very welcoming, are they?'

I laughed without any real humour.

'Riley's nice,' I said. 'But she's on a shoot today.'

Jen looked out at the office again and shuddered.

'Can we wait to do the introductions until she's back?'

A burst of laughter from outside made her raise her eyebrows in surprise and we both looked to see Damo coming past Vanessa's desk, carrying a paper tray with three coffees on it, and a box of doughnuts. He threw the box at Vanessa and she caught it, smiling. I was pleased to see she could actually smile.

'Doughnuts,' I hissed to Jen. 'I should have brought doughnuts.'

If only I'd known that was all it would take to make Vanessa smile, I'd have bought everything in Krispy Kreme.

Damo burst into the office and dumped the coffees on the table.

'Jen!' he said, sweeping her into a hug. I watched her head rest on his broad chest and felt a brief flare of envy that I immediately pushed aside. Professional, remember?

We all sat at the round table by the window and Damo and Jen looked at me, waiting for me to wow them with my amazing idea to save Mode.

'So like I said to Jen, we're theming the issues,' I said.

'Back to Basics was not great, but that wasn't surprising because it was a very last-minute decision. I feel a bit more in control now. Our next issue's theme is Body Confidence and we're theming the whole mag. Fashion, beauty, everything. We've got an interview with a plus-size fashion blogger, our cover star is Hayley Hanwell – that model who was attacked by her ex-boyfriend and whose face is scarred …'

Jen looked less than excited. I could almost hear her thinking, 'I gave up being editor for this?'

Undeterred, I ploughed on.

'We planned a vintage issue,' I said. 'And then Emily, my workie, gave me a pile of old issues …'

Jen looked faintly more interested. Damo slurped his coffee. I pulled out the issue of Home & Hearth I'd been looking at and held it up.

'This is amazing,' I said. 'Amazing. It's got so much in it.'

'It's a pie,' said Damo.

'Yeah, the cover's not great,' I admitted. 'But it's so well planned. It's got short pieces, humour, meatier features on some quite controversial issues … and this was aimed at housewives. The early issues of Mode are even more relevant.'

I looked past the others out into the office.

'They've got everything we haven't.'

Jen made a face.

'You got that right,' she said.

'So I want to recapture all this energy,' I said. 'Magazines are expensive, I understand that, so we need to give our readers a lot of content. A lot of good, worthwhile content.'

'You want to turn Mode into a news magazine?' said Jen in disgust.

'No,' I was annoyed that she wasn't getting it. 'Of course not. I'm not saying ditch fashion and beauty, or celebs – I love all that. I'm just saying young women are interested in more than shoes. They're intelligent. They're engaged. If we can tap into that, we're set.'

'You need to get digital on board,' said Jen. 'If you want to be newsier, then the web team is the place to start.'

'You're right,' I said.

'So we're still doing the themes?' Damo checked.

I nodded.

'Still theming, but I want us to think bigger, better, more off the wall,' I said. 'Different cover stars. Campaigns. Weightier features.'

Jen – finally – looked interested.

'I think this could be really exciting,' she said. 'It's what we've been talking about for years.'

I smiled. She was right. We'd always moaned about how young women were underestimated and undervalued.

'Hopefully it'll get the team's energy back and get them buzzing again,' I said.

I paused.

'And I have to be honest, our sales figures are dreadful,' I said. 'This is our last chance to turn things around. But I really think we can get people talking about this. We can get coverage in other publications. If we get the right cover stars we can syndicate those interviews. If we run some campaigns we can get lots of press ...'

Jen was smiling again, much to my relief.

'I think you're right,' she said. 'What's the PR department like here?'

I shrugged.

'Not sure,' I said.

'I know them,' Damo said. 'Felicity Jenkins is in charge. She's a great girl.'

I rolled my eyes inwardly. Of course Damo knew her.

'Could you ring her?' I said. 'Give her a heads up. Get her on board?'

Damo nodded.

'Sure,' he said.

I looked from him to Jen.

'So we're doing this?' I said.

They both nodded firmly and I grinned.

'Great,' I said. 'So now for the hard bit – getting the team on board.'

Chapter 16

I'd given a million presentations in my career, given talks at schools, hosted awards ceremonies, and run company meetings. But I was more nervous that morning than I'd ever been before. I wanted this to work so badly and I wasn't stupid – I knew with a shoestring budget, a skeleton staff and hardly any money, the odds were against us.

We gathered in the big meeting room at one end of the office. I perched on the wide windowsill at the top of the room, Jen by my side like a lucky mascot, and looked at the team. Emily looked at me expectantly, but everyone else was ignoring me. Riley – who was back from her shoot – and Damo were deep in conversation at the other end of the table and I felt a flicker of annoyance. Or was it jealousy? Either way, it bothered me.

I cleared my throat. No one looked up.

'Right,' I said loudly. A couple of people dragged their eyes up to me. Vanessa carried on doodling on her pad.

'As you know, things are tough,' I began. 'But I'm convinced Mode has a future and I'm determined we're the people to shape it.'

Someone sighed, but I carried on.

'We need to attack this on all sides. With distribution, pricing and with some really brilliant content.'

I didn't quite say 'tah-dah!' but I meant it.

There was a small murmur of interest, which I took as a good thing, but Pritti grimaced.

'What's the point?' she said. 'The magazine's closing anyway, what's the point of relaunching?'

I'd had it with negativity. I glared at her.

'The point,' I said, icy cold, 'is to make sure the magazine doesn't close. I know this is going to be hard. But everything that's worth doing is hard. It's a brilliant opportunity for you all – you're all great and this will lead to bigger and better things. But I need you all to put your heart and soul into it or it's not going to work. Are you all with me?'

You know that bit in Jerry Maguire when Tom Cruise writes that email and asks who's with him and no one stands up except Renee Zellweger? Yeah, it was like that. Without Renee.

Everyone just stared at their feet except Emily, who gave me a quick sympathetic grin.

I'd brought the pile of old issues into the meeting with me. Now I handed them out and I was gratified to see the first glimmers of interest in the team as they started to flick through them.

'You'll be able to see straight away just how much there is in these magazines,' I said.

'It would take you days to read all this,' said Riley, who was turning pages rapidly trying to find the fashion section.

'Exactly,' I said. 'I want to really give our readers something to talk about. I want them saying "oh I read this thing in Mode …" and I want them to feel like they're taking something away from our magazine.'

'We don't want to be preachy,' Jen said, and I gave her a quick grin. 'We just want to get people thinking.'

'I want cover stars who actually have something to say, rather than just promoting their latest film,' I said. 'Vanessa, Joanna

Fuller is perfect for that. See if you can interview her in the House of Commons and find out what it's like being a twenty-five-year-old female MP in a world of old men in suits.'

Vanessa nodded firmly.

'Humour's important too though,' I said. 'We don't want to be boring. There are loads of fab female comedians around – maybe one of them could write a column for us? Or someone might even make a cover star.'

'What about that woman who won the baking show?' Jen said. 'She could do some cookery features.'

'Great, yes,' I said. This was it – we were really getting somewhere. 'And we could do with getting a health expert and a fitness guru on board too. But they have to be people who really know what they're talking about. I don't want a reality star who's done a fitness video.'

Riley was leafing through the fashion pages and talking urgently to Pritti, the beauty editor, who was scribbling furious notes. Damo was listening to her ideas and pointing to something on the page as she talked. I caught Jen's eye and she winked.

'It's going to work,' she said in a low voice. 'This is brilliant.'

Emily caught my eye.

'You should speak to Suze Williams,' she said. 'I bet she'd have loads of ideas.'

'Oh wouldn't it be amazing to pick her brains?' I said.

'Whose brains?' said Jen.

I leafed through my papers and found the photo of the first Mode team. I showed it to Jen and pointed to the short-haired, smiley brunette at the end of the line. 'Suze Williams. She was editorial assistant when the magazine launched and she went on to become Mode's editor, but I'm not sure what happened to her after that.'

'She'd make a great feature herself,' Jen said. 'I bet she's got some brilliant stories to tell.'

'I Googled her but it's weird,' I said, opening my laptop. 'She was editor for about ten years, then she just disappeared in the late seventies.'

I typed her name into the search engine.

'Did she go to America maybe?' Jen suggested, peering over my shoulder.

'Doesn't look like it,' I said. 'Wiki just says she left Mode in 1979 and then it doesn't say what happened to her.'

Emily was on her phone, scrolling through search results.

'There's a mention of her here on this romance novels website,' she said. 'At least it might be her. It mentions a romance novelist called Susannah Harrison and then in brackets it says Suze Williams.'

She showed me the screen on her phone and I shrugged.

'It's plausible,' I said. 'Writing is writing and Harrison could be her married name, or a pen name.'

I typed Susannah Harrison into Google this time and found an author's biography on her website. She had written almost a hundred romance novels – the most recent one had been published last year so she was obviously still working.

'It says she lives in a village in Kent, with her dog,' I said.

'Does it say her real name is Suze Williams?' Jen asked.

I shook my head.

There's no mention of Suze Williams,' I said. 'But there is a contact-me form ...'

'Fill it in,' said Jen. 'We could really do with her expertise.'

'What if it's not her?'

She made a face.

'Then we keep looking.'

Quickly I wrote a message explaining who I was and what we needed and pressed send. Then I looked up at the team, who were all now crowded round Pritti, Riley and Damo, swapping ideas for features. Even Vanessa was adding some ideas and – I blinked in surprise – she was even smiling.

Jen squeezed my arm.

'You're a really good editor,' she said. 'And this is going to be a really good issue. It's going to be remembered for a long time.'

I squeezed her back.

'You think so?' I said.

She nodded and I sighed.

'I just hope it's enough to make the magazine work.

You're a really good editor,' she said. 'And this is going to be a really good issue. It's going to be remembered for a long time,' I said, and he said.
'You think so?' I said.
She nodded and I sighed.
'Just hope it's enough to make the magazine work.'

Chapter 17

After the meeting Damo went to sort out some last bits on Homme, Jen went back to her office, and my team all went for lunch. Without asking me to join them. Oh well, I had lots to do anyway.

I sat at my desk and thought about what I'd ask Suze Williams if I managed to get in touch with her. It would be amazing to get her take on modern magazines, I thought. Then, more gloomily, I wondered what she'd think of our most recent sales figures and whether she'd think we were a lost cause.

The phone on my desk rang, startling me out of my miserable musings.

'Hi Fearne, it's Kinga on reception,' she sang as I answered. 'Your mum is here for you.'

I laughed.

'Think you've got the wrong person,' I said. 'My mum's not here.'

But then I heard Mum's voice as she spoke to Kinga.

'I'll go straight up,' she said. 'Which floor?'

'Third,' Kinga said, as I said: 'No!'

Too late. Mum was here? What on earth for?

Fixing a smile on my face, I went to wait for her by the lift, trying not to grimace as the doors opened and she stepped out.

I had inherited Mum's hair and very little else. She wore her blonde waves shorter than me, above her chin in loose curls, and her colour was now more platinum than honey. Today she was wearing dark brown slim trousers, with flat leather Chelsea boots, a pale pink blouse and a loose brown slouchy wrap. She looked younger than her sixty-five years and very stylish.

'Darling,' she said, kissing me on the cheek then holding me at arm's length to look me up and down. 'What funny shoes.'

I was wearing blinding white Adidas trainers – hardly clown shoes – but I forced myself to smile, ignoring her comment.

'Mum,' I said. 'What are you doing here?'

'It's reading week for my students,' she said, with a wave of her hand. 'There are no lectures, so Daddy and I are having a day in town. I told you this.'

'You didn't,' I said.

Mum looked unapologetic.

'Oh I must have forgotten,' she said. 'It's been frantic at work and the bloody Today programme are never off the phone.'

'There's no downtime in economics, eh?' I muttered.

Mum gave me a sharp look.

'Where's Dad?' I said, before she could tell me how things were looking on the FTSE and what the pound was doing against the dollar.

'Oh he sends his love,' she said. 'He decided to pop in and see some old friends in Chambers.'

My dad had been a barrister before he retired. Now he pottered happily round his study in the attic of the big Oxford house where I'd grown up, writing legal textbooks and giving occasional lectures at the university. Rick, my brother, was also a barrister, and had an eye on becoming an MP one day. My love of fashion, magazines and the Kardashians made me something of an outsider at family parties. But it would have been nice to see my dad all the same.

'He's not coming?' I said, trying to look like I didn't care.

'I thought I'd take you for lunch,' Mum said, neatly sidestepping my question. 'He might pop in for coffee.'

'Lunch?' I said. 'Sorry, Mum. I can't come for lunch. I'm swamped.'

Mum looked over my shoulder at the empty office behind me and raised an arched eyebrow.

'I'm the boss,' I said. 'I have to set an example. I can't just skive off.'

'Set an example to whom?' Mum said.

'Fine,' I said, grudgingly. 'Let's go.'

We went to a smart restaurant on Wardour Street – I'd never been there before but Mum said she'd heard good things about it.

'I'm sorry about my daughter's shoes,' she said in a conspiratorial fashion to the waitress who showed us to a table. 'I know they're not strictly in keeping with your dress code.'

'Mum,' I hissed, amazed that I could manage a team and handle a budget and still be shown up by my own mother. 'It's fine.'

The waitress, who looked like she could not care less what I had on my feet, sat us down and handed us some menus.

'I think I used to come here in the sixties,' Mum said, looking round with a frown as we handed our menus to the waitress. 'It was a bit dingier back then.'

'Really?' I was relieved she'd taken her attention away from me.

'I was studying in London of course,' she said, thoughtfully. Mum had – obviously – gone to LSE and liked to remind me of it at every opportunity. 'And I used to come to Carnaby Street to look at the shops. I remember going to a party round here once. It was this amazing flat with a roof terrace and someone got cross about Bob Dylan and threw his record out of the window …'

I grinned. Finally some common ground.

'I've found a photo from that time. It's of the team that launched Mode,' I said. I leaned down and dug about in my bag for the picture of Suze Williams and the rest of them.

'What's Mode?' Mum reached for a breadstick.

I was pleased I was still bent over so she couldn't see my face. I'd found the photo but I gave myself a second to take a few deep breaths before I sat up again.

'Mode is the magazine I edit,' I said, through gritted teeth. 'It was the first magazine that was aimed just at young women and it launched in 1966. It was groundbreaking at the time, and it's been very successful ever since.'

I paused, aware I was reverting to type and trying desperately to impress her.

'It was fairly political back then – covering all sorts of women's issues. I'm trying to get back to those roots.'

Mum nodded politely.

'Because I'm in charge,' I added. 'And I don't think we should ignore young women's opinions.'

'That's it,' Mum said in triumph. And I beamed at her, pleased she was finally listening to what I had to say.

'Bands used to play here,' Mum said, gesturing with her breadstick. 'There was a stage over there, but the bar's in the same place, that's what made me recognise it. Oh we had some good nights out here.'

I stared at her.

'Great,' I said. 'Glad you had fun.'

'Sorry, darling. What were you saying?'

Mum dragged her gaze from the far wall of the restaurant and back to me.

'I want the magazine to cover more women's issues,' I said. 'Current affairs and how they'll affect young women. Engage with them more.'

I looked around for inspiration. A woman at the next table had shopping bags round her feet.

'Like how Brexit might make Zara more expensive,' I said.
Mum blinked at me.

'Who's Zara?' she said.

I sighed.

'Or something about the next American president,' I said
vaguely.

Mum smiled.

'Well done, darling,' she said, the way she congratulated her
cat when it ate all its dinner. 'Let me know if you want me to
write anything for you.'

I twisted my lips into a smile.

'Thanks,' I said. 'I will.'

The rest of lunch was easier, because I didn't try to talk. Mum
told me about the play she and Dad were going to see. She asked
if I'd read a piece Isabelle – my brother's girlfriend – had written
for the New Statesman and I lied and said I had. I'd actually seen
it on Facebook and read the introduction, so I could say enough
to start Mum off.

As she debated the pros and cons of Isabelle's arguments with
herself, I drifted off. I wondered if Mum's path had ever crossed
with Suze Williams's in the sixties. I couldn't imagine they hung
out in the same places. Mum had always been very career-driven,
spurred on – I always thought – by her desperation to leave the
Midlands market town where she'd grown up far, far behind. The
same sort of drive that got me out of Oxford, lovely though it
was, and down to London, via Sydney.

Mum was looking at her watch.

'I don't know what's happened to your father,' she said. 'I'll
have to meet him at the theatre.'

She started gathering her bits.

'You get off,' I said, almost aching with relief. 'Lunch is my
treat.'

Mum gave me a sympathetic glance.

'You don't have to do that, darling,' she said. 'I know things are tight for you. All those years when you were doing internships.'

'Long time ago,' I said. 'Honestly, my treat.'

'Thank you,' she said graciously. We kissed goodbye.

It was only when she'd gone that I discovered she'd left two twenty-pound notes on the table.

Chapter 18

1966

Suze wasn't fine.

The party was in an attic flat above a shop on Wardour Street.
Suze didn't know who lived there, and she didn't know whose
party it was.

'Is it a birthday party?' I asked as we walked along the road.
I could hear guitars playing in a bar across the road and three
girls, wearing identical baker boy hats on their identical long
straight hair, stood outside smoking.

Suze gave me a withering look.

'It's just a party,' she said. 'This is it.'

It was a door between two shop fronts and it had been propped
open with a shoe. I followed Suze up the narrow stairs, stepping
over a guy with long curly hair who was smoking a joint, and a
couple who were entwined so closely I could barely see where
one ended and the other began.

Suze, of course, knew lots of people though I was quickly
beginning to realise that she knew much more about other people
than they knew about her. She led me into the main room where
guests were standing around chatting, next to a trestle table

groaning with bottles of booze and a huge bowl with a ladle in it. One girl, who had straight black hair, right down to the hem of her – very short – skirt, was dancing with her eyes closed. Suze ladled some of the liquid from the bowl into a glass and thrust it into my hand.

'Here,' she said.

'What is it?' I smelled my drink. It was a lurid pink and had a whiff of aniseed.

Suze shook her head.

'Some sort of punch,' she said. 'Dunno what's in it.'

She drained her glass and refilled it.

'Come on,' she said. 'Don't be so square.'

I sipped gingerly at the strong drink and wondered if I could swap it for a beer without her noticing. I wasn't a big drinker – living with Dad had made me cautious about what it could do.

I wasn't sure if it was the booze, but there was something slightly wild about Suze tonight. It made me wary and I was very aware that I barely knew her. But I also felt a bit guilty. I'd more or less forced her to tell me about how she'd ended up in London and everything that had happened to her, and I wondered if that was the reason for her funny mood.

It was a good party – I thought. I'd never been anywhere like that before. Two men sat by the record player, choosing which songs to put on and people were dancing everywhere – even in the kitchen. A fog of smoke hung over the room and my eyes stung as I peered at everyone. Some of the girls were wearing gorgeous clothes and I saw one guest, who had a chic Mary Quant style bob and stark white lips, wearing a dress I'd been drooling over in Biba's window for weeks. It was like an assault on all my senses, my ears rang from the music – and from the arguments when one guy tried to put on a Bob Dylan record and the other one took it from the turntable and threw it out of the window. My tongue throbbed from the sweet punch, and the cloying stench of marijuana stuck to my hair. It was exhilarating and frightening.

I went to the toilet and shut the door, glad there was a lock. I was out of my depth here. For all my sassy girl-about-town persona, at heart I was just a little girl from the suburbs. I glanced at my watch, half-hoping I'd still have time to get the last train home but it was too late.

I flushed and washed my hands and opened the door. Two girls fell into the bathroom – they'd obviously been leaning against the door – and laughed uproariously. I stepped over them and went to find Suze.

She wasn't in the room with the music, or the kitchen. I opened the door to the bedroom and hissed her name, but there were just some guys in there, passing round a joint and playing a guitar – very badly. Had she gone home without me? What would I do? Beginning to panic, I went back into the living room.

'Nancy?'

I turned round. On the sofa in the corner, was George. He was sitting on the arm of the couch, his arm draped casually along the back. Sitting next to him was a girl wearing a long knitted waistcoat. She had a cloud of blonde curls and bright blue eyeshadow.

'George,' I said, gratified to see how he leapt to his feet as soon as he saw me. The girl he'd been talking to shut her eyes and started to snore softly, sitting upright on the sofa.

'I didn't expect to see you here,' he said. 'Not your usual hang out?'

'I came with Suze,' I said. 'But I've lost her and I'm meant to be staying at hers.'

'Have you been outside?'

'No,' I said, surprised. 'I didn't even know there was an outside.'

George tugged at my sleeve.

'I'll show you,' he said.

I followed him through the kitchen and out the back door onto a metal fire escape. We climbed a few stairs and came out onto a roof terrace.

'Wow,' I said. I pulled the sleeves of my dress down over my fingers – it was cold out here and I had no idea where my coat was.

It was a square, concrete space, with metal railings all around. But the view was amazing. I could see right down to the Houses of Parliament and across the rooftops of Soho.

'It's great, isn't it?' George said. 'I always want to photograph it but night-time pics never come out like I hope.'

'It's amazing,' I said. 'I love London at night – I always think it's like two cities. The daytime London and the night.'

I leaned on the railing and looked out into the darkness.

'It would be a good feature, I think,' I said, half to myself. 'Visit the same street in London at different times of the day and see how it changes.'

'That's a great idea,' George said. 'One of the Sunday papers would love that. I'll do the pictures.'

I dug about in my small shoulder bag for the notebook and pen I always carried with me.

'I'm writing it down,' I said, scribbling furiously. 'I'm going to pitch it on Monday.'

George laughed.

'Always working,' he said. I looked up at him and grinned and he held my gaze for a fraction too long. Then something caught his eye behind me and he looked away.

'There she is,' he said, nodding behind me. 'Suze. She looks a bit worse for wear.'

She was standing in a group of people, swaying slightly.

'Suze,' I called.

Suze whirled round. Her eyes were wide and glazed and I thought she didn't see me at first. Then she focused on me.

'Naaaaancy,' she said, wrapping her arms round my neck. 'Nancy, come and dance.'

'No,' I said, peeling her off me. 'I think it's time we went home.'

'Don't be such a bore,' she said, squinting at me. She stumbled and George caught her before she fell.

'George,' she said. 'Did you come to see Nancy?'

George grinned.

'Of course,' he said.

'I knew it,' Suze said, jabbing George's chest with a pointed finger. 'I knew you liked her. Didn't I know it, Nancy?'

I was mortified. I couldn't look George in the eye.

'Sorry,' I muttered. 'She's drunk.'

'She's more than drunk,' George said in my ear.

I was shocked but not surprised, really.

'Suze,' I said. 'Have you taken anything?'

Suze laughed sleepily.

'Only a tiny little Valium,' she said. 'I like how they make my head go all floaty.'

I groaned, feeling terrible. Suze was full of bravado, but now I realised just how fragile she really was. Obviously telling me what had happened to her had stirred up some memories that she was now trying her best to block out.

I gave her a hug, feeling how thin she was.

'I'm sorry,' I whispered in her ear. 'You'll be okay, Suze. You'll be fine.'

I looked at George over the top of her head and he understood what I was asking.

'Let's get her out of here,' he said.

'Come on, Suze,' I said, pulling her arm. 'Let's go.'

Thankfully, she let me lead her back down the metal staircase and into the flat. I found my coat, draped over a sleeping figure in the bedroom – I couldn't tell if it was a man or a woman – and carefully George and I steered Suze down the narrow steps and out onto the street.

'Thanks,' I said to George. 'I'll take her home – it's not far.'

'Let me help,' George said.

My fears of George being shocked by Suze's living arrangements were outweighed by my worries about getting Suze home in one piece.

'Okay,' I said. 'I'd appreciate it.'

With one of us on each of Suze's arms, we made slow progress down Wardour Street and eventually onto Peter Street. I found Suze's key in her pocket and unlocked the door.

'Shut it,' she slurred as we went inside. 'Shut it properly.'

I padlocked the door and showed her. She nodded approvingly and I exchanged a glance with George. Suze must be really frightened those guys would come back if she worried about it in the state she was in.

I helped her upstairs and into the living room. She slumped onto the bed and within seconds she was asleep. I pulled off her shoes, covered her in the thin blanket that was draped over the headboard, and sighed.

'Drink?' said George. I'd almost forgotten he was there.

He was holding out a small bottle of gin.

'Where did you get that?' I said.

'I pinched it from the kitchen at the party,' he said.

I gasped in mock horror.

'Thief,' I said.

George grinned.

'Got this too,' he said, producing a bottle of lemonade from his bag.

I laughed. I walked over to the counter that acted as Suze's kitchen and picked up two mugs.

I gave one to George and he slopped gin into first his, then mine. I peered into them and poured half of my gin into his mug, then I topped them both up with lemonade.

I threw myself onto the sofa and raised my mug to him.

'I guess we'd better get rid of those stolen goods, then,' I said. 'Cheers.'

Chapter 19

2016

When I got to the office the day after I'd met Mum for lunch – at the crack of dawn, obviously – I was amazed to see Damo already there. He was sitting at his computer, staring intently at the big screen.

"Sup," he said, without taking his eyes from the page he was looking at, as I passed.

"Sup?" I said, hoisting my gym bag further up my arm. "Sup? What are you, fifteen?"

Damo laughed.

'Good morning,' he said in an affected posh British accent.

I grinned.

'Better,' I said. 'What are you doing here so early?'

Damo pushed his chair away from his desk and leaned back so he could look up at me.

'I'm designing,' he said. 'I'm excited about this anniversary issue and I wanted to get started on a bit of a redesign. But we've got the current issue to finish as well, so I thought I'd come in early so I didn't get behind.'

I stared at him, open-mouthed.

'Oh don't look so surprised,' he said. 'I'm a bloody good designer and you know it.'

'When you want to be,' I said. 'On your terms.'

Damo looked uncharacteristically pissed off, his usual Aussie beach bum demeanour slipping for a second.

'I realise it probably eases your guilty conscience to paint me as a layabout loser,' he said, pushing his hair back from his face. 'But you know that's not true.'

I grimaced. He had the measure of me, all right. Always had.

'Sorry,' I whispered. 'It's just strange having you around.'

I felt a squirming in my stomach that could have been hunger but was more likely guilt. Or, I thought, as I looked at his firm jaw, set in annoyance, it might have been lust.

Shaken, I slapped him on the back like he'd just scored an excellent goal in a five-a-side football match.

'Keep up the good work,' I said cheerily. 'Show me what you've got later.'

Then I dived into my office.

'Well, Fearne, you handled that beautifully,' I muttered, dumping my gym stuff in the corner and switching on my computer. 'Keep up the good work. He's not running a 10km.'

'You left your coffee on my desk.' Damo had followed me into my office and I cringed all over again.

'Thanks,' I muttered, as he handed me the cup. 'I do appreciate you being here, you know.'

Damo grinned at me.

'No you don't,' he said. 'But you will.'

'Jen said she's going to hand in her notice today,' I said, changing the subject in a hurry. Since when did Damo make me feel so damn uncomfortable?

'Is she on three months' notice?' Damo asked. 'We'll have made all the changes before she can start.'

I shook my head.

107

'Just a month,' I said. 'She'll be here in time for the next issue.'

Like I'd willed it happen, my phone buzzed on my desk.

'That'll be her,' I said. 'Hope she's calling to say it's done.'

'Jen,' I said, as I pressed the button to answer the call. 'Are you with us?'

There was a silence on the other end, so long that I thought we'd been cut off. I took the phone away from my ear and looked at the screen – still connected.

'Jen?' I said again.

'I'm not coming,' she said.

I sat down heavily in my chair. Damo looked puzzled and I gestured for him to leave. He frowned but he didn't argue. He slunk out and shut the door behind him.

'What do you mean, you're not coming?'

Jen sighed. I could picture her twisting a piece of her hair round on itself as she talked.

'Vicki, the editor of Grace, is leaving,' she said.

'No. Way.' I was pleased – having her gone would make things easier for us. 'That's great news. Who told you?'

'The publisher,' Jen said. 'When he offered me the job.'

For a minute I didn't understand what she was saying to me. 'What job?'

'I'm the new editor of Grace, Fearne,' Jen said.

'You're the …' I was still bewildered.

'I'm Grace's editor. I start in a month.'

'But you're my deputy,' I said. 'You agreed.'

'That was before this came up,' she said. 'I can't turn it down. It's an amazing opportunity.'

I winced. She was repeating my own words back to me. The words I'd used when I'd run out on her and our plans for The Hive to take the job at Mode.

'How long have you known?' I said slowly.

'A week or so.' Jen sounded a bit sheepish. 'But they didn't officially offer it to me until yesterday afternoon.'

108

'All the meetings we had,' I said. 'All our ideas. You know exactly what we're planning.'

'Well, yes,' said Jen. 'I suppose I do.'

'I trusted you,' I said.

Jen snorted down the phone.

'Really?' she said. 'Just like I trusted you when you ran out on me?'

'Is that what this is about?' I said. 'Are you getting your own back?'

'Yes,' said Jen, her voice laced with sarcasm. 'That's what this is all about. I've worked really hard and won the job as editor on Britain's best-selling women's monthly magazine just to get revenge on you.'

I couldn't speak.

'What would you have done, Fearne. Honestly? In my position, what would you have done?'

I bit my lip.

'I'd have taken the job,' I said quietly.

'Well there we go,' said Jen. 'I learned from the best. Good luck with Mode, Fearne. I hope it works out for you.'

She hung up.

Carefully I stood up from my desk, shut my office door and twisted the blind pull to shut it. Then I went back to my chair and sat down with my head in my hands.

Just when I thought I was getting somewhere, this happened. It was a disaster. A setback so huge I wasn't sure we'd be able to come back from it.

Unable to decide whether to be furious or hurt, I switched on my computer and opened my emails. Going through some mindless press releases would distract me and let me work out how I was feeling.

I drummed my fingers on the desk as I scrolled through. It seemed fury was winning at the moment. I couldn't believe Jen would be so traitorous, so untrustworthy, and so …

I paused in my angry thoughts because I had an email from Susannah Harrison.

'Oh thank god,' I breathed. If she'd come on board and help us turn the magazine round, then perhaps it wouldn't matter that Jen was telling the team at Grace all our plans.

I took a slurp of flat white and clicked on the email to open it.

I half expected it to say Susannah Harrison had never heard of Suze Williams – that was how well things were working out for me – but it didn't say that. Instead, it said: 'Thank you for your interest. I'm afraid I can't help with your article. Please don't contact me again.'

I breathed out slowly. That was a fairly brutal brush off but, I thought as I read through it again, it didn't say we'd got the wrong woman. If it had, I'd have shrugged my shoulders, made a few more attempts to track down Suze and then given up. But it didn't. And that intrigued me.

I rooted around on my desk and found the photo of the first Mode team. I stared at Suze Williams. She was turned slightly away from the camera, a notebook clutched to her chest, and she was laughing. Then I called up the author biography on Susannah Harrison's website once more.

'Susannah lives in a village in Kent with her dog, Cooper, and enjoys taking long walks,' it said.

That didn't sound like the Suze in the picture, even if she'd be in her early seventies now. She didn't look like the sort of person who'd enjoy living in a village in Kent with a dog. And yet she hadn't said it wasn't her.

I got up and went to the door of my office.

'Damo,' I said. 'Can you help me?'

He loped into my office and looked at me, enquiringly.

'What do you think of this?' I said, showing him Susannah Harrison's email.

He read it, then he gave a quick nod.

110

'It's her,' he said. 'Definitely.'

I was thrilled.

'That's what I thought,' I said.

'Wonder why she's lying,' Damo said. 'That's interesting.'

'I know,' I said. 'Isn't it? I really want to find out.'

Damo gave a mock sigh.

'Oh I feel for poor Susannah,' he said. 'You're not going to leave her alone now, are you?'

I stared at him.

'This is for the good of Mode,' I said – perhaps a little over-dramatic. 'Jen's dropped us right in it.'

He gave me a questioning look.

'She's dumped us for Grace,' I said.

'Shit.'

'So it's vital we find bloody Suze Williams,' I said. 'Our jobs are on the line, Damian.'

He laughed.

'It's not because our jobs are on the line,' he said. 'It's because you're nosy and you can't resist a mystery.'

I was so pleased we'd gone back to our easy banter that I ignored the dig.

'I'm going to find her,' I said.

'Good luck with that,' Damo said, looking dubious. 'It's not easy to find someone who doesn't want to be found.'

He left me to it and I opened Google again.

Susannah Harrison village Kent, I typed. Up came several results, none of which were right. I scrolled through them slowly, seeing results from ancestry websites for someone called Susannah Kent who died in 1989, a school called Harrison Village Primary, and other annoying links between the words, until I came upon some minutes from a parish council meeting in 2010. There, buried deep among plans to clean up the war memorial, and arrangements for the summer fair, was the name Susannah Harrison.

'KP suggested local author Susannah Harrison might be approached to open the fair, but GT pointed out that she plays very little part in village life and is not likely to be amenable to the idea.'

That was her. I looked at the top of the page – the village was called Summerhurst. I pulled up a map and found it easily. It was tiny, but it was just the other side of Sevenoaks so it wasn't far away.

I switched the view on the map to photos and studied the pictures carefully. There were a few houses, a shop, a cafe and a pub. I didn't have Susannah Harrison's address but I reckoned someone there would know where she lived.

I sat for a few minutes, tapping my fingers on my desk, pretending that I wasn't about to do what I was about to do.

Then I picked up the early issues of Mode, my plans for next few issues and the photo of the staff from 1966 and stuffed them all in my bag.

Casually, like I was just popping out for a coffee, I sauntered out into the main office, and slunk over to Damo's desk.

'Can you hold the fort?' I muttered.

He looked up at me.

'Going to track down the mysterious Susannah,' he joked. Then he saw my face.

'Oh god, you are,' he said. 'Leave the poor woman alone.'

'I can't,' I said. 'I want to know why she doesn't want to know.'

Damo sighed. He pushed back his chair and picked up his bag.

'What are you doing?' I said.

'Coming with you.'

'No,' I said.

'She might be a crazy serial killer,' Damo said. 'The whole village could be. It might be like the Wicker Man.'

'It's in Kent,' I pointed out.

He shrugged.

'Still coming.'

'I need you here,' I said. 'You're in charge.'

'Ness?' Damo shouted to Vanessa, who was just taking off her coat. 'Can you take charge for a couple of hours?'

She flashed him a dazzling grin.

'Of course,' she said.

'Right,' Damo said. 'All sorted. Let's go.'

We stared at each other for a minute and I cursed myself as I looked away first.

'Fine,' I said. 'But don't talk to me.'

'No problemo,' said Damo. 'Onwards.'

Chapter 20

'See,' said Damo, as we climbed out of a taxi an hour or so later. 'Exactly like the Wicker Man.'

I grinned.

'Exactly,' I said.

Summerhurst was a sweet village on top of a hill. The taxi had dropped us by the pub, which overlooked a green. But it wasn't the old-fashioned, traditional place I'd expected. The pub – which was closed because it was still early – was painted in a chic grey, with a menu to rival any restaurant in town, and next door was a retro-style café. There were little boutiques, a deli, an artisan bakery and a mini Waitrose. It wasn't even ten a.m. so the shops were either closed or just beginning to open, though the café was busy.

'Coffee?' Damo said.

I nodded and followed him inside.

The place was packed – mostly with mums and babies – but we found a table near the window and sat down with flat whites.

'So we need a plan,' I said.

Damo chuckled.

'Why are you so desperate to find this woman?' he said.

I shook my head.

114

'Not sure,' I said. 'It's just with Jen leaving us in the lurch, I feel like she's our only hope.'

'She's not,' Damo said, seriously. 'She's really not. You're doing a good enough job by yourself.'

I looked down at the table top, uncomfortable with his compliments.

'Plus,' I said. 'I wasn't actually that bothered about tracking her down until she sent the email asking me to stop. Then it was all I could think about.'

Damo laughed again.

'Sounds about right,' he said. 'Contrary.'

'I'm not contrary,' I said. 'I'm nosy. And she worked on the first ever issue, Damo. The one I've read over and over trying to find its magic ingredient. And she went on to be Mode's longest-serving editor, and then she disappeared. That's got to be worth finding out more about. What if she's got a brilliant idea to save the magazine?'

'S'pose,' he said. 'How are we going to find her?'

'Well,' I said, lowering my voice. 'I thought we could have a walk round the village, and see if any of the houses look like they might be hers …'

Damo gave me a look that suggested I was crazy, then he got up and walked to the counter.

'G'day,' I heard him say, playing up the lost-Aussie-tourist thing. 'We're from Susannah Harrison's publishers down under. We're here for an important meeting with her and my colleague here has lost her address.'

I glowered at him, but the waitress was looking sympathetic as Damo leaned across the counter, all the better to show off the muscles in his tanned arms.

'Don't suppose you know where to find her, do you?'

The waitress leaned over too, so her face was close to Damo's. She was a pretty redhead with alabaster skin like Nicole Kidman's.

'She doesn't like visitors,' I heard her say. 'She's a bit prickly.'

'Oh don't we know it,' Damo laughed. 'The things we've had to promise her to get her to invite us round for a cuppa. The woman's a bloody nightmare.'

I put my head in my hands, wondering what on earth he was doing. But two seconds later he was back, with an address and a little map drawn on a napkin.

'Bingo,' he said.

I took the napkin in awe. Scrawled beneath the map was a phone number, the name Melissa, and a little smiley face. I showed it to Damo and he grinned.

'Still got it,' he said.

I snatched it back.

'Looks easy enough to find,' I said. 'Ready?'

Damo nodded.

'Ready,' he said.

We found the house without any trouble whatsoever. It was a small cottage at the end of a lane, with a well cared-for garden all around it – exactly where you'd imagine a romance author to live.

Together we walked up the path and I knocked on the door. There was no reply and I looked at Damo. I'd not considered that Susannah, or Suze, or whatever her name was, wouldn't be at home.

'Let's go back to the café and give it half an hour,' Damo said. 'She might just be walking her dogs or something.'

Despondent, we walked back towards the village green.

'I bet she's on holiday,' I said.

'If she's not there when we go back, we'll put a note through the door,' Damo said. Nothing ever got him riled up or gloomy – apart from me leaving him hanging in the middle of Sydney, of course. 'Then she knows how serious you are.'

I nodded.

As we turned the corner onto the main road through the village we passed a woman with a neat steely grey bob. She was carrying a Waitrose hessian bag and she had a small dog on a lead. She gave us a brief smile to acknowledge us and carried on walking the way we'd come.

We carried on a few steps and then I stopped and looked back at the woman.

'You go on,' I said to Damo. 'I'll catch you up.'

Damo looked at me and I smiled.

'Go on,' I said. 'Get me a tea will you?'

'That her?' he said, tilting his head towards the woman.

'She looks familiar,' I said. 'I just want to check.'

I turned and walked quickly after the woman and caught up with her just as she reached her garden gate.

'Excuse me,' I called.

She turned and smiled.

'Are you lost?'

I shook my head.

'No,' I said. 'I'm Fearne Summers. I emailed you? I'm the editor of Mode magazine …'

Straight away the woman's smile dropped.

'I asked you not to contact me,' she snapped. 'I'm not interested.'

'But you are Suze?' I said. 'Suze Williams?'

She looked sad for a minute.

'I've not been Suze Williams for a long time.'

She walked through the gate and shut it so it formed a barrier between her and me. But she didn't move. Instead she looked like she was going to say something. I waited, but she didn't speak so I jumped in.

'Mode's in trouble,' I said in a hurry. 'I've got a year to save it. I'm relaunching on a shoestring budget and I've been reading the first ever issue …'

I looked at the woman's face. She wasn't wearing any make-up but her hair was well cut and her clothes looked expensive. Those romance novels must be doing well, I thought. But it wasn't surprising. She'd been brilliant at Mode magazine, I imagined she was just as good at writing books.

She gave me a brief smile, though she still looked sad.

'We caused quite a stir with that issue,' she said.

My hopes raised, just a little bit, I ploughed on.

'I know,' I said. 'I want to cause a stir with ours too. That's why I thought you could help.'

The little dog barked at me and I took a step backwards.

'I found this picture,' I said, pulling the photograph out of my bag and handing it to her. 'I'd love to do a proper interview with you about launching Mode, too. Really I want any help you can give me.' I gave a little self-conscious giggle. 'I'm just a bit out of my depth and I so want to make it work.'

Susannah – Suze – stared at the photograph for a second, a little smile on her lips. The dog barked again and she bent down and took off its lead. It bounded away round the side of the house and into the back garden, I assumed. A cacophony of barking came from the direction he'd run in.

'He likes to chase the rabbits,' she said. 'But he's so loud about it, they all scarper before he gets a chance to catch them.'

I didn't care.

'Will you help me?' I asked. Begged, really. 'Will you help me save Mode?'

Suze smiled her sad smile again, and shook her head.

'I'm so sorry,' she said. 'I can't.'

Chapter 21

1966

'I am exhausted,' I said, slumping onto the wooden bench. 'But I think we've really got something good.'

George sat down next to me, cradling his camera like a baby. 'It's great,' he said.

We had spent all day working on the 'day in the life' feature that I'd had the idea for on the rooftop at the party.

With a bit of help from Rosemary, who seemed to have taken me under her wing and had even given me a day off from the magazine to work on this article, I'd approached one of the Sunday supplements. To my surprise they'd commissioned me to write a feature based around a park bench in Soho Square. So George and I had spent the day hanging round the garden and pouncing on everyone who sat down. I'd interviewed – and George had photographed – a group of kids from the nearby primary school and their teacher, a gardener, some office workers on their lunch, two women who worked in a fabric shop close by, and finally – as the sun went down – I spoke to two men. They were obviously a couple but, not surprisingly, were guarded about their romance at first. When I said I didn't have to identify them in the piece, they spoke candidly about how they'd met, told me how much a change in the law surrounding homosexuality would mean to them, and bickered good-naturedly about their plans for the future. I was enthralled and I knew it would be the perfect end to my piece. George photographed them from behind so they could stay anonymous, with their heads close together silhouetted against a street lamp, and they went off together, promising to look out for the article.

It was properly dark now and getting chilly, even though there had been a whiff of spring in the air during the day. I shivered and pulled my coat round me a bit tighter.

George looked at me.

'You did really well,' he said. 'I've worked with writers a lot more experienced than you who can't chat to people as easily as you do.'

I blushed, surprised how much his words meant to me.

'Everyone's got a story,' I muttered.

'I reckon the editor at the paper will want more like this,' he carried on. 'You could do park benches all over London. All over the country, even.'

I laughed.

'I could be the park bench correspondent,' I said. 'It would be good though. I've really enjoyed today.'

George nodded.

'Me too,' he said. He put his hand on top of mine. 'Me too.'

I felt the thrill in my stomach that I always felt when George touched me and reluctantly pulled my hand away. I'd not told him about Billy, though I knew I should. But we'd been working together more and spending time together, and I'd not quite got round to 'fessing up that I had a fiancé – probably for all the wrong reasons.

'What time do you need to be back?' George said, putting his camera into the case and starting to gather his things.

'I should probably get a train in an hour or so,' I said. 'But I need to pop in to see Suze first.'

'I'll walk back with you,' he said.

We strolled slowly back towards Peter Street, chatting about the people we'd met that day. As we went to cross Dean Street, though, I tripped over an uneven paving stone and George caught me just as I was about to tumble into the road.

'Careful,' he said. His arms were round me and I suddenly realised I didn't want him to let go.

I looked up at him. His brown hair fell across his eyes and I reached up and brushed it away. Then, not really thinking about what I was doing, I tilted my head up to his and kissed him.

Kissing George was very different from kissing Billy. Billy's kisses were dry and cautious, and left me wondering what all the fuss was about. But as George and I stood there, on the kerb, wound round each other, I understood. My heart pounded in my chest and my legs felt weak.

'Let's go out,' George said eventually, smiling down at me. 'Let me take you out.'

'Yes please,' I said, not caring about how tricky that would be with my dad and Billy, and everything really.

Hand in hand we walked back towards Suze's place so I could leave my notes there. I knocked firmly on the wooden panel that covered the door and George kissed me again.

'I'll let you know when I've developed the pics,' he said. 'I'll bring them round to Mode.'

'Okay,' I said, unable to stop smiling. 'I'll see you then.'

Hands in his pockets, he wandered off. I watched him go, grinning.

'What's up with you?' Suze had finally unlocked the door and was standing, hands on hips, on the step like I imagined some dads did when their daughters stayed out too late.

'Up?' I said, sailing past her and up the stairs. 'There's nothing up with me.'

Suze locked the door behind me and followed me into the lounge, looking at me suspiciously.

'You spend all day with George and now you come back with your head in the clouds?' she said. 'What happened?'

I threw my notebook onto my side of our shared desk, then twirled round and threw myself onto the sofa.

'I kissed him,' I announced.

Suze jumped up and down and clapped her hands.

'Finally,' she said. 'Did he kiss you back?'

'Yes,' I said. 'Of course he kissed me back.'

'Was it nice?'

'It was wonderful.'

Suze shoved my legs off the sofa and sat down next to me.

'It's all coming together,' she said. 'Our lives are beginning.'

Normally I laughed at Suze's over-dramatic declarations, but today I had to admit she had a point.

'Today went really well,' I said.

'I know,' she said, making a kissing face. 'You told me.'

I laughed.

'No, I meant the interviews,' I said. 'It's going to be a great article. Did you finish your piece for Viva?'

Suze nodded. She'd managed to make some brilliant contacts – people she'd met at another one of her endless parties, as far as I could tell. She knew a receptionist at a recording studio, a runner at a production company, lots of secretaries at BBC Television Centre – and she'd talked her way into Viva magazine. The editor – a man called Marcus who I found terrifying and who Suze said was a 'pussycat' – had asked her to write a series of pieces about up-and-coming bands, films, TV shows – anything that people would be talking about in the months to come. Suze was in her element. Her first piece was in the new issue of Viva and she'd been writing another about a gangster film that was coming out at the end of the year. She'd even interviewed the lead actor – a guy called Roy – who was, she assured me, going to be a big star.

Meanwhile, I'd also been getting lots of commissions alongside my regular work at Mode and Rosemary had been giving me more writing too. I was secretly hoping I'd be promoted to writer soon and she'd employ someone else to type up recipes and order envelopes.

My savings book – my running away fund – was looking very healthy and Suze and I talked a lot about getting a flat together. I knew it was what I wanted to do, but the thought of telling my dad I was moving out made me tremble.

'So are you going to tell him?' Suze asked now.

'George?' I said, suddenly feeling miserable as I considered telling him that I was engaged to another man. 'I should, I know. I have to be honest.'

Suze shook her head as though I was being very slow.

'Not George,' she said, carefully. 'Tell Billy. Tell Billy you've met someone else and you can't marry him. Or just tell him you can't marry him, it doesn't matter why.'

I stared at her.

'Dad would be furious,' I said. But even as I said it, I wondered if it was true. It depended on how much Dad had drunk and if he listened when I told him. Either way, though, it wouldn't be great. Either he'd be angry and probably give me a smack to show me what he thought, or he'd be silent and uninterested and prove just how little he cared.

'He might throw me out,' I added. 'Or make it impossible for me to stay.'

Suze shrugged.

'So live here,' she said. 'It wouldn't be for long. We've almost got enough money for a flat anyway.'

I felt a rush of excitement and fear.

'Okay,' I said. 'I'll do it.'

Chapter 22

I thought about what Suze had said all the way home on the train. I knew I couldn't carry on living this crazy double life. I was lying to Billy, and to George, and to Dad, and it was a terrible way to behave. I had to decide what I wanted – whether it was suburbia and marriage and a family with Billy, or my career and possibly a relationship with George. And I had to decide quite soon.

Billy was waiting for me outside the house, sitting on the garden wall, still in his mucky overalls from the garage.

'Didn't expect to see you,' I said.

'Just popped round,' he said. 'I was surprised you were at work so late.'

I looked at my watch.

'It's half eight,' I said. 'Dad not in?'

Billy shook his head.

'I knocked but he's not there,' he said. 'Must be down at the George.'

I groaned. Dad had probably come home after he'd shut the shop, discovered I wasn't there and his dinner wasn't on the table, so he'd gone out again. Now he'd be drunk when he came home. I'd have to make sure I was out of his way.

I pulled my keys out of my bag and opened the front door. Billy followed me inside and I tried to hide my irritation.

'I've got a lot to do, Bill,' I said. 'Dad needs dinner.'

He gave me a little half-smile.

'I wanted to see you, Nance,' he said. 'I've barely seen you for days.'

I felt guilty and cross at the same time.

'Sorry,' I said. 'I'm just busy, that's all.'

Billy put his arms round me and I froze, thinking about George.

'You won't have to work so hard when we get married,' he said. 'I'll look after you.'

I pushed him away gently.

'You can start now,' I said, making a joke to hide how uncomfortable I felt. 'There are potatoes that need peeling, but wash your hands first. Do you want to stay for dinner?'

Billy nodded.

'Your dad might be back soon,' he said carefully. I'd never told Bill about Dad's sudden angry moments, and he'd never asked, but I sometimes wondered if he knew how I got my bruises.

'He might be,' I said.

Billy rinsed his hands under the kitchen tap, scrubbing his fingernails with a kind of self-conscious concentration.

'Get an early night, won't you?' he said, fake-casually. 'Get upstairs as soon as I've gone.'

I didn't look at him. Just squeezed his arm so he knew I was grateful. He was a good man. He was. And once I'd thought he would be my salvation. But now I knew we wouldn't make each other happy. I'd not be the wife he wanted – or deserved – and I would be resentful and glum, knowing there was much more waiting for me elsewhere.

I pulled some leftover stew out of the fridge and dumped it in a pan to warm through. Billy whistled as he peeled the potatoes and I put them on to boil. Then he sat down at the kitchen table.

'Put the kettle on, Nancy,' he said. 'This is nice, ain't it? Us

125

being here, together. It's like a little taster of how it'll be when we're married.'

I filled the kettle and switched it on, trying not to think that he was right. This was a glimpse of what my life could be like. Billy home from work, sitting at the table in his dirty overalls, asking me to make him tea, while I cooked. Despite myself, I shuddered as I got the teapot down from a cupboard.

'Goose walk over your grave?' Billy laughed.

I opened my mouth to speak but no words came out.

'Nancy?' he said. 'Are you okay? You're being a bit strange. What's going on?'

'Nothing,' I said in a bright voice, gripping the teapot. 'Just work, you know. And wedding plans. Nothing much.'

'You're at work a lot,' Billy said, almost accusingly. 'More than you said you would be.'

'It's just busy right now,' I said truthfully. 'I'm getting more responsibility and things are going very well. They like me there, Bill. I'm good at what I do.'

Billy leaned back in his chair and regarded me.

'Oh la-di-da,' he said. 'Don't you be getting bigheaded.'.

His expression changed a bit. Became more serious.

'And don't let your dad hear you talking like that. He's expecting you to work in the shop, isn't he? This job is all well and good, but you've got other things to think about.'

I made a face.

'What if I don't want to work in the shop?' I said, surprising myself.

Billy gave me a fierce look.

'Is that what this is all about?' he said. 'You think you're above it all do you? Better than your dad and me. Now you're working in London?'

'That's not what I meant,' I said.

'There's nothing wrong with working in a shop, Nancy. It's a good business, that newsagent. Your dad's worked hard.'

'I know,' I said. 'I'm not la-di-da. I'm just enjoying doing something else, that's all.'

Billy's expression softened a bit.

'Look, Nance,' he said. 'I know your dad's a bit difficult sometimes. And I understand if you're nervous about working in the shop with him. But he's a good bloke, deep down.'

I snorted. Undeterred, Billy carried on.

'I just think it's worth you working in the shop for now,' he said. 'We might want to take it over one day.'

'What about the garage?' I said. Billy was a proper grease monkey and never happier than when he was underneath an engine. I couldn't imagine him getting up at the crack of dawn on a Sunday morning to sort out a pile of Telegraphs.

He grinned.

'We can have an empire,' he said. 'Or we'll sell the shop and expand the garage. Who knows? The world is our oyster.'

He chuckled but I felt the walls closing in on me.

'Beckenham's our oyster,' I muttered.

Billy pretended he hadn't heard.

'It's good to keep your options open, Nancy. And if that means putting up with your dad for a while longer, then I reckon it's worth it.'

He got up and came over to where I leaned against the Formica counter and gently put his hand on my tummy.

'Anyway, let's hope we'll have lots of little ones before too long and you can just stay at home and look after them.'

The stew was bubbling madly and relieved to have an excuse, I turned away from him.

'Dinner's ready,' I said.

Billy watched me carefully but he didn't say more. Instead he sat down at the table as I dolloped stew and potatoes onto three plates, covering Dad's with foil and putting it in the oven. Then I almost threw Billy's in front of him and looked down at my own. The thin gravy slopped over the side of the plate and the peas were wrinkled. I felt nausea rise up in my throat.

'I don't feel very well,' I said. 'I think I'd better go to bed.'

Billy looked surprised.

'What about dinner?' he said, a lump of beef hanging from his fork, halfway to his mouth.

'Eat,' I said. 'Let yourself out.'

I blew him a kiss and fled upstairs, pausing at the front door to pick up a letter from Dennis that I'd missed on the way in.

Upstairs, I pulled on my nightie and crawled under the duvet feeling shaky and sick. I felt like I'd been in a cage and though I'd once seen Billy as the one to open the door and set me free, I now realised what he was offering me was another prison.

I tore open Dennis's letter, hoping his funny tales about the boys he taught would make me feel better, but instead of his usual pages of neat handwriting, he'd simply scrawled on one sheet torn from an exercise book.

'Nancy!' he wrote. 'The headmaster needs a secretary. I've told him all about you and he says he'd love to meet you. Come and stay, flutter your eyelashes at him and the job's as good as yours. We could get a place together and Dad can't complain if I'm looking after you. What do you think? Let me know as soon as you can. Telephone me at work. Dennis.'

I stared at the letter. Once it would have been welcome – another escape from my life with Dad. But not now. Not now I had Suze, and George, and a career. I adored Dennis but living with him wasn't the answer either.

Stuffing the paper under my pillow, I closed my eyes. I'd made my choice.

Chapter 23

2016

Generally speaking I wasn't a crier. I was a coper. When things went wrong, I gritted my teeth, put my head down and got on with it, until they went right.

But it had been a difficult couple of months and Suze – or Susannah, or whatever her name was – turning me down was the final straw.

'I'm sorry,' she said, walking up the path to her cottage, still holding tight to the photograph of the first Mode team. 'I really can't help you.'

She opened the front door and flashed me a small apologetic smile over her shoulder.

What I meant to do was thank her politely, turn on my heel, find Damo and come up with a new plan. What I actually did was wail: 'Please don't shut the door!'

Startled, she stopped and stared at me. I tried to smile but I couldn't. I felt tears hot in my eyes and even though I blinked I couldn't stop them falling.

'It's supposed to be the best job in the world,' I said, gripping on to the rails of the iron garden gate like a prisoner, my voice quivering. 'But it's all gone wroooooong.'

Suze looked like she was going to say something, but she didn't. Encouraged, I opened the gate and followed her up the path, but she gave me a quick sympathetic grimace and stuffing the photograph into her pocket, she shut the door.

Embarrassed and annoyed and horribly aware that I wasn't acting like the editor of Mode was expected to act, I discovered that once I'd started crying, I couldn't stop. I sat down on the doorstep of the cute cottage, pulled my knees up to my chest and wept.

After a while, the little dog bounded up to me, licked the knee of my Whistles trousers, which were soaked with salty tears – the horror – and then scratched at the front door.

Interested, I raised my head. Suze said the dog could get in the back door, right? So why was it trying to get in here? Was she standing on the other side, listening to me crying my eyes out?

I wiped away a tear and took a breath.

'It's called imposter syndrome,' I said, in a tone that suggested I was simply carrying on a conversation, albeit a bit of a teary one.

'I wrote a feature on it for my old magazine – imposter syndrome. It's that feeling that you're going to be found out. That you're faking it. That one day soon, someone's going to track you down and tell you there's been a terrible mistake. You're not supposed to be editor of Mode. How ridiculous. Clear your desk and get out.'

I stopped and listened. There was no response from the other side of the door, but I thought I heard a floorboard creak. The little dog had sat himself on the step next to me, so he obviously thought it was worth carrying on.

'I think with me it goes back to my parents,' I said, giving little laugh. 'Doesn't it always? Nothing I did was ever good enough for them. It still isn't. They don't value creative talent – writing

isn't a job in their eyes, unless you're writing text books or articles for The Economist. I should have been in banking, or law,
or done anything that makes a lot of money and sucks out your
soul ...'

I took another deep breath.

'I've spent my whole life trying to get this job,' I said. 'I have
always wanted to be editor of a glossy magazine and I worked
really hard to get here.

'I've worked long hours. I've worked at weekends. I've got not
social life to speak of except in the summer when I spend every
Saturday at other people's weddings, trying to avoid being set up
with one of the ushers. And now all those brides are having
babies, and I've not even had a boyfriend for years ...'

I shifted slightly on the step.

'And when I did have a boyfriend, I dumped him for the sake
of a job.'

It might have been my imagination, but I thought I heard
movement on the other side of the door. Hoping Suze was on
the other side and I wasn't losing my mind, I went on.

'As for friends,' I said, with a hollow, mirthless laugh. 'I'm not
sure anyone likes me very much.'

I thought of Jen's face when I told her I didn't want to launch
The Hive like we'd planned.

'I've treated my best friend dreadfully,' I said. 'I let her down
and abandoned all our plans just because this job came along
and I didn't want to miss out. And she forgave me. At first.'

I took a breath.

'She came to some meetings, heard all about what we were
planning – and then she took a job as editor of Grace magazine,
which is the reason Mode is doing so badly.'

I paused for a minute as I thought about just what a massive
problem Jen going to Grace was.

'And I couldn't get cross with her, of course, because she's
basically done exactly what I did to her.'

The floorboard on the other side of the door creaked again.

So, it's been a long road,' I said. 'I've dumped boyfriends, treated my friends like shit, and given up anything remotely resembling a social life for my career. I've done all that to get this job at Mode. So when they approached me I was thrilled. The publisher emailed and asked me to have lunch with her. I couldn't believe it – it was all so easy. I've always believed that to make it in life you have to work really hard – that's why I hate the X Factor and shows like that. Those people just want success given to them. They're not interested in grafting.'

Aware I was babbling, I tried to focus on my point.

'Anyway, when Lizzie asked me to lunch, I thought that was it. All my hard work had paid off. And it seemed like that at first. It really did. I was pleased with myself. Smug, even. I'd made all those sacrifices and now it was coming together.

'But on my first day, they told me the magazine was sinking and they'd really only brought me in to close it.'

I felt myself close to tears again.

'They've only given me a few months to turn it round,' I said breathlessly. 'I've got no budget, an unenthusiastic team and one brilliant editorial assistant, and now the person I trusted with my ideas has gone to run the competition. It's like climbing Mount bloody Everest wearing flip flops. But even though it seems hopeless, I'm not giving up. I'm going to do this, I am. I just need a bit of help …'

On the other side of the door, I heard the sound of a lock turning. The little dog gave me a triumphant look, barked once, then ran off round the side of the cottage.

I stood up, slowly, feeling my knees crack because I'd been curled up for too long.

Eventually, after what seemed like forever, the door opened and Suze stood there.

'Imposter syndrome?' she said.

I nodded.

She bit her lip, making her look very young despite her steely grey hair.

'I know all about that.'

'Will you help me?' I said, desperate for her to agree. 'Please?'

She stepped back away from the door so I could go into the cottage.

'What do you need?' she asked.

Chapter 24

While Suze made tea, I texted Damo to tell him I was going to be at least an hour and to head back to the office if he wanted. Then I settled down on the over-stuffed sofa and looked round. It was quite a small room with a low ceiling but it wasn't dark in the slightest. The walls were painted a warm white and the wooden floor was stained a light oak colour. The sofa I sat on was also white, with a blue stripe, and opposite me was a wing-backed chair upholstered in a gorgeous flowery fabric. The whole room was like an advert for countryside chic. Suze obviously had exquisite taste.

The alcove to the side of the open fire was lined with shelves which were brimming with books. I got up and went to look. Suze – Susannah Harrison – had written most of them.

'I always feel like I'm showing off having them in this room,' Suze said, coming into the room with a tray of tea. 'But I can't have too many books upstairs in the study because the floor's not strong enough to hold the weight.'

I fought the urge to look up and check the ceiling wasn't about to come down.

'It's a beautiful house,' I said. 'It's very quiet.'

Suze smiled. She sat down on the sofa and poured tea into two cups.

'Milk?'

I nodded.

'I wanted a complete change from London,' she said. 'But I'm near enough to visit once in a while.'

'Why did you give up magazines?' I asked. I hadn't meant to be so direct, but I couldn't square the Suze I was talking to now – in this quiet, stylish cottage – with the bubbly sixties fashionista in the picture Emily had found. 'Did you always want to write romances?'

Suze laughed.

'God, no,' she said. 'I wrote the first one almost by mistake. It was like I was writing the story of how I wanted my life to turn out. But then a contact who worked for a publisher read it, she offered me a deal and I decided to give it a go.'

I must have looked doubtful. I couldn't understand why anyone would give up editing the most famous women's mag in the country, at the most exciting time in magazines, to write what I saw as throwaway romantic novels.

'Don't dismiss what I do,' Suze said mildly but with a definite barb in her tone. 'Romantic fiction sells by the bucket-load. I may not be in the running for the Booker Prize but I make a good living. A very good living.'

I gave her a rueful smile and sat down next to her.

'Sorry,' I said. 'I'm so consumed by Mode that I can't see anything else.'

'I was like that once,' Suze said, handing me a cup of tea. 'I understand.'

'Do you miss it?'

'Not any more,' said Suze, offering me a biscuit. 'I did at first, of course. I missed the whole life. It was such a wonderful time …'

She trailed off, lost in her memories, then shook her head and looked at me.

'I'm not sure I can help you much,' she said.

135

I pulled all my papers out of my bag and thrust them at her.

'I've got nine months to save the magazine,' I explained. 'I want to make people talk about it, but with my tiny budget it's not easy. So I need to do something that will grab everyone's attention. We've been planning to theme the issues, but now Jen's gone to Grace so they'll be a step ahead of us and I think we might need to do something else. I'm sort of desperate.'

Suze was sorting through the bundle I'd given her. She pulled out my battered copy of the first issue and gazed at it in wonder.

'I worked on this,' she said. 'Oh it was such hard work – but what fun we had.'

She began turning the pages, and I bit my lip so I wouldn't talk and interrupt her train of thought. I wanted her to tell me what she remembered.

'I slept under my desk one night,' she said, giggling and looking like the girl in the old photo. 'I didn't even live that far away but it was just easier to curl up on the floor with a blanket because we'd worked so late.'

I grinned. This was what I wanted.

'We thought we weren't going to finish in time. Our editor, Margi, was like a thing possessed, calling in favours, getting help from anyone she could. But we did it. And it was wonderful.'

'I love it,' I said. 'It's got such energy.'

'Energy?' Suze said, resting her hand on one of the open pages.

'Yes, that's it, exactly. It almost had a life of its own.'

There was a pause.

'That's what I need to get back,' I said. 'Mode is tired. My team are fed up. I need to bring back that energy and give it some life. We're planning a vintage theme for the anniversary issue, but I'm not sure that's enough to really capture the spirit of those early years.'

Suze looked distinctly unimpressed, which was pretty much how I felt.

'I've read the issue over and over,' I said. 'It's just so brilliant and even though it's fifty years old, lots of the articles are still relevant today.'

I took the magazine from Suze and flicked through it until I found the feature on illegal abortion. 'This one, for example,' I said. 'You could write that today and it would still work. You could base it on Northern Ireland – abortion's still illegal there …'

I tailed off as my thoughts took over. Could we do exactly that? Write updated versions of the articles that were in the first issue?

Suze was watching me, a smile on her face.

'Idea?' she said.

'Maybe.' I tapped my fingers on the cover of the magazine. 'What if, instead of doing a vintage issue, we relaunch Mode with a version of the first issue?'

Suze made a face.

'A fifty-year-old magazine isn't going to win over the readers,' she said. 'Even their grandmothers wouldn't remember our first issue.'

'I don't just mean re-printing it as it was,' I said. 'I mean giving it a twenty-first century twist.'

'Go on,' said Suze, giving me an approving look.

Slowly I tried to put my idea into words.

'We could stick to the themes of each article, broadly,' I said. 'As with the illegal abortion feature …' I began leafing through the issue, explaining how we could update each story. Suze listened intently and it struck me that she perhaps missed magazines even more than she'd realised.

'Good,' said Suze. 'That's good.'

I smiled and turned on to the next feature.

'I could commission someone to write about why they don't want kids,' I said. 'This feature here, about why the writer never wants to be a mother, is just as relevant as it was then. Shocking in a different way, perhaps, but still relevant.'

Suze had a strange expression on her face.

'Are you okay?' I said.

'Nancy Harrison wrote that piece,' she said.

I looked at the name on the byline and nodded.

'Yes, Nancy Harrison,' I agreed. 'Oh, Harrison? As in Susannah Harrison. Are you related?'

Suze had gone quite pale.

'Not related,' she said. 'Not as such.'

'Friends?' I said.

She made a funny jerky movement that could have been a nod but equally could have been her shaking for no.

'Friends?' she said. 'I suppose so.'

'So Susannah Harrison is …?'

'When I needed a pen name,' Suze said slowly, as though she'd never said these words in this order before, 'I thought of Nancy and I used her surname.'

'Are you still in touch with Nancy?' I asked, wondering why talking about this mysterious writer from the sixties was having such an effect on Suze. 'Did she mind that you'd used her name?'

'In touch with her?' Suze said, giving a tiny laugh. 'That's a good one.'

I had no idea what was going on.

'Where is Nancy now?' I asked. 'Where's Nancy Harrison?'

'Oh she's dead,' Suze said. 'Dead.'

I was mortified. No wonder she was acting so strangely if one of her friends had just passed away.

'I'm so sorry,' I said. 'Was it recent?'

Suze stared at me.

'Recent?' she said. 'Not at all. Nancy died in 1966.'

Chapter 25

1966

'Just tell him,' Suze said to me impatiently a week or so later. We were having lunch at Bruno's. She was treating me with the proceeds of another article she'd written for Viva.

'Just bloody tell him you're not getting married.'

'I will,' I said. 'I will. It's just hard to say the words. He's nice, my Billy. He doesn't deserve me breaking his heart.'

Suze rolled her eyes and sipped her Coke.

'You need to put yourself first,' she said.

I shook my head.

'Billy's not done anything wrong,' I said. 'I need to be gentle.'

Suze looked put out.

'You've not done anything wrong, either.'

'No,' I said. 'Yes. Maybe. I don't know. I just feel so guilty.'

Suze leaned over the table and pushed up the sleeve of my blouse, too fast for me to pull my arm away. I had a row of bruises on my wrist from where Dad had grabbed me the night before.

'Your dad?' Suze said.

'He didn't mean it,' I said. 'He'd had one too many and

139

misjudged how hard he'd gripped when he asked me to get him another beer from the fridge.'

'I'd hate to see how hard he hits when he does mean it,' Suze said. 'Look, I know you think you owe Billy, but I don't see him helping you get away from your father.'

I shrugged.

'He doesn't know,' I said, knowing he did really.

'You need to make the break,' she said. 'Get out of your dad's house and get rid of Billy.'

'I know,' I said. 'You're right. I'm not arguing with you. I'm just saying it's hard. I'm scared.'

'We're doing well,' Suze said. 'We're making money. We're getting our names out there. We could rent somewhere now.'

'It's all a bit haphazard though,' I said, finding it hard to be as positive as she was. 'A bit here and a bit there. If we just had proper writing jobs we'd be set.'

'You mean if I had a proper writing job,' Suze said. 'You already have one.'

I grinned.

'I've got a typing-recipes job,' I said. 'But I'm really hoping Rosemary might promote me to writer soon.'

'And then I could come and type recipes,' Suze said.

I raised my eyebrow.

'You'd last five minutes typing recipes,' I said. 'Why don't you ask your friend at Viva for a job?'

'I'm going to,' Suze said. She popped a tomato into her mouth and signalled to Bruno for the bill. 'I'm setting up an interview that he'll be so impressed with that he'll be begging me to work with him.'

'Oh yeah?' I said. I was slightly envious of Suze's amazing knack at making contacts and her easy confidence when it came to asking people for interviews.

'Who with?'

'That would be telling,' she said, pulling some notes out of her

140

bra – Suze never carried a purse – and laying them down for Bruno, whose eyes were almost popping out of his head. 'I have to dash.'

She blew me a kiss and wiggled out of the booth. Bruno watched her go admiringly.

'That girl is making waves,' he said.

'I believe you're right,' I said, giggling.

I wandered back to work, still wondering who Suze's interview was with. Could it be Cilla Black? Tom Jones? The Beatles, even? Nothing would surprise me.

I sat down at my typewriter and rolled in a fresh sheet of paper, trying not to think about Suze wowing Paul McCartney when I was typing up a recipe for something called stargazy pie.

'Nancy?' Rosemary called me across the office. 'Can I have a word?'

I felt a surge of adrenaline. Was this it? Was she about to promote me? Would stargazy pie be the last recipe I ever typed?

Rosemary shut the door to her office behind me and I felt nervous all over again as I sat down, clasping my hands together so they stopped shaking.

'Nancy,' she said. 'I just wanted to catch up and let you know how impressed I've been with your work.'

I beamed at her.

'In fact, I was boasting about you to a friend of mine, Margi Matthews, the other day,' she carried on. 'And it's backfired on me a bit ...'

My hands started shaking even more. I wasn't sure where she was going with this. But she was smiling, so maybe it wasn't bad. Concentrate, Nancy ...

'Margi is editor of a magazine in New York, called Mode,' Rosemary was saying. 'It's a magazine aimed at young women. It's quite ...' she paused and gave me a wry smile. 'Quite modern.'

'Good,' I said. I still wasn't sure what that had to do with me.

'I've been asked to take over as editor,' she said.

'In New York?' I said, excited for her. 'Oh well done, that's good news. I'll miss you though.'

I was telling the truth – I had really appreciated Rosemary's help with my career so far.

Rosemary smiled. 'There's a vacancy in New York because Margi's coming to London,' she went on. 'She's launching Mode in Britain. Most of her team is in place but she needs a junior writer.'

My head started to spin.

'I thought of you straight away,' Rosemary said. 'You're exactly what she's looking for – young, talented, keen.'

I couldn't speak. I simply stared at Rosemary, trying to work out if what she was saying was real or if I was dreaming.

'What,' I stammered. 'What should I do?'

'It's not going to be easy,' Rosemary said, briskly. 'I'm not the only person Margi's spoken to for recommendations, so there are going to be lots of girls like you going for this job. But you've got just as much chance as them.'

'Should I write?' I said.

Rosemary handed me a sheet of paper.

'It's all here,' she said. 'You need to put together some of your best articles and write a covering letter, too. I'm happy to have a look at it before you send it off.'

'Thank you,' I said. 'I really appreciate your help with this.'

Back at my desk I couldn't stop smiling. This was it. Things were happening – just like Suze said.

Oh.

Suze.

My stomach fell into my white PVC boots.

I had to tell Suze about the job. How could I not? But then she'd want to apply too. And with her fabulous portfolio of interviews and all the articles she'd written for Viva, she was bound to be chosen instead of me.

I put my head in my hands. What on earth should I do?

'Penny for them.'

I looked up to see George standing next to my desk. Immediately I blushed. I'd not seen him since we'd kissed because he'd been sent away on a job the next day.

'Hi,' I said. 'Are you bringing some pictures for Rosemary?'

'No,' he said. 'For you. The day-in-the-life pics.'

He put them on my desk with a flourish.

'Oh George,' I said, leafing through them. 'These are wonderful. Is the paper pleased?'

He looked proud.

'Very,' he said. 'They've commissioned me to do some more stuff.'

Thrilled, I jumped up and threw my arms round him.

'That's so great,' I said, all awkwardness forgotten. 'I've had some good news, too.'

I filled him in on everything Rosemary had said and he grinned at me.

'This is perfect for you,' he said.

'I know,' I agreed. 'There's just one problem.'

'Suze?' he said.

'Suze.'

I screwed my nose up.

'I have to tell her about it,' I said. 'But I'm being mean because I don't want to. She's better than me, George. What if she gets the job and I don't?'

George gave me a good-natured punch on the arm.

'She's not better than you,' he said. 'She's a good writer but you're great. She's got some good ideas – but so do you.'

'She's got bloody Beatles interviews in her portfolio,' I said gloomily – and untruthfully.

George shrugged.

'Your portfolio is good too,' he said. 'And you've got Rosemary on your side. I'd say it's a pretty even match. And you never know, they might have more than one job going.'

I looked up at him.

'You think I can do it?'

He nodded.

'I know you can,' he said.

Chapter 26

In the end, though, I didn't have to tell Suze anything. She already knew.

She was waiting for me outside the office when I left work later.

'I have to go home today,' I said. 'I can't be late. I promised Dad I'd be home for dinner. He's got some friend coming and I've got to get things ready.'

'I've got huge news,' she said, ignoring me.

I stopped and looked at her.

'Me too,' I said. 'Bet it's the same news.'

Suze gave me her blinding smile.

'Mode,' she said. 'Mode's coming to London.'

She gripped my arm.

'We're going to get jobs there,' she said. 'I've got it all worked out.'

I giggled, despite myself.

'I do need to go home,' I said. 'But walk with me to Charing Cross and tell me your plan.'

Arm in arm we sauntered through Soho, Suze gabbling nineteen to the dozen.

'So Marcus told me about the job,' she said. 'He's friends with the editor in America ...'

'So is Rosemary,' I said. 'She told me the same thing.'

'Amazing,' Suze breathed. 'It's all coming together.'

'Except,' I pointed out. 'There's only one job.'

I took a breath.

'You're bound to get it,' I said. 'Your contacts are great.'

'You'll get it,' Suze argued. 'You've got more writing experience and you've written for quite a few magazines now.'

'I almost didn't tell you,' I said quietly. 'I thought if I didn't tell you I'd have more chance.'

Suze waved her hand as though my confession meant nothing at all.

'Oh I know,' she said. 'I thought the same. But we're a team, right? We work together. Two heads are better than one.'

'Rosemary said they only needed one junior writer,' I said. 'But George reckons they might need more. If we can impress them enough.'

'Exactly,' said Suze, dragging me across the Strand in front of the number 15 bus. 'We'll make them see they need both of us. My contacts and your writing skills. We're a team.'

'Rosemary said I was to write a cover letter and send some examples of my work,' I said. 'Is that what Marcus told you?'

'Yes,' said Suze. We paused outside the station. 'That's easy enough to do – we can do that now and send it off. But I've been thinking about when we go and meet this Margi.'

'Meet her?'

Suze looked impatient.

'Yes, she'll want to meet us,' she said. 'We'll get an interview. Of course we will.'

I grinned at her optimism.

'So why don't we give them more?'

'More?'

'I thought we could do a dummy magazine – both of us together. We can mock it up with features and interviews we've already done. We've probably got enough between us to fill a

146

whole mag and if not, we can write some more. We can write some stuff that we'd like to read – like we talked about, remember?'

I thought back to the first night in Suze's squat, when we imagined our ideal magazine, and felt a thrill run through me.

'Do you think we can do it?' I said. 'We've not got much time – Margi's coming to London in a month.'

'We can definitely do it,' Suze said. 'More than that, we have to do it. We're in the right place at the right time, Nancy. We need to grab this opportunity with both hands.'

She clasped my hands.

'This is our moment,' she said. 'The only way to make our dreams come true is to work bloody hard and do it ourselves.'

'It's going to be tough,' I said, half to myself. 'I'll have to tell Billy and Dad that we're working on a project or something, so I can stay late every evening.'

Suze grinned.

'That's the spirit,' she said.

'I bet George would help us,' I said, warming to the idea. 'He can help with layouts and pictures. We're good at words, but it would help to have someone arty on board.'

'Perfect,' she said.

'And when we send our letters this week we should both mention each other,' I pointed out. 'If we're a team we should say so.'

Suze laughed in delight.

'That's what I thought,' she said.

I bounced on the balls of my feet, like Suze did, feeling a surge of excitement.

'This is it,' I said. 'You're right, Suze. This is it.'

She flung her arms round me and squeezed.

'A new life,' she said.

A thought struck me.

'What will I do about Billy?' I said.

'Just break it off,' Suze said, like she was talking about something as straightforward as making a cup of tea, not breaking an engagement and shattering Billy's heart. 'Tell him you've met someone else and you can't marry him.'

'Urgh,' I said. 'You make it sound so easy.'

'It is easy,' Suze said. 'You won't have time to see him anyway, because we're going to be working evenings and weekends.'

She gave me a sly glance.

'And you'll be spending lots and lots of time with George ...'

I nudged her.

'Don't,' I said. 'Don't tease me.'

'Lots and lots of time for talking to George,' she said, giggling. 'And for laughing with George. And for kissing George ...'

I groaned.

'Oh goodness,' I said. 'I need to break up with Billy.'

Suze looked at me.

'You really do,' she said.

I looked at my watch.

'My train,' I said. I gave her a quick hug.

'We're a team,' I called over my shoulder as I dashed across the station to the platform. Suze gave me a thumbs up.

As I changed my clothes and wiped off my make-up in the tiny train toilet, I wondered if my days of living my double life were at an end. If I could get a job on Mode, and get a flat with Suze, everything would be so different. I imagined us working hard in the day – wearing fabulous clothes of course – and spending our nights at parties and concerts. Hanging out with pop stars and actors. Laughing with John Lennon.

'Oh John,' I'd say. 'I'm flattered, I really am. But I've got a boyfriend. His name's George. He's a photographer.'

It sounded perfect. It was so far away from working in the shop with Dad and marrying Billy that I almost ached with how much I wanted it. But I knew it wasn't going to be easy.

For once, though, things worked out. As it turned out, Dad's friend was a local business contact – a man called Graham, who ran a chain of estate agents. Dad may have had a drinking problem and a temper, but out of the house he could charm the birds from the trees when he wanted to. He was very good at his job and a popular member of the local businessmen's association – which was what Graham had come round to chat with him about.

Knowing Dad would want to make a good impression, I saw my chance as we sat down to eat.

'And how is your job going,' asked Graham. 'It's insurance, isn't it?'

I nodded, hoping he wouldn't ask me anything complicated.

'I'm learning a lot,' I said. 'I've actually been asked to work on an important project.'

'What kind of project?' Dad grunted.

'Next year's budgets,' I said. 'Learning how to do financial projections will be very useful for when I work in the shop.'

I had no idea what a financial projection was, but I was hoping it sounded confident enough to impress Graham – and by extension, Dad.

Graham smiled.

'It is useful,' he said. 'But I thought you were getting married.'

I bristled.

'Not for a while,' I said cheerfully. 'I'm going to make myself useful to Dad first.'

I gave Dad a sweet smile and forked up some mashed potato.

'This project is going to really change things,' I said. 'It's going to be very hard work. I'll have to work evenings and maybe weekends too.'

'What about the shop?' Dad said. 'I need you at weekends.'

'I can do both,' I said. 'I'm not afraid of a bit of hard work.'

Graham was nodding approvingly.

'I like a grafter,' he said. 'You've got a good one here, Frank. Even if she is a girl.'

Dad patted my hand.

'She's an asset, my Nancy,' he said. It was the nicest thing I'd ever heard him say about me, and it hurt to know he was only saying it to impress his friend. 'She's got a bright future.'

Chapter 27

2016

I was almost lost for words.

'Nancy Harrison died in 1966?' I stammered.

'She died before the first issue came out,' Suze said.

'How sad,' I said helplessly. I wasn't one for girly chats and outpourings of emotion and I wasn't really sure what I should be saying.

'Do you still miss her?' I said.

Suze gave that funny little laugh again.

'Not at all,' she said.

We both sat side by side in awkward silence for a few minutes. I was wondering how I could make my excuses and get the hell out of there – it had been a very bad idea.

'This was a very bad idea,' Suze said suddenly, looking much older again. 'I am sorry.'

I couldn't help myself – I started to giggle.

'That's exactly what I was about to say,' I said. 'A very bad idea.'

Suze giggled too.

'Disastrous,' she said.

We were both laughing properly now.

'I'm not sure why I thought this would be the right thing to do,' I said in between laughter, and realising I was seconds away from crying again – this job had turned me into an emotional wreck. 'Everything else to do with Mode has been a bloody misery from the off.'

'You don't mean that,' Suze said. 'I heard what you said about making sacrifices.'

'I do,' I said. 'I mean every word. I'm even working with my bloody ex-boyfriend. Why would anyone ever think that's a good idea?'

Suze chuckled again.

'I should probably just get on a train, go to the office and tell Lizzie that it's over,' I said, back to being morose again now our laughter had died down. 'It makes no sense to keep the magazine going when it's inevitably going to close. It's not fair on the team.'

Suze patted my hand.

'It's Mode,' she said.

'Yes.'

'Think of all the women who have read it,' she said. 'Think of all the women who read one feature in Mode over the years and recognised themselves, or their situation, or their hopes and dreams.'

'I was one of them, once,' I said.

'And your dream was to edit the magazine,' Suze pointed out. 'And now you're doing it. Surely you're not just going to give up?'

Supple as a snake, she suddenly slid off the sofa and sat cross-legged on the floor beside the coffee table.

I blinked in surprise.

'I always used to work on the floor,' she said. 'When we were starting out, we'd spread all our features on the floor. I always thought it was the best way – so we could see what fitted together.'

'You and the team at Mode?' I asked, settling down next to her.

'No,' she said. 'Before I got the job. When it was just me and …'

She paused then she smiled at me.

'Just me and Nancy,' she said.

She was quiet for a second, then she clapped her hands and made me jump.

'Right,' she said. 'Show me what you've got.'

While Suze made yet more tea, I carefully laid out photocopies of the features from the 1966 edition of Mode across her cream carpet. Then we talked through each one, discussing how it could be brought up to date and how we could approach them. I jotted down all the ideas on Post-it notes and stuck them on each page.

Eventually, Suze and I stood and looked at the pulled-apart magazines, mugs in hand, and sighed.

'Oh. My. God.' I said. 'I've got so much to do.'

I felt hopeless. Relaunching the mag was a huge job. I couldn't possibly pull it off in the time we had.

I looked at Suze, expecting her to look horrified at the sheer scale of what we were attempting, but she didn't. Her cheeks were flushed and she looked excited.

'It's too much,' I said.

'It's difficult,' Suze agreed, bouncing on her toes like a little girl. 'But it's not impossible. Not at all. It's going to be a lot of fun.'

'You think?' I was doubtful.

'I know,' she said. 'I've done this before, remember? Working on the first issue of Mode was one of the best experiences of my life. There was no rulebook – we were writing the rulebook. It was just so much fun.'

I rolled my eyes.

'Well, unfortunately, I've got a rulebook,' I said, but Suze was already shaking her head.

'You don't,' she said. 'You don't.'

She clutched my arm in excitement.

'Because you can't make things any worse,' she said.

I grimaced.

'Thanks for reminding me.'

'No, this is brilliant,' she said. 'It feels good when you've got nothing left to lose.'

I started to catch on to what she was saying.

'If I do nothing – change nothing – Mode will close,' I said slowly. 'So doing anything at all has to be better than that.'

'Exactly,' Suze said, her face flushed with triumph. 'So take some risks. Do whatever you want to do. Rewrite the bloody rule book that we wrote in 1966.'

I started to feel her enthusiasm rubbing off on me.

'No one had ever done a feature on illegal abortions,' Suze said. 'Obviously the papers had covered it in a kind of po-faced way, but no one had ever spoken to the real women who were out there, having abortions and risking their lives in the process. We did.'

I nodded.

'We did a feature about sex,' she went on. 'Actual sex. In a time when women weren't really supposed to enjoy it. A year or so later we did lots of features about being gay – when the law on homosexuality changed. We were breaking rules left, right and centre. People wrote whole newspaper articles about how we were proving that the moral code of Britain was in decline. Our editor had to go on the news, more than once, to defend what we were doing. But we kept doing it.'

I couldn't imagine going on Newsnight to tell Kirsty Wark why I published a feature on abortion, but I did feel butterflies at the thought of breaking rules and making our mark on British culture.

'Okay then,' I said, let's do this.

I ended up spending the whole morning and quite a lot of the afternoon with Suze as we pulled apart and re-imagined every feature in the 1966 issue. She was full of ideas and surprisingly

154

clued-up on current trends in magazines. She was less savvy with digital plans but once I'd explained how the magazine fed into the website and vice versa, she was totally on board.

'What about the cover?' she said. 'We used models in those days, but it's all celebrities now.'

'Do you know Amy Lavender?' I said. Suze nodded. 'She'd be brilliant. She's gorgeous and she even looks a bit like your original cover model. We can style her in a sixties-inspired outfit.'

'She's really fun, isn't she?' Suze said, thoughtfully. 'I remember seeing her on that dancing show. So why don't you get someone to film your cover shoot?' she said. 'They're always a hoot if you have the right model. You can edit the film and put it on the website.'

Impressed with Suze's ideas, I added that one to my already bulging notebook. I'd been so right to come. Suze's energy was amazing and I was already plotting to get her to the office to inspire my jaded team.

'Let's go for lunch,' I said, looking at my watch and realising with surprise that it was already three o'clock. 'A very late lunch. My treat.'

Suze nodded.

'I'm starving,' she said. 'All this planning has taken it out of me.'

She hurried off to get her coat and I fished my phone out of my bag. I had five missed calls from Damo, a couple from Emily, and even one from Vanessa. I fired off texts to them all, explaining where I was and how brilliant it was.

Emily replied straight away.

'Amazeballs,' she wrote. I rolled my eyes. 'Ask her if she'll do an interview. Ask her if I can interview her about being editorial assistant on the first issue. I can compare her life then to mine now.'

That was a brilliant idea, I thought. Emily really was a find. She'd be editor of Mode one day – if I didn't manage to close it first. As Suze came back into the room, wearing a classic beige mac and a gold scarf, I took a chance.

'There's another feature we want to do,' I said, shoving all my papers back into my bag and picking up my own coat. 'Sort of a "day in the life" of our editorial assistant, Emily.'

Suze nodded.

'And she'd really like to compare her life with yours,' I went on. 'She can interview you, and write it up. We'll shoot you together. It'll be really interesting.'

But Suze had gone pale.

'No,' she said. 'Absolutely not. I left that life behind a long time ago. I don't want to be a part of it.'

'But it'll be great,' I said. 'Shoots are loads of fun. We'll get your hair and make-up done, and a stylist, not that you need one ...'

Suze was taking off her coat.

'I'm sorry Fearne,' she said. 'I'm Susannah Harrison now. I can't go back to being Suze Williams. There's too much at stake.'

'Your books?' I said, not understanding.

'Not really,' she said. 'People. People are at stake.'

I stared at her open-mouthed.

'I'm so sorry, I've just remembered I've got plans for lunch,' Suze said. 'It was lovely to meet you.'

She started bustling me towards the front door.

'It was lovely to meet you too,' I said, not sure what was happening.

Suze opened the door and I stepped out.

'Suze,' I said.

'Susannah,' she corrected.

'Susannah. Can we meet again?'

She looked at me for a second, all sorts of emotions showing in her beautiful face. Then she shook her head.

'I don't think so,' she said. Then she shut the door.

Chapter 28

I wasn't completely sure what had just happened. One minute we were laughing and making plans for lunch, and the next I was on the doorstep on my own.

Stunned into stillness, I stood there for a minute or two, then I rang the bell. I heard the little dog barking but Suze didn't come. 'I have spent too long on this sodding doorstep today,' I muttered to myself. I pushed all my papers and notes into my canvas bag, picked up my handbag, spun round and left.

Now the shock of being turfed out of Suze's cottage was wearing off I was starting to feel angry. How dare she slam the door in my face? Who did she think she was?

I stewed about it all the way back to Sevenoaks in a cab, then I stewed even more when I discovered a branch had fallen down on to the line and all the trains were delayed. And when I eventually made it back to the office, past six o'clock, clutching a sandwich and a coffee, and discovered the whole team had already gone home, I was furious.

I marched into my office and threw my bag of notes in the corner. There was a pile of page proofs on my desk to read and though I'd been checking my emails all day, I felt out of the loop and out of sorts.

Working at Mode felt like an endless cycle of excitement and disappointment. I felt so helpless and as though nothing I did was ever going to work out.

Peeling the wrapper off my sandwich, and feeling very sorry for myself, I settled down at my desk to read the pages.

'How are you doing?' Damo's voice made me jump.

He wandered into my office, picked up the other half of my sandwich and sat down.

'I thought you'd gone home,' I said.

'Gym,' Damo said through a mouthful of chicken and avocado. 'Just came back to pick up my keys.'

I shrugged, not remotely interested in his fitness regime.

'How was Suze?' he said, reaching for my coffee to wash down my sandwich. I slapped his hand away.

'That's mine,' I said. 'She was lovely and completely bewildering.'

'What do you mean?'

'Long story,' I said, throwing my sandwich packet in the bin.

'I'm not going anywhere,' said Damo. He flashed me his most winning smile. 'Fancy a drink?'

I had planned a hot date with my pyjamas, a large bar of chocolate and the season finale of The Good Wife, but what the heck. I nodded. Vigorously.

'Yes please,' I said. 'More than one, in fact.'

Damo grinned again.

'Last one to the bar's a loser,' he said.

We went to the pub next door to the office. Damo bought me a bottle of beer, which I'd actually not drunk since I left Oz but it had been a strange sort of day so I didn't argue, and then he settled down opposite me.

'Spill,' he said.

I swigged my beer.

'It was brilliant,' I said. 'She was so switched on. We went through the whole mag, and she gave me some amazing ideas. I was starting to think about asking her to come on board as an editorial consultant or something ...'

'So why was it confusing?' Damo asked.

'As soon as I mentioned us doing an interview with her, she shut down,' I said, glugging some more lager. 'She wouldn't even consider it. Then she shoved me out of her house and shut the door in my face.'

'Ouch,' said Damo. 'You obviously upset her.'

'Well, yes, I realise that,' I said. 'But how? All I said was we wanted to do a "day in the life" comparing how Emily lives now and how she lived when Mode launched.'

Damo frowned.

'That was it?'

I nodded.

'Apart from a bit early when she'd talked about a friend who died just before the magazine launched, she was fine all day,' I said.

'Was her friend working on the mag too?'

I nodded.

'She wrote a couple of features in the first issue,' I said. 'Nancy Harrison, her name was. Suze took her surname as a pseudonym when she started writing.'

'Oh that's sad,' Damo said. 'Maybe you just brought back some bad memories for her. The time you'd be asking about – the launch of the mag – must have been when her friend died.'

I slapped my hand to my forehead in horror.

'Oh of course,' I said. 'There's me breezing on about comparing rents and what they had for lunch, and she'd have been thinking about her friend.'

Damo shrugged.

'So call her and apologise,' he said. 'It's not the end of the world.'

'S'pose,' I said. 'I feel bad, though. She's helped me so much.'

'So send her flowers, then call her and apologise,' Damo said.

159

'You made a mistake, that's all. Don't beat yourself up about it.'

'I'm making a lot of mistakes lately,' I said, staring down the neck of my bottle. 'In the time I've been working at Mode, I've gone from being this completely together, successful woman to a disaster.'

'That's not true,' Damo said, holding my gaze for a fraction too long until I looked away. 'You were never together.'

Despite myself I laughed, then groaned.

'Oh but it is true,' I said. 'I'd got it all sorted, you know? And now it's falling apart.'

'You'll get it back,' Damo said. 'You always do. You're Fearne Summers, editor extraordinaire. You're winning at life.'

'Hardly,' I snorted. 'My career's gone to shit, I live on my own with only some dying houseplants for company, I annoyed my best friend so much that she treated me just as badly as I'd treated her and I can't even blame her, and …'

I stopped. What I'd been about to say was that working with him, spending time with him, was reminding me what we'd had. And that I'd carefully packed my memories of him away in a part of my head labelled Sydney 2009. Back in the UK it was easy to rewrite my past and pretend my relationship with Damo had just been an extended holiday romance – something that belonged to a different me, like wearing flip flops to the office or spending Christmas Day on the beach with a load of other ex-pats. It – and he – had all seemed so far away from London. But now he was here. In my office and in my head and acting so normal, and it was messing with my compartmentalising.

'And?' Damo said.

'Pardon?'

'Your career's gone to shit, you're a sad loner, you've pissed off Jen, and …?'

'There was no "and",' I said hurriedly.

'It sounded like there was an "and".'

'No,' I said. 'No "and".'

Damo looked at me a bit strangely.

'No?'

'No.'

I forced myself to smile.

'Isn't that enough?'

'I guess,' Damo said. But he didn't look like he believed me.

'So as I was saying,' I said. 'Everything's ruined.'

Damo leaned forward. A bit of his hair flopped into his eyes and I fought the urge to push it back. Instead of looking at his face, I focused on his arms. His tanned, well-muscled arms ... okay that didn't help. I looked up at his face again.

'It's not ruined,' he said. 'It just looks that way. You have to look at things differently.'

'Like there's no such thing as problems, just opportunities?' I said, my voice heavy with sarcasm.

'No,' said Damo, picking up my empty beer bottle. 'By getting drunk.'

Chapter 29

1966

I had honestly never been so happy.

Every day I worked at Home & Hearth as usual. Then I dashed out of the office and headed straight to Suze's where we worked on our articles for a couple of hours. It was really hard to create an entire magazine when there were only two of us. Suze was right, we had written a lot of features between us, but we didn't have nearly enough. We also had to write all the other pages in the magazine – contents, and news pages, and fashion spreads, and all sorts. It was exhausting, it was never-ending, I was worried we wouldn't finish in time for Margi arriving in London, and I was absolutely and completely loving every minute.

I'd hardly seen Dad. He went to the shop early in the morning – before I left to catch my train – and he was often in bed by the time I got home. Each morning I prepared his dinner and left it in the fridge with some instructions about what to do with it. It was mostly sandwiches, or cold meat and salad and boiled eggs, but I'd not had any complaints. He left his dirty plate on the worktop each evening and I washed it up when I got home. I got the impression that Dad was happier when he didn't see me and

I wondered – not for the first time – if he just couldn't cope with being around me. I looked more like my mum every day so I must have been a constant reminder for Dad.

Suze and I were working really hard – but we were having a lot of fun, too. I stayed with Suze at the squat some nights and once we'd finished our work, we went to parties. London was like a wonderland where everything was changing and no one played by the rules any more. For the first time I felt as though I was part of it and it was everything I'd dreamed about.

Suze had been working some lunchtime shifts in Bruno's café, where she eavesdropped on everyone's conversations. As a result she knew about every television show that was being written, who was recording a new album, where bands were playing – everything.

We shamelessly exploited all her knowledge and turned up everywhere. People began recognising us.

'There's SuzeandNancy,' they'd say, making our two names into one. I was never sure anyone knew which of us was Suze and which was Nancy. I knew we looked alike, with our slight builds and dark hair – mine long and Suze's short. And it didn't seem to matter who was who.

'SuzeandNancy said Michael Caine is going to this party tonight ...' we'd hear people say. Or 'SuzeandNancy will be watching Dusty Springfield sing later,' or even 'SuzeandNancy are coming to watch the play so it must be good ...'

It was as though we were winning. For years – decades – centuries even – older people had made the rules. They'd dictated what was in the news, what people wore, what we talked about, what we watched or listened to or read. But not any more. Now it was the young people who were making news. The Beatles were more popular than Jesus, and everyone was talking about our music and our films and our books – Suze and I were determined to get them talking about our magazines, too.

And then there was George.

The day after Suze and I decided to make our own magazine to wow the bosses at Mode, I went to see him in my lunch hour. I found him perched on the bonnet of Frank's car, which was parked on Carnaby Street, smoking a cigarette and chatting to a man with a handlebar moustache and who was wearing a cape. I raised my eyebrow at George as the man said goodbye and he laughed.

'He's a brilliant photographer, but he is a bit eccentric,' he said. 'He loves that cape. Watch him swirl it when he goes round the corner.'

We both looked as the man whipped his cape round as he turned into Beak Street, and collapsed into giggles.

'Here to see Frank?' George asked, jumping off the car and brushing off his trousers.

'No,' I said. 'I'm here to see you. Suze and I have a favour to ask.'

'Interesting,' said George with a grin. He offered me his arm. 'Shall we walk and talk?'

I looped my arm through his and we strolled off down Carnaby Street, towards Oxford Circus.

'Suze and I have decided to throw everything at getting a job on Mode magazine,' I explained. 'We're making our own magazine and we wondered if you could give us a hand with some layouts.'

George looked pleased.

'Me?' he said. 'Really? But I'm a photographer.'

'I know that, silly,' I said, chuckling. 'But you've got a good eye, haven't you. You're artier than we are – we're just good with words.'

'I'd love to,' he said, squeezing my arm. I felt a shiver run right through me. It was so right, walking arm in arm with George. I didn't feel awkward or embarrassed like I did when Billy took my hand. I was proud and I wanted to see people I knew and have them see me and George together, like a unit.

We reached the end of Carnaby Street and turned right onto Great Marlborough Street.

'So,' George said, ultra-casual. 'I suppose we'll have to spend a lot of time together.'

'Yes,' I said. 'A lot of time. Every day, I think. Will it be awful for you?'

George stopped walking and pulled on my arm so I turned to face him.

'It's going to be terrible,' he said, bending to kiss me. Immediately my legs turned to mush again – he had such an effect on me, it was incredible. I let myself relax into his kiss for a moment, then I pulled away.

'George,' I said.

'Uh-oh, that sounds bad,' he said, studying my face. 'I didn't like how you said my name.'

I grinned.

'It's not bad,' I said. 'Well, it sounds bad, but it's not, honestly. It's just complicated.'

I threaded my arm through his again and we carried on walking.

'I'm engaged,' I said.

George stopped again and stared at me. I could see he was hurt and it made me feel awful so I hurried on.

'I'm breaking it off,' I said. 'I don't want to marry him. I don't want to marry anyone. I didn't mean to get engaged.'

'It was an accident, was it?' he said.

I shrugged.

'It was, a bit,' I said.

I sat on a bench close to where we stood.

'Can I explain?' I asked.

Reluctantly, George sat down next to me. He looked wary.

Slowly, I started to tell him what my dad was like, how my mum had died and how Dad drank and lashed out because he was grieving.

165

'When I was younger, I just wanted a way out,' I said. 'Billy was part of that.'

George nodded. His lips were pressed together into a thin white line.

'He didn't even ask me to marry him, not properly,' I went on. 'It was just assumed that's what we'd do. I thought marrying Billy would save me but now I know it won't. I have to save myself.'

George nodded again.

'Go on.'

'Suze and I are going to get a flat,' I said. 'And I'm going to break up with Billy. I don't want that life. And I don't want Billy.'

George watched a bus rumble down Great Marlborough Street.

'What do you want?' he said.

I took his hand, thankful he didn't resist.

'I want to work at Mode,' I said. 'I want to live in a flat with Suze and I want you to be my boyfriend.'

George gave me a small smile.

'What about Billy?' he said.

'Billy's a nice man,' I said. 'He's a good person and he'll make a lovely husband for someone. But not for me.'

George played with my fingers.

'When are you going to do it?' he said.

'I'm going to see him tonight,' I said, making my mind up on the spot. 'I really like you George and I want us to be together. But Billy hasn't done anything wrong. It wouldn't be fair for me to be with you while I'm still engaged to him.'

George smiled properly now.

'You're a softie, Nancy,' he said. 'Lots of girls wouldn't care. They'd have blokes all over London. But not you.'

I shook my head.

'I tell lies every day,' I said. 'My dad doesn't even know I work on a magazine. He thinks I work in insurance.'

George laughed.

'Amazing,' he said, sounding quite impressed. 'Nothing will stand in your way, will it?'

'Nothing,' I said, astonished at how bold I was being. 'I want to work on Mode. I want to live with Suze, and I want you to be my boyfriend.'

'Then who am I to stand in your way,' George said. He stood up again. 'I would love to be your boyfriend, Nancy. Just as soon as you break poor Billy's heart.'

'Oh don't,' I said, hunching my shoulders. I looped my arm through George's again, and we began walking back towards my office. 'I'm dreading it.'

George looked right at me.

'This is the start of your new life,' he said. 'It starts here.'

Chapter 30

Breaking up with Billy was harder than I'd imagined it could be. He was terribly upset and I felt awful.

We were in the park, sitting by the bandstand watching a group of teenage boys who were pretending to be the Beatles.

'I don't understand,' he said, looking at me with bewildered eyes. 'We had a party. People bought us presents.'

We actually hadn't opened the presents yet. They were all still in a pile on the dressing table in my bedroom.

'We'll send them back,' I said. 'The presents don't matter.'

'It was all arranged,' Billy said.

'It wasn't,' I pointed out. 'We hadn't set a date.'

Billy glared at me.

'But I gave you a ring,' he said. 'We agreed.'

I had taken my ring off earlier and put it back in the small velvet box from the jewellery shop on the high street. I'd been gripping it in the pocket of my mac, and now I took it out and handed it to him.

'Sorry,' I said, trying not to mind that he hadn't said anything about love. 'You'll realise this is the best thing to do.'

'For who?' Billy said. 'For you?'

I watched one of the teenage boys do a passable impression of Paul McCartney's tilty head, then I looked at Billy.

'Yes, actually,' I said. 'For me.'

He stared at me, eyes narrowed.

'And you're the only one who matters, are you?'

'No,' I said. 'But the world's changing, Billy. I want more than just being a wife and a mother.'

He shook his head.

'What do you want?'

'I want it all,' I said simply. 'I want a job and a flat and friends. There's so much happening out there – music and films and television and magazines – and I want to be a part of it.'

I waved my arm in the vague direction of the Crystal Palace tower and beyond it, the centre of town.

'It's all so exciting,' I began. But Billy was gazing at me, understanding spreading across his face.

'You're not interested in accounts,' he said.

I looked at my feet.

'You're not spending all this time learning about book keeping, are you?'

I grimaced, wondering what to say.

'Is there someone else?' Billy said. 'Is that what all this is about? You're not spending any time with me, so there must be someone else.'

'No,' I said, trying not to think of George. 'Of course not.'

Billy looked at me through narrowed eyes, clearly suspecting me of lying. Which I was, I supposed, in a way.

'Then it's your job,' Billy said, in a flash of uncharacteristic insight. 'You're lying about your job.'

Reluctantly I nodded.

'I don't work for an insurance company,' I admitted.

'Do you work at a magazine?' he said. He knew how much I

169

loved the mags my dad sold, so it wasn't a huge jump for him to make.

I nodded again.

'I do.'

Billy was silent.

'I would have told you,' I said. 'But I didn't want you to be part of my lie.'

'Which one?' he said.

'Pardon?'

'Which magazine?'

'It's called Home & Hearth,' I said. 'It's for housewives.'

'Those terrible housewives,' Billy said, raising an eyebrow. 'The ones you can't bear to think of ever being like.'

'I mostly type recipes,' I said, making a face. 'I should be a wonderful cook by now.'

Billy almost – almost – smiled.

'What about if I said I didn't mind,' he said. 'I'm a modern man. I would be proud to have a wife who worked.'

I stared at him.

'What do you mean?'

'I mean, let's just carry on as we are. You can go to work and we'll plan the wedding and when we're married, you can keep working.'

I forced myself to smile.

'You're such a nice man,' I said. 'You really are. But it wouldn't work, Bill. I need to be part of it all. It's long hours …'

'Like this project,' he said suddenly. 'The one that means you're always at work. Is that what you mean?'

'There's a chance of a job on a new magazine,' I told him. 'It's going to be for young women, like me. But there will be lots of writers going for it so my application has to be perfect.'

'Writers?' Billy said. 'You're a writer, are you?'

I nodded.

'I've written some pieces for Home & Hearth, and I've just done a series for the London Post. Suze …'

I broke off, feeling strangely that I didn't want to discuss Suze with Billy.

'Who's Suze?' Billy said.

'She's my friend,' I said. 'She's written for Viva. She's going to interview the Beatles.'

Despite himself Billy looked impressed.

'So she works with you, does she? Suze?'

'Not yet,' I said. 'But we're hoping we'll both get a job on Mode – that's the new magazine. Then we can get a flat together.'

Billy's face was flushed.

'You've got it all worked out,' he said, his voice cracking slightly. 'It sounds great.'

I felt a wave of guilt again.

'I really am sorry,' I said. 'I would only make you miserable if we got married. I think you're a lovely man,' I continued. 'And I think you'll make someone a wonderful husband. But not me, Billy. I'm not the right woman for you.'

Billy's jaw was set. He stared straight ahead.

'So that's it, is it?'

'Sorry,' I said again. 'I just wanted to be honest with you.'

He gave me a grimace that I thought was supposed to be a smile.

'Bye then,' he said. He went to stand up but I caught his hand.

'Billy,' I said. 'There's something else.'

He laughed, a short sharp bark that had no humour in it.

'Oh, what else?' he said. 'What now?'

'I need you to keep this secret,' I said. 'I thought perhaps we could just tell everyone we decided we were too young to settle down? I'm …'

I took a breath.

'I'm scared of what Dad might do if he finds out.'

171

Billy's eyes softened a tiny bit.

'How long are you planning to keep this up?'

'Not much longer,' I said. 'We've been saving up, Suze and me, and we've almost got enough to rent a flat together. Once I can leave, I'll tell Dad.'

'You're set on this?' Billy said. 'This new life?'

'I'm afraid so,' I said. 'But I don't want to rock the boat before I have to. That's why I don't want Dad to know all this yet. So please, please, will you just go along with the story that we're too young?'

There was a pause. My heart was beating so hard that I thought Billy must be able to hear it pounding. Then, eventually, he nodded.

'All right,' he said. 'I'll go along with it.'

He looked sad for a moment.

'We'd have had a good life, Nance,' he said.

I nodded.

'I know,' I said. 'But it wouldn't have been enough.'

I leaned over and kissed him gently.

'Bye, Billy,' I said.

He got up and I breathed a sigh of relief. Maybe he wasn't that upset after all. But as he went to walk away, he paused and looked back.

'My mum always says pride comes before a fall,' he said. For the first time I saw real anger in his face. 'You're so full of your-self, Nancy Harrison. Thinking you're better than all of us with your fancy clothes and short bloody skirts, and your magazines.'

'That's not what I think,' I began, but Billy carried on.

'You're a liar,' he said, as though he'd just worked it out. 'You've been lying to me for months, since the beginning.'

'No,' I said. 'No, that's not how it was. I didn't mean all this to happen, Billy.'

He looked at me for a minute, then his face crumpled.

'I thought we were going to be happy,' he said. I could see

tears glistening in his eyes and I felt terrible. 'I thought we were going to be like my mum and dad.'

I shook my head.

'We wouldn't be happy,' I said. 'I wouldn't be happy.'

'Selfish,' he breathed, but I shook my head again.

'I'm not selfish,' I said honestly. 'I'm just trying to survive.'

But Billy wasn't convinced. He didn't look like he hated me any more. Instead, I saw disappointment mixed with the tears in his eyes and strangely, that was worse.

'Fine,' he said, with a resigned shrug of his shoulders. 'Fine. You do what you want. But don't expect me to keep your stupid secrets. Good luck with your amazing life. I hope it's bloody miserable.'

He walked away without looking back.

I sat on the bench for a while longer. I was shaking a bit because I realised I'd hurt him very badly, and I was nervous that he'd meant it when he said he wouldn't keep my secret. But I realised what I mostly felt was relief. Sometimes I worried that I was a horrible person because I knew Billy was right. We could have had a good life. But I had been right too – it wouldn't have been good enough for me and I wouldn't have made him happy in the end.

The boys had given up their Beatles impressions and were playing football instead. One of them ran over close to where I sat to pick up the ball.

He grinned at me, and raised my spirits a tiny bit.

'Dump him, did you?' he said.

I laughed.

'Sort of.'

He nodded.

'Best thing,' he said, pushing a lock of hair out of his eyes and fixing me with a serious look. 'Just have fun.'

He booted the ball over to his friends and ran off.

'Oh don't worry,' I said to myself. 'I'm going to.'

Chapter 31

I sat in the park, feeling a strange mixture of exhilaration and dread. I did really like Billy and I hadn't meant to upset him. I thought about catching up with him and asking if he really meant he would tell Dad about my double life. Surely not? He knew what Dad was like, didn't he? Upset as he was, he wouldn't cause me harm. Would he?

It started to rain so I got up and headed for home, wishing I was wearing the PVC coat I'd pinched from the fashion cupboard at work, instead of my sensible mac. By the time I reached our front door I was drenched. I glanced at the shed wondering if I should rescue tomorrow's clothes that I'd already stashed there – the roof wasn't very watertight. Deciding I'd rather not risk arriving at the office wearing a knee-length skirt, I pulled my hold-all out and went inside.

'Nancy?' Dad called from the lounge as I shut the door behind me. I froze. I'd not been expecting him to be home yet. Had Billy caught up with him already?

Trembling, I threw my bag into the cupboard under the stairs and went to find him.

Dad was in his usual chair, watching Z-Cars, a glass of whisky in his hand.

'Turn that down, Nancy,' he said. I felt another lurch of fear. What did he want? I went to the telly and turned it down, then I sat on the sofa waiting.

'Did you have your dinner?' I asked.

'Yes, very nice,' he said. I wondered if he even remembered what he'd eaten.

I took a breath.

'Have you seen Billy?' I asked.

Dad frowned.

'Thought you were with him,' he said. He laughed – a sound I rarely heard any more. 'Have you lost him?'

I forced myself to smile.

'No,' I said. 'Just thought he might have called round.'

Dad obviously wasn't interested. He cleared his throat.

'I've been nominated for small businessman of the year,' he said.

'That's good,' I said, thrown for a second at how differently this conversation was going than how I'd expected. 'Congratulations.'

Dad picked up a bunch of papers from the arm of his chair.

'I've got to fill in this form,' he said. 'I've got to be honest with you, Nancy, I can't make head nor tail of it.'

He handed it to me and I scanned it. Lots of questions about his role in the community and his approach to business – nothing too tricky.

I looked up at Dad.

'Will you do it for me?' he asked. 'Type it up all nice on your typewriter.'

Now wasn't the time to remind him my typewriter was 'in for repair' at Suze's place. Instead I grinned, giddy with relief that he hadn't spoken to Billy or found out that my job in insurance was nothing of the sort.

'Why don't we do it together now,' I said. 'I'll jot down all your answers and I can type it up in my lunchbreak from work tomorrow.'

It was the longest Dad and I had spent together for years. We

175

went through his form and came up with some pretty good answers for every question. Dad may have been a bully but there was no doubting his business sense, that was for sure.

'You've got a way with words,' he said approvingly, as he read through our final draft of question four. 'It's all those magazines you read.'

I nodded.

'I like writing,' I said.

Dad looked at me.

'You and your brother, you've both got brains,' he said. 'Of course my father was a clever man.'

I said nothing. My granddad had died when I was little and I didn't have a lot of memories of him, but I did remember spending most of our visits to my grandparents' house hiding behind Mum's legs because he was so grumpy and unpleasant.

'You're wasted in insurance,' Dad said. 'You should be a writer.'

I stared at him, open-mouthed. Had he really said that? I wondered what he'd do if I said, *actually Dad, that's exactly what I am.*

Dad slapped his hand on the arm of his chair as though he'd just told a terribly funny joke.

'A writer,' he repeated, laughing. 'That's a good one. My daughter, a writer.'

I forced myself to smile.

'Dad,' I said, thinking now was as good a time as any. 'I split up with Billy. The wedding's off.'

Bracing myself, I waited for him to get angry. Instead, though, he shrugged.

'His uncle's annoyed because he wasn't nominated for the award,' Dad said. 'Twit.'

'So you don't mind?' I said, unable to believe my luck.

'What, that you're not marrying that twit's nephew?' Dad said. 'Not at all. And it'll save me a few bob, too, won't it? If I don't have to fork out for the wedding.'

176

'It will,' I said. 'So let's do question five, shall we?'

We carried on answering the questions together until we'd done the whole form. Dad didn't mention Billy again, so I didn't bring him up either. I hoped he and Billy's uncle would continue their feud – it would certainly make life easier for me.

And maybe, I thought, as I got into bed that night, maybe life was going to get easier now. Billy was dealt with – relatively painlessly as well. And Dad was actually being nice to me. Perhaps if the job on Mode worked out, I could tell him the truth about where I worked. If I was moving in with Suze anyway, it wouldn't matter if it took a while for him to get used to the idea of me writing for a mag and not working in the shop with him.

I fell asleep while I was imagining bringing George home with me for Sunday lunch. Dad would shake his hand and not even make one single rude comment about the length of his hair or the narrowness of his trousers. And I'd show him the latest issue of Mode, he'd flick through it and exclaim at how many features I'd written.

'I'm so proud of you, Nancy,' he'd say. 'You've really made something of yourself.'

But of course, life never works out as you planned, does it?

Chapter 32

2016

I woke up with a start, my heart pounding. There was someone in my flat. I could hear them rattling around in the kitchen.

I sat up, realising my head hurt, and with another shock, remembered I wasn't in my flat – I was at Damo's. Oh what had we done? I remembered us drinking each other under the table, and then staggering through the cobbled Soho streets looking for a cab. And I remembered Damo telling me I couldn't go home alone in the state I was in, and saying I could stay at his. And then I remembered nothing.

Gingerly, I put my hand out and felt the other side of the bed. Empty. Dizzy with relief – and hangover – I peered under the duvet and saw I was wearing all my underwear, one sock, and an Iron Maiden t-shirt that was definitely not mine but which hung halfway down my thighs and which was undoubtedly not sexy.

There was a grunt from the side of the bed and I glanced down to see Damo – at least I assumed it was Damo – huddled in a sleeping bag, with just the very top of his head poking out. He'd obviously slept on the floor. And the noises I'd heard were clearly his flatmate.

It was Saturday so I didn't have to go to work but I did have to get out of there. I couldn't face an awkward morning-after conversation with Damo – not with my head pounding the way it was.

I slid out of bed, gathered my clothes, and headed for the bathroom hoping I wouldn't come face to face with Damo's flatmate, whoever he was.

I showered in four seconds flat, then put on my clothes and brushed my teeth with my finger. I couldn't do much with my hair so I just twisted it up. I had sunglasses in my bag, so I'd wear those home and hopefully they'd disguise my bloodshot eyes.

Hoping Damo was still asleep and his flatmate was still busy in the kitchen, I unlocked the door, slunk out of the bathroom and came face to face with a goddess. She was about six foot tall, legs up to my armpits, wavy long sunkissed blonde hair, and a broad perfect smile. And she was holding a cup of coffee.

'Oh shit,' she said, in an Aussie accent. 'I thought you were Damo. I made him this.'

I gave her a weak smile.

'He's asleep,' I said. 'I was just leaving.'

She held out the coffee.

'Want this?' she said. 'I've already got one.'

I weighed up my need for coffee against my desire to be out of that flat. Coffee won. I gave the goddess a grateful grin and took the mug.

'Thanks,' I said.

'Come in the kitchen,' she said, turning round and walking down the hall. She was wearing a vest top and some battered old running shorts – I didn't know if she'd been running or if that was her pyjamas but I did know she looked astonishing in such a horrible outfit. The short shorts showed off her tanned, slim, well-muscled legs and the vest flattered her broad shoulders.

179

'I'm so pleased Damo's met someone,' she said as she sat at the small kitchen table. 'He's a miserable bugger when he's single.'

'Known him long?' I said, wondering who she was.

'Not really,' she said. ''Bout a year. He's friends with my sister's husband's buddy from uni. So when he needed a place in London, Vally – that's my sister – said he should contact me, because Sylv – that was my old flatmate – had just moved out and I needed someone to share the rent. Vally likes him being here because she says he keeps me out of trouble, but we're really boring most of the time. Vally just thinks I have this incredible life because I'm in London and she's back home with a husband and a baby ...'

She paused for breath and I drained my coffee.

'Another one?' she said.

I nodded and she poured some more into my mug.

'So where did you meet Damo?' she asked.

'Work,' I muttered. 'Few years ago.'

'Not this new job?' the goddess asked. 'That's a shame, I'm dying to find out more about this Fearne he's working with.'

I froze, coffee cup halfway to my lips, but thankfully she didn't seem to want an answer.

'She's the reason I'm glad he's met you,' she continued. 'She totally broke his heart. Abandoned him on a round-the-world trip. Just sneaked out one night when he was asleep and went home.'

I fought the urge to tell her it wasn't quite like that – that we hadn't started our round-the-world trip when I bailed – but I settled for just arranging my face into a shocked expression.

'Scottie – that's Vally's husband – he said that Mike – that's his mate from uni – says that Damo never really got over Fearne. And then he comes to London and starts a new job and things start going well. He starts dating and he loves his job and it's all great.'

180

She swigged her coffee.

'And then, he bumps into Fearne and it all goes to shit.'

I sat up a bit straighter.

'How so? I said, sounding terribly English and uptight.

'Oh she calls and he goes running,' the goddess said, stretching her legs out onto one of the other kitchen chairs. 'He had a great job, but she asked him to quit so he could work with her – and it sounds like it's a dead-end project if you ask me, not that I know much about magazines because I work for a bank, but you can normally get a feel of something, don't you think?'

Stunned by the way this conversation was going, I could only nod.

'Anyway, he quits his job, he spends every waking hour working with Fearne, and you just know that spending all this time with her has rekindled his feelings for her. It's a bloody disaster, that's what it is. So that's why I was so pleased that he'd brought you home.'

I stared at her and she made a face.

'Oh shit,' she said. 'I've said too much, haven't I? I always talk too much. Vally's always saying to me, "Madison, you talk too much" and she's right, even though I'd never tell her that. Have I put you off him? Please don't run off. He's such a nice guy and he really deserves a nice girl.'

'I have to go,' I said. 'Thanks for the coffee. Tell Damo I'll call him later.'

'You will?' she said, her beautiful face breaking into a broad smile. 'Oh thank god.'

She followed me down the hall towards the front door and opened it to let me out.

'Thanks,' I said, still a bit shell-shocked by everything she'd said. 'It was nice to meet you.'

'Nice to meet you too,' she called as I walked down the path. 'Oh, what's your name?'

I paused by the garden gate, which was hanging off one hinge, and thought about lying, but my head hurt and I was too tired to be creative.

'My name?' I said.

Madison nodded.

'It's Fearne,' I said.

Madison's eyes widened in horror and I felt a bit bad.

'Sorry,' I said, meaning it. 'Tell Damo I'll call.'

Chapter 33

1966

I walked to work the next day like I was walking on air. My eyeliner had gone just right, despite the train coming to a juddery halt as I started to apply it. My hair was pulled back into a ponytail and for once, my fringe had stayed heavy and straight instead of kinking. The sun was shining, which was enough to put anyone in a good mood after weeks of rain and spring was in the air – about time as we were well into April now. I was wearing a black pinafore dress over a thin white polo neck sweater and I felt sassy and stylish. I was meeting George for lunch and I was going to tell him I'd broken up with Billy. Life was good.

I flew through my work that morning. I typed up Dad's entry, stuck it in an envelope and posted it straightaway. I hoped he'd win – he had been in such a good mood last night that I even thought a win could completely change his personality.

At lunchtime I checked my hair in the mirror in the ladies, redid my lipstick, and feeling slightly nervous, I headed to the studio to see George.

Suze was working a shift at Bruno's and as I passed she dashed out.

'Are you going to see George?' she said, gripping my arm with one hand, while she balanced some empty coffee cups on the other. 'Come and see me on your way back to work. I want to hear everything.'

'Not everything,' I said, smiling. 'Some things are private.'

I blew her a kiss over my shoulder as I sauntered down the road towards Carnaby Street, feeling the eyes of a group of mods on me as I passed. I deliberately swung my hips a bit more while I walked, feeling sophisticated and a bit saucy.

And my luck carried on when I reached the studio and discovered George was alone.

'Hello,' I said, when he opened the door. 'I wondered if my boyfriend might be free for lunch?'

George grinned at me.

'You did it?' he said. 'How did he take it?'

'Not great,' I said, walking into the room and sitting down on the sofa. 'He's upset and angry and he threatened to tell my dad about my job. But I reckon he'll calm down. He'll probably meet someone else straight away.'

George came over and sat next to me.

'Like you did, you mean?' He played with the end of my ponytail.

I smiled in what I hoped was a sophisticated, sexy fashion.

'Stop talking about Billy,' I said. 'And kiss me.'

With no reason to stop this time, our kisses were deep and slow. I loved the weight of George on top of me and the feeling of his hands on my skin.

'Where's Frank?' I gasped at one point. 'Is he due back soon?' George was kissing my neck, making me shudder with pleasure.

'Glasgow,' he said. 'He's not due back until tomorrow.'

All the feelings that I'd never felt with Billy were hitting me at once. I wanted George so badly it was like an ache.

He slid his hand up my thigh and I shifted slightly so he could go higher.

'Are you sure?' he whispered.

I nodded.

'I've never been surer of anything,' I said.

Afterwards, we lay on the sofa together, our legs entwined, and shared a cigarette.

'I need to go back to work,' I said.

'Phone in sick.'

I giggled.

'I can't,' I said. 'Rosemary knows there's nothing wrong with me.'

'See you later?' George said as I started to get dressed.

'Suze and I are going to that Rolling Stones party,' I said, hardly able to believe I was being so casual about hanging out with bona fide pop stars. 'It's to celebrate their new LP and Suze is interviewing them. She sorted it all out with some friend of a friend of hers. Can you do some photos?'

George nodded.

'Well of course I bloody well can,' he said. 'I've always wanted to meet the Stones. What time is it?'

'I'll pop in and ask her on my way back to the office.' I pulled on my shoes and picked up my jacket. 'I'll give you a ring and tell you all the details. Meet you at Suze's later?'

George blew me a kiss as I headed down the stairs and I grinned.

I walked along Carnaby Street with a swagger. I wondered if everyone could tell what I'd just done, if it was written all over my face. I hoped Rosemary wouldn't know – I was terribly late coming back from my lunch break and I'd have to make up an excuse.

I ducked into Bruno's as I passed. It was quiet now the lunch rush had passed. Suze was wiping down a table at the back of the café and I waved from the door. She stopped cleaning and gave me a beaming smile.

'So?' she said.

'Oh, nothing much to report,' I said, keeping my face sombre. 'I've just been for a quick lunchtime cuddle with my boyfriend.'

Suze squealed and hugged me.

'I bet it wasn't a cuddle,' she said, giving a dirty chuckle. 'You naughty girl.'

'A lady never tells,' I said, blushing. 'He's coming tonight to do some pics, but I couldn't remember what time it was.'

'About eight-ish, I think'

'Nervous?' I teased.

'It's the bloody Rolling Stones,' Suze said, bouncing up and down. 'I'm almost passing out with fear, Nancy. What if I say all the wrong stuff and they laugh at me?'

I laughed.

'Why on earth would you think that?' I said. 'You're a brilliant interviewer. You'll be telling jokes to Bill Wyman after five minutes.'

Suze made a face.

'But there will be loads of music journalists there. They're all very serious.'

I shrugged.

'So?' I said. 'You're a different sort of journalist. You'll be asking about their girlfriends, and where they buy their trousers, who's going to win the World Cup, and what they think of Harold Wilson.'

Suze nodded. Then she gripped my arm excitedly.

'Do you feel it, Nancy?'

I peeled her fingers off one by one.

'I feel a bruise coming,' I said. 'Feel what?'

Suze sniffed the air like a Bisto Kid.

'Change,' she said. 'I can feel things changing. It's all happening.'

I grinned. Suze might have been a bit like an untrained puppy in the way she bounced through life, but she had a point. Spring had arrived, and London was full of energy. Everywhere felt new and young and exciting and we were part of it.

A little bubble of laughter popped out of my mouth.

'It's happening,' I said. Suze and I hugged again. I glanced at my watch.

'Oh god, I have to get back to work,' I said, turning my head as someone came into the café and the bell over the door tinkled.

'So I'll meet you at your place later and we can …'

I looked back at Suze and broke off when I realised she'd vanished.

Startled, I looked round. She was lying along the long seat on one of the banquettes next to where she'd been standing. She reached out and tugged my skirt.

'Don't look at me,' she hissed. 'Pretend you're on your own.'

'Can I sit anywhere?' the customer called. He was a man in his early thirties with short, mod-style hair and a checked shirt.

'Distract him,' Suze murmured. 'Distract him so I can get into the kitchen without him seeing me.'

I had absolutely no idea what was going on, but I couldn't see that I had much choice. I walked towards the customer, smiling broadly.

'I don't work here,' I said. 'But let me just get Bruno for you. Why don't you sit here …'

I bustled him into a chair, which faced out into the street, his back to where Suze cowered, and gave him a menu. Out of the corner of my eye, I saw Suze scamper into the kitchen.

'I'll get Bruno,' I said to the customer. Then I headed after Suze, determined to find out what on earth she was up to.

Chapter 34

Confused about why Suze had left me to deal with the customer at Bruno's while she hid, I went to hunt for her. She wasn't in the kitchen but Bruno was there, unloading a crate of onions.

'You've got a customer,' I said, nodding towards the front of the café. 'Where's Suze?'

'Out the back,' he said. He wiped his hands on a tea towel and made a funny face at me. 'She is looking crazy.'

He had that right.

Suze was leaning against the back wall of the café, smoking a cigarette. Her already pale face seemed several shades lighter and tinged with green, and her eyes were teary.

'What's happened?' I said, bewildered and worried. 'What's going on?'

Suze took a huge draw on her cigarette, tilted her head up and breathed the smoke up into the air.

'That man,' she said, gesturing with her fag. 'That man in the café is one of Walter's mates.'

I frowned.

'Walter?'

'The man I met when I first came to London,' Suze said. 'The one I nicked the squat from.'

188

'Really?' I said. 'Are you sure?'

Suze gave me a withering look.

'Of course I'm sure.'

I thought about the man in the café. He looked like a normal bloke. Nice shirt. Smart shoes. Short hair. Nothing like the drugged-up louts I'd imagined when Suze had told me about when she first moved to London.

'You haven't seen them for three years,' I said. 'You might have made a mistake.'

Suze gave a short, sharp laugh.

'Oh believe me, I won't ever forget their faces,' she said. 'For a while, after they left, I saw them every time I closed my eyes.'

She smiled a sort of hopeless smile.

'I knew Walter would find me eventually,' she said.

'Walter's inside, though, isn't he?' I said. 'Locked up?'

Suze shrugged.

'Dunno,' she said. 'He was. But he might be out by now.'

'You said you didn't think he'd come back.'

'I don't,' she said. 'Not really. It was just frightening to see Vic out there.'

'Do you think he was looking for you?'

Suze shook her head.

'Actually, I don't,' she said. 'It's probably just an unfortunate coincidence.'

'A narrow escape,' I said.

Suze nodded, a grim look on her face.

'I hope so,' she said. 'But I think he saw me.'

'Do you think he recognised you?'

She shook her head.

'Probably not.'

I took the cigarette out of her hand and inhaled.

'So?' I said. 'Then he won't come back. Will he?'

'I hate when you do that,' she said.

'Are you all right?' I asked, remembering how crazy she'd gone

189

when we talked about Walter and his friends the night of the party in Wardour Street. Would seeing Vic again send her off the rails?

Suze smiled, a weak smile.

'I'm fine,' she said. 'I think I'll tell Bruno I'm not feeling well, and I'll go home for the afternoon. I'll hide out in the squat like I used to.'

'Oh Suze,' I said. 'I'm not sure that's the answer. But if it makes you feel better, then stay at home all afternoon. I'll come round after work.'

Shit. Work. I was so late coming back from my lunchbreak; it was almost three o'clock.

'Lovey, I have to go,' I said. 'Rosemary's going to have my guts for garters. Are you all right?'

Suze smiled.

'I'm fine,' she said. 'Go.'

'I'll meet you at yours after work,' I said. 'Big night tonight.'

'The biggest,' Suze said. 'Go on.'

I pulled her into a tight hug.

'Vic's no one,' I said into her ear. 'You're fine. You're great, in fact. And tonight you're interviewing Mick Jagger.'

Suze squeezed me back even tighter.

'Thank you,' she said.

I kept my head down all afternoon, working really hard to stay on Rosemary's good side and I was pleased that the hours flew by. At six o'clock, when most people had gone home, I headed for the fashion cupboard where our fashion editor, Lucy, had laid out some outfits for me.

'Wear the checked dress,' she said. 'It's perfect for tonight.'

I pulled it on – it was black and white dogtooth check with long sleeves and thick white cuffs. The skirt was very short with a pleat in the front. I loved it – it was fashionable and professional at the same time. I paired it with white tights and my favourite white shoes with a strap. Lucy helped me with my hair, brushing it straight and spraying my fringe to make sure it stayed flat, and my make-up.

'Not bad,' I said, when she finished, turning this way and that to see how I looked from all angles in the mirror.

'You have to look good for Mick Jagger,' said Lucy.

'I won't be going anywhere near him, thank goodness,' I said, picking up my bag and wondering if I dared risk going without a jacket. It wasn't raining, but there was still a chill in the air despite the recent spring sunshine we'd enjoyed. 'Suze is doing the interview. I'll probably pass out with excitement if he so much as says hello to me.'

'Get his phone number for me,' Lucy called as I left and I giggled.

When I got to Suze's, George was waiting outside. He looked really trendy in a suit jacket with a striped top underneath. He was holding a piece of paper with handwriting scribbled on it – a note from Suze obviously.

'She's going to meet us there,' he said. He gave me a kiss and I shivered with pleasure. I almost suggested not going to the party at all and just going back to George's for the evening, then I remembered it was Suze's big night.

'Where is she?'

George shrugged. He handed me the note.

'Nancy!' it said, in Suze's scrawl. 'Something came up. See you at the party.'

'Well that's not very enlightening,' I said.

'Typical Suze,' George said. 'She'll explain later.' He screwed up the note and lobbed it into the bin, and together we strolled along Berwick Street.

The party was in a basement nightclub on Oxford Street. It was dark and it took a while for our eyes to adjust to the light as we went down the stairs.

'Oh, wow,' said George. 'This is cool.'

For the first time since my new London life had begun, I felt a bit suburban and out of my depth. It was cool. It was really cool. There was a black and white checked dancefloor, where some beautiful people were dancing to a Rolling Stones song, that I assumed was from the new LP.

Around the edge of the dancefloor, lots of even more beautiful people stood sipping cocktails. I had no idea what was in them, but I really wanted one.

As if by magic, a waitress walked past with a tray of drinks. George took two and handed me one and I gasped as I noticed the Stones sitting in a corner booth.

'There they are,' I said, trying not to stare at Mick Jagger's long, long legs and tight trousers. 'Oh I'm desperately envious of Suze and completely terrified for her at the same time.'

George laughed.

'Can you see Suze?' he asked, looking round. 'I can't.'

I squinted through the people and smoke but I couldn't see her either.

'Maybe she's not here yet,' I said. 'Let's have a wander round.'

We weaved our way through the crowds, sipping our drinks, and I began to feel more like I belonged there. I saw a few people I knew. George saw even more people he knew – honestly, that man knew just about everyone in London – and I drank in the atmosphere.

'This is where I wanted to be,' I murmured to myself. 'This is what it was all for.'

I stood, leaning against the wall, half-listening to George talking to a singer from another band that I hadn't heard of, and half-looking for Suze who still hadn't appeared. Mostly, though, I was watching how the beautiful people acted. How they stood. How they talked. How they danced. I was going to be like them one day.

By the table where the Stones sat, a tall willowy girl stood up. She was wearing the miniest skirt I'd ever seen, and her jet-black hair reached almost to her hemline. She bent down and whispered something in Keith Richards's ear and he gave her a cheeky smile. Then – to my absolute horror – she stood up and pointed at me.

'Who's she?' I hissed to George as she came towards me.

'That's Gloria Brown,' he said. 'She's the Stones' publicity person. She sorted out the interview for Suze, I think. Through that girl Suze knows at the studio. It must be time for Suze to do her thing.'

'But Suze isn't here,' I said, panicking. 'What should I tell her?'

'Hi,' said Gloria. 'Suze Williams, right? And George Mann? The guys are ready for you now.'

'Just go with it,' George said under his breath. 'We can't miss this chance. Everyone mixes you and Suze up anyway.'

I gripped my hands together to stop them shaking and gave Gloria what I hoped was a winning, sophisticated smile.

'Lovely to meet you,' I said. 'Lead the way.'

And I walked across the dancefloor to interview the Rolling Stones.

Chapter 35

2016

I had two choices, I thought as I travelled home on the train – Damo lived in Hackney, I discovered when I left his place, which was fortunately quite easy for me to get home from. I thanked my lucky stars he hadn't moved somewhere further away.

I slumped in a seat and went through my options as the train rumbled towards south London.

My first option was to fall apart. Things had gone wrong. Really wrong. Like Madison said, I'd broken Damo's heart for the sake of my career. And I'd thrown away all the work Jen and I had done on The Hive and trampled all over her feelings too, and that had really come back to bite me on the bum. In fact, that career I was so keen on? That hadn't exactly worked out as I'd planned either. Option one was tempting. I really, really wanted to crawl under my duvet and stay there all weekend. And then run away from Mode, from Damo, from Jen – go back to Oz perhaps, or try New York …

And yet, there was option two. And that was to make it work. To rebuild my relationship with Damo and maybe Jen too if that wasn't past saving. To relaunch Mode and make it a huge success.

To launch The Hive, which I was certain would be a massive hit. To finally prove to my bloody mother that my job was worthwhile. That I could do something important, even if it wasn't economics or law.

That option sounded a lot less fun, and much, much harder. But it also sounded more like me. I was Fearne Summers. I worked hard and I got results.

'Yeah!' I said.

'What's that, love?' said the man sitting next to me.

'I don't give up,' I told him as the train pulled into Crystal Palace.

'Good for you,' he said.

I worked all weekend. First, I texted Damo to say thanks for putting me up, then I turned my phone off so I wouldn't get distracted. I cleaned my flat from top to bottom. I made green juice and even managed to drink some of it before pouring it away and going for Diet Coke instead. And I stayed up late and put together a proper plan for relaunching Mode with a twenty-first century version of the first ever issue.

I wrestled with my budget, working out what we absolutely had to spend money on and what we could do in-house. I planned what was going on which page and pulled together all my notes on the features that I'd made at Suze's house. She had given me some brilliant ideas and made me look at some things in a different way. We'd have to commission some writers and I hoped Vanessa would pull it out of the bag. We had a budget for one big name, or a couple of cheaper writers, and then it would be in-house all the way but I'd let her sort that out. I thought the whole team would enjoy pulling together all the articles. And I knew Damo would make them all look amazing, with or without glitzy photoshoots.

Once I'd done that, I got out my diary and pencilled in a meeting with Vanessa and Lizzie to discuss Vanessa's ideas for selling the mag in different places. And I drafted a press release about the relaunch. Should we have a party, I wondered? In fact, could we have lots of parties in shopping centres across the country to really take the magazine to our readers? We'd just need DJs and some goodie bags. It needn't be too expensive.

I scribbled notes and ideas furiously, determined to make Mode's relaunch as good as it possibly could be.

Could we have a big celeb-filled party if we got a sponsor? Would there be time to arrange it? If we got the right guests we could get lots of coverage.

And while I was thinking about celebs, I emailed Amy Lavender's agent and asked if she'd be our cover star. Her story was all about rebirth – from failed soap star to national treasure – and she was bloody gorgeous, too. It was one area where I was going to divert from the original Mode but it was definitely the right idea.

Finally, on Sunday evening, I ordered a Chinese takeaway, poured myself a glass of wine, resisted the pull of Netflix, and sat down to look at The Hive. I had an idea that we could somehow combine the work we'd already done with all the effort we were putting in at Mode. But that wasn't really my motivation. I kept thinking about Suze and her friend Nancy, who'd died. The way she talked about working with her friend and how they'd really helped each other, had reminded me of how I used to work with Jen. I missed that and I missed her. I felt like I had to at least try to put it right. Perhaps showing her I was still serious about The Hive would go some way to doing that.

I worked late, slept well, and headed to the office bright and early on Monday morning, raring to go.

When everyone arrived, I called them into a meeting ready to explain what I wanted to do.

When Emily found the old issues, she'd told me that the entire first issue of Mode was on the company server. So on Saturday I'd rung our printers and sweet-talked them into producing enough duplicate copies for the team. They'd been waiting for me on my desk when I arrived and now I handed them out to everyone. I was gratified to see the first glimmers of interest in the team as they started to flick through them.

'I met Suze Williams on Friday,' I said, glossing over the bit where she threw me out of her cottage. 'She had some amazing ideas and together we came up with what I think is a great way of relaunching Mode with a bang.'

I took a breath.

'We're going to recreate the first ever issue to coincide with the magazine's fiftieth anniversary,' I said.

There was silence. The team all stared blankly at me.

'So we're just going to copy this?' said Vanessa, her lip curled up. I gave her a sharp look – I was making inroads with her, of course, but she still had a tendency to be negative. But she carried on regardless. 'It doesn't seem all that innovative.'

I thought for a minute.

'Think of it as looking back to move forward,' I said. 'We're going to be inspired by the features in this issue, but we're really just using them as a starting point and updating them for women now.'

I stood up and opened the magazine at the feature about illegal abortions – the one that had given me the idea in the first place.

'For example,' I said. 'This was written before abortion was legal and it's fairly shocking. Have a read.'

There was silence while everyone scanned the article. Riley tutted loudly.

'Terrible, what people went through,' she said. 'And it's relatively recently.'

'But abortion's legal now,' Vanessa pointed out. 'We're not going to get a feature on some backstreet Vera Drake.'

I nodded.

'So we need a different take on it,' I said.

Vanessa chewed her lip.

'It's still illegal in Northern Ireland,' she said slowly.

I grinned.

'Exactly,' I said, thrilled we were thinking along the same lines.

'I've got a friend from uni who had to come to England. It was pretty traumatic for her.'

'I've heard of people buying abortion medicine on the internet,' Emily added. 'I think women have been arrested.'

'So that's how we'd write that feature,' I said. 'We need to look at each article in turn and think about how we'd approach them now. Like this one here, on why the writer – Nancy Harrison – doesn't want to be a mother. We could get someone to write a twenty-first century take on that.'

Vanessa was – finally – nodding.

'So same basic ideas, but given our own twist,' she said. 'We can't do the whole mag like that though.'

'We can't?' I said. I'd sort of hoped we could.

She shook her head.

'No,' she said. 'We'd need to explain what we're doing – maybe in the ed's letter – and then we'd probably need some other features about the differences between then and now too.'

Emily jumped in.

'What about my interview with Suze Williams?' she said. 'My day-in-the-life thing – comparing then and now?'

I made a face.

'Leave that one with me,' I said. 'We might need to come up with something else.'

Damo had been very quiet the whole time, listening carefully and drumming his fingers on his thigh. Now he grinned.

'You're on to something here, Fearne,' he said. 'We can have a lot of fun with this.'

He pulled the first issue towards him.

'There's not a lot of colour inside,' he pointed out. 'So obviously we'd do that differently. But I'm thinking we could drop in a pic of the original feature on each page so people know what they're comparing.'

'And we could put the whole first issue online,' Emily suggested. I flashed her a smile – that was a great idea.

We threw around more suggestions, and Emily wrote them all up on the huge whiteboard at one end of the room. I felt really positive for the first time since I'd started at Mode and I was pleased that finally the team were all working together. I just hoped it was going to work.

When I eventually got to my desk I trawled through my emails from the weekend – ninety per cent were rubbish but one caught my eye. It was from Suze. My heart thumped as I clicked to open it.

'I'm sorry if I over-reacted,' she wrote. 'I enjoyed meeting you but I don't want to be involved in the magazine and I can't do the interview. If I can help over the phone, please don't hesitate to give me a call. I would like to help you relaunch Mode, which has a special place in my heart. But please don't use my name anywhere in the issue.'

I stared at the email for a while. I was pleased Suze was willing to help because the ideas she'd had on Friday were so brilliant that I couldn't imagine doing it without her now. But her reluctance to be officially involved and the way she'd shut down any suggestion of it, had intrigued me.

'Maybe she just gets upset when she talks about her friend,' Vanessa suggested later when I filled her in.

'That's what Damo said. But I get the impression it's more than that,' I said. 'She was so adamant. Almost nervous.'

'It's a long time since she worked in magazines, perhaps she's lost her confidence.'

I nodded slowly and pulled at my ponytail.

'Yeaaah,' I said.

'But you don't think so?'

'She virtually threw me out of her house,' I said. 'She wasn't shy, or worried about being out of touch. She was determined that no one would find out she was involved in the magazine.'

'But she writes novels,' Vanessa pointed out.

'Under a pseudonym.'

'Maybe she did something bad,' Vanessa said, leaning forward. She was eating porridge, which may have been a really late breakfast or an early lunch, and she dropped a lump on my desk then wiped it up hurriedly when she saw my face. 'Maybe she did something so terrible, she had to leave Mode and go and hide away in the countryside.'

'That could be it, you know,' I said. 'That's exactly how she acted – like she was feeling guilty about something.'

'Maybe she murdered her friend,' Vanessa said.

'I have some sympathy for her in that case,' I deadpanned and Vanessa laughed. I was pleased we were joking together again.

'Seriously, though, it might have something to do with Nancy Harrison,' I said, thinking back to how Suze had acted when I was in her house. 'She was funny about her.'

'So Google her,' Vanessa said, sucking on her spoon. 'Google Nancy Harrison and find out how she died and what happened. Find out if Suze was ever a suspect.'

'I don't have time to investigate a silly mystery from fifty years ago,' I said. 'I've got a magazine to save.'

'But you're going to do it anyway, right?'

'Hell, yes.'

Chapter 36

1966

It was one of the best nights of my whole life. I'd not prepared any questions, obviously, so when Gloria introduced me to the band I was terrified. I thought my voice wouldn't come out right. But then Brian Jones threw his head back and fixed me with a wide stare from under his thick blond fringe.

'You're not going to ask us about our influences, are you?' he said. 'Because I don't think I can make up any more shit.'

I grinned.

'No,' I said. 'I want to know where you buy your trousers, what you think of Harold Wilson, and who you want to win the World Cup.'

Brian laughed. So did the rest of the band. And suddenly I relaxed. These lads may have been pop stars but they were just like any other young men, deep down.

We chatted for ages about everything and nothing and I got enough to make a brilliant feature. I hoped Suze would agree to me writing it up for Viva instead of her – I was sure she would – and I thought I could write it all a different way for our dummy

Mode issue, too. That would be a real coup and it would show what great contacts we – well, Suze really – had.

George snapped some candid pictures while we were chatting, and then he wandered off with the boys to do a proper shoot for half an hour, leaving me talking to Gloria – who turned out to be a hoot.

'They keep me on my toes,' she said, grabbing a cocktail from a passing waitress. 'It's like herding cats. I get them all together in the right place to talk to a journalist and I turn my back for five seconds and Bill's buggered off to talk to a girl, or Keith's at the bar. I need to get a dog lead and put them all on it.'

She pushed her hair back over her shoulders and gave me a dazzling smile.

'So this is for Viva, right?'

I nodded.

'Viva first,' I said. 'But there's a new magazine launching called Mode and we're hoping ...' I paused. 'I'm hoping to get it in there, too.'

'Oh how thrilling,' said Gloria. 'Are you working on this new magazine, then?'

'I bloody hope so,' I said. 'It's going to be really exciting – quite forward-thinking and all about the stuff women like us are interested in.'

'It sounds great. Good luck with it all,' Gloria said. She dug about in her bag and gave me her card. 'If you need anything from the boys, just let me know. We can always make time for friends.'

'Thanks,' I said. 'I'll give this to ...' I broke off. I had been going to say that I'd give the card to Suze, but why should I? Gloria was my contact. I was the one who'd done the interview and impressed her. I smiled and put the card into my bag.

'I'll give your details to George too,' I said. 'He's such a great photographer – I'm sure you'll be interested in using him again when you see the pictures.'

202

'Talk of the devil,' Gloria said, nodding over my shoulder. George was coming back from the side room where he'd been shooting the band, deep in conversation with Mick Jagger.

'Did it go well?' Gloria said.

'It was great,' George said. 'They're all very professional.'

Mick laughed and I wondered what had gone on. George always seemed to have a huge amount of fun when he was photographing bands.

He slipped his arm round my waist and whispered in my ear. 'Shall we go?'

I nodded.

'We have to get on,' I said to Gloria, implying we were terribly busy and important instead of actually planning to go back to George's flat and make the most of being alone. 'Thank you so much for setting this up.'

'Any time,' she said. 'Good luck with the magazine.'

George slung his arm across my shoulders as we walked out into the night air and I shivered, regretting not bringing a coat after all.

'That was amazing,' I said, my ears ringing in the quiet after the noise of the club. 'I really felt part of something, you know?'

'We are part of something,' George said, waving his arm around to take in Soho, London, Britain – the world. 'Everything's changing and we're leading the way.'

I threw my arms up in the air and whooped.

'It's all happening,' I said. 'It's really happening.'

Laughing and playfully shoving each other, we walked back towards Soho. As we turned into Wardour Street, some movement up ahead caught my eye.

'Look,' I said, pointing to the shadows cast by the street lights. 'Is that Suze?'

I squinted at the figure ahead of us, leaning against a doorway, lighting a cigarette. As the match flared, I saw it was definitely Suze.

'Suze,' I cried, rushing towards her. 'Where the bloody hell have you been?'

Suze looked round slowly, and gave me a broad smile.

'Nancy,' she said. 'I was just coming to meet you at the party.'

'The party's over,' I said. 'I did the interview. It's finished.'

'Really?' said Suze. She was acting so strangely, her movements were slow and she seemed like her head was in the clouds. She was clearly drunk but there was something else too. 'Oh that's a shame.'

She staggered slightly and I caught her.

'Suze,' I said, quite cross that once again I was picking up the pieces. 'Are you drunk?'

'She's drunk and stoned,' said George. 'Have you been smoking weed?'

Suze smiled at him, a peaceful, calm smile.

'I have,' she said. 'I like it.'

All my hopes for a night with George disappeared as, like a trained army, he and I took one of Suze's arms each and started walking with her towards her place.

When we finally got there – after trying to stop Suze going into every pub we passed – she slumped on the sofa and ignored the glass of water I'd handed her.

'This is what happens,' she said. 'This is my life.'

I exchanged a glance with George.

'It's not what happens,' I said, sounding a bit like my old headmistress. 'It's what you make happen. No one made you go out and get smashed tonight. That was all your doing. It's no one's fault but your own.'

Suze narrowed her eyes at me.

'It's their fault,' she said. 'Those bastards.'

'Walter and Vic,' I said, remembering the man in the café earlier. 'This is about them?'

Suze started to cry and I suddenly felt awful for being cross with her.

'Sweetheart,' I said. 'What's the matter? You're doing so well.'

'I saw Vic,' Suze said. 'And I was so scared. I was so frightened he'd seen me too and that he'd find me. Or he'd go and tell Walter. And he'd find me.'

'They've gone,' I said. 'You've had a horrible, horrible time but it's over now.'

I gripped her hand and she looked into my eyes.

'It's over, but I can't stop remembering,' she said simply. 'And the only way I've found to stop remembering is to get drunk. And when getting drunk doesn't work, I smoke marijuana. Or take a Valium. And back when I first moved to London – when I was part of that life – taking Valium didn't work either, so I took other stuff. But I stopped. And it wasn't easy. And I don't want to go back, Nancy.'

She was crying properly now, big messy tears. Her hair was tousled and her eyeliner was halfway down her face. I felt so sorry for her. I pulled her into my arms and stroked her hair like she was a toddler who'd fallen over and I was her mum.

'It's going to be okay,' I said. 'It's all going to be okay. You've got me now, and George, and lots of friends. We're all going to look out for you. And those bastards aren't going to come back. Vic can't have seen you today – you moved so fast. And even if he did catch a glimpse of you, he won't be certain.'

Suze wiped away a tear from her jaw with the heel of her hand. 'Do you think?' she said.

'I know. Men like them are bullies and cowards and they always choose the easy route,' I said. 'There's no way he'd put in the effort needed to find you.'

Suze nodded, though she didn't look convinced. Her eyes were drooping and I gently guided her to the bed and helped her lie down.

'Thanks Nancy,' she said. 'You're my best friend.'

Chapter 37

I woke the next day in Suze's bed, where I'd crept after George left in the early hours. We'd talked late into the night about Suze and her reaction simply to seeing this Vic.

'What if he does come back? I asked George. 'I'm scared about what she might do.'

George smiled sadly.

'Frank had a friend like Suze,' he said. 'He was a really talented photographer but there was something inside him that he couldn't live with. He drank and he took drugs just to silence that inner voice.'

'That's not like Suze,' I pointed out. 'It's not something inside her, it's not something that's wired wrong or her hormones or anything like that. It's something that happened to her.'

'Maybe she should see a shrink,' George said.

I made a face.

'Really?'

'Might help,' George said. 'Give her some ways to cope with everything that happened to her.'

'S'pose,' I said. 'What happened to Frank's friend?'

'He died,' admitted George. 'But like you said, what was wrong with him wasn't the same as what's up with Suze.'

206

We talked back and forth, trying to work out how we could help Suze. I was adamant that if we could just get jobs at Mode, and a flat together, then things would be all right.

'It will solve all our problems,' I told George. 'I'll be away from my dad, and Suze will have something else to think about and her life won't be so … chaotic … and I'll be around to look after her.'

But George wasn't sure.

'I'm just worried this is bigger than we think,' he said. 'And I'm worried that this man could come back at any time and she'll go off the rails again.'

'I think the trouble with Suze is that she's never had anyone,' I said. 'Apart from that teacher who wanted to take her in, no one's ever really cared about her. I need to show her that we're here for her.'

George nodded.

'You've got a good heart, Nancy Harrison,' he said.

'I'll speak to her tomorrow,' I said. 'I'm sorry our night together didn't work out.'

George leaned over and kissed me.

'It doesn't matter,' he said. 'We'll have hundreds of nights together. Thousands. Millions even.'

When he'd gone, I pulled on a nightshirt and climbed into bed with Suze. She was out for the count and didn't even stir and I was dead to the world a few seconds later. It had been an exhausting day.

When I woke up, though, Suze was nowhere to be seen. I washed my face and got dressed and as I was pulling on my tights, Suze came home.

'You're awake,' she said. 'Good. I've got breakfast.'

She had bacon rolls from Bruno, and some of his best, strongest coffee. She laid it all out on her rickety table and grinned at me.

'Help yourself,' she said. 'It's an apology.'

I sipped the coffee, which was scorching hot, and shook my head.

'You don't have to apologise,' I said. 'I know how much seeing Vic shook you up.'

'Well a thank you then,' said Suze. 'I don't know what I'd do without you. Was Gloria annoyed that I didn't turn up at the party?'

'She didn't know,' I said, taking a bite of my roll. 'No one ever knows which of us is Suze and which is Nancy. So she assumed I was Suze, and it was easier not to explain.'

'Was it a good interview?'

'It was fantastic,' I said, excitedly. 'They're so nice and funny, and so keen to talk about something other than music. It'll make a great piece.'

There was a pause.

'When are you going to write it?' Suze said.

I grinned.

'I'd really like to do it today, while it's fresh in my mind,' I said. I reached out and took her hand. 'That's if you don't mind.'

Suze shook her head.

'Of course I don't mind,' she said. 'It makes no sense for you to do the interview and me to write the article. Viva won't mind, as long as you hit the deadline.'

'Once I've done the Viva piece, I'll write a slightly different one for our Mode application too,' I said.

'It's all coming together,' Suze said. 'As long as I don't ruin it all.'

'You won't ruin it. Why would you?'

'If Vic comes back, I'm not sure I can cope,' Suze said simply. 'I just can't deal with it all.'

'Of course you can cope,' I told her. 'You've coped all along. You're much stronger than Vic or Walter, or anyone else who's been horrible to you along the way.'

Suze looked doubtful.

'Oh Nance, I'm not sure I am. I'm not like you.'

I took her hand across the table.

'You're much stronger than me,' I said. 'You left, didn't you? I'm still there, avoiding my father and changing my clothes on the train.'

Suze gave me a weak smile.

'You're the bravest person I know,' she said.

'I've come to realise that the only person you can really rely on is yourself,' I said.

'And each other,' said Suze.

We looked at each other for a minute. She was right. As much as she needed me, I needed her. We balanced each other out and we understood each other. I knew Dennis cared about me, and wanted to protect me, but he didn't really 'get' me the way Suze did. His idea of looking after me meant me typing up school timetables in Leeds where he could keep an eye on me.

'We're going to make this work,' I said suddenly. 'Because we have to.'

Suze smiled.

'It's our only chance,' she said.

'I'm going to move in. Today, if that's okay?'

'Of course it's okay,' she said. 'Are you sure?'

I nodded firmly.

'I'll go home, get my stuff and move in,' I said. 'Dad's being really nice just now. I think maybe he's turned a corner.'

Suze frowned.

'Don't go when you know he'll be there,' she said. 'There's no point in making him cross.'

'He'll be fine, honestly.'

But she shook her head.

'Don't,' she said. 'Go and get your stuff when you know he's not there. It's not worth the risk of upsetting him.'

'All right,' I said, to stop her worrying. But I kept thinking about how Dad had said I should be a writer, and how calm he'd been when I told him about Billy, and I started to hatch a plan.

'I'm sure you're right,' I said.

Suze grinned and squeezed my arm.

'We'll be flatmates,' she said. 'Well, if you can call this a flat.'

'I call it home,' I said.

We smiled at each other for a minute, then Suze clapped her hands.

'Shall we get on? We've got lots to do if we're going to finish our magazine this week.'

'Okay,' I said. 'I'll write up the Stones interview first. Then we can lay out the dummy issue and see how it's all fitting together.'

'Great,' said Suze. 'Great.'

Suze was right, we did have a lot to do. Our version of Mode was taking shape but time was tight. We'd written all the features now, apart from the Stones interview, but that was the easy bit – the bit we knew about. Now we had to make it into something that resembled a magazine and that was going to be a lot harder because it wasn't anything we'd ever done before.

We had to lay out the articles so they looked right, add the pictures, and make sure the features followed each other in a logical order. We had to get the pace of the magazine right, so short features followed longer, meatier reads. It was going to be a challenge and we only had a week left before Margi arrived in London and we had to wow her with our efforts.

For now, though, I had to write this Rolling Stones interview. I settled myself down at Suze's desk, took the cover off my typewriter and wound a clean sheet of paper in. Then I opened my notebook. I knew how I wanted to begin – with Brian Jones begging me not to ask him about music – and I was sure the whole piece would flow once I'd got started.

'I don't want to talk about the new album,' Brian Jones says *when I arrive to talk about the Rolling Stones' new album ...* I

typed. Then I looked at Suze. She was crouching on the floor, trying to add pictures to a feature on the hottest new TV stars.

'Suze,' I said. 'You are okay, aren't you?'

She gave me one of her special, dazzling smiles.

'I'm fine darling,' she said. 'I'm absolutely fine.'

But she wasn't. And, as it happened, nor was I.

Chapter 38

It started with the haircut. I decided I was going to cut my hair
before I went home to get my things. I knew there was a chance
I'd back out of leaving home – after all, I'd done it many times
before. So I wanted to make sure I'd completely committed to
my new life.

Suze and I worked on our magazine most of the day, taking
the smallest of breaks for lunch. Then, at about three o'clock, I
said I had to go.

'I'm going to go and get my stuff,' I said.

Suze squealed in excitement.

'I'm working at Bruno's in a bit,' she said. 'Can you take
the dummy mag with you? I don't want to leave it here just
in case ...'

In case Vic came back, she meant. Though why she thought
he'd be interested in our Mode application, I had no idea. I picked
up the magazine anyway, though, and put it in my bag.

'Will your dad still be at the shop?' Suze asked.

I nodded, truthfully. He would still be there now, but I had
somewhere to go first. Anyway, I was still – naively – confident
that even if he was at home, he'd be fine about me leaving.

I hugged Suze goodbye and wandered down to Carnaby

Street. It was Saturday afternoon and it was buzzing. I smiled at the energy of it all, grinning at the girls standing around looking beautiful and the men standing around watching them. I had no time to stand around, though. I knew where I was going – a hairdresser I'd walked past many times on my way to George's studio. I hurried along the road towards it, then paused as I got to the door. Inside they were playing The Yardbirds loudly and inside two girls stood chatting to an older woman wearing a beautiful dress with large flowers all over it.

Without stopping to think, I pushed open the door. I was going to cut off all my hair – perhaps not quite as short as Suze, who wore hers in an Audrey Hepburn elfin crop. I was thinking more like Twiggy or Mary Quant. But either way it was going to mean I couldn't hide my double life any more.

In the end, I got a Twiggy. The hairdresser pointed out my rounded chin – Suze's was more angular – and said Mary Quant's blunt bob wouldn't do much for my face.

'You need a side parting,' she said.

I nodded and tried not to cry out in alarm as she picked up my ponytail and cut it off in one slice of her scissors.

She handed it to me over my shoulder and I gasped.

'New look,' she said.

'New life,' I added.

It was going to take a bit of getting used to, I thought, as I walked to the station later, looking at my reflection in shop windows as I passed.

My hair had been long, brushing my shoulder blades even when I wore it in a high ponytail. Now it stopped just below my ears. It parted above my left eye, and my blunt fringe had been swept across my forehead. I looked very different. Much more like Suze, actually, I thought, peering at myself in a car windscreen as I crossed St Martin's Lane. And very trendy. I was pleased. And nervous. What was Dad going to say?

213

For once I didn't change my clothes when I got on the train, or wipe off my thick eyeliner. I stayed in my mini dress and left all my make-up on. But as I got off the train at my stop, I felt my bravado start to desert me. What if Dad had been drinking already? It was after six o'clock now. He would've had time for a drink or two since the shop closed. For the first time in my life, I hoped he'd gone to the pub and was settling in for the night. I could grab the few bits I needed, scribble him a note, and leave. Suze was right, there was no point in antagonising him – not when I was so close to escaping.

'Come on, Nancy,' I said out loud. 'Worst case scenario, Dad will shout a bit. It's not a disaster. It's not the end; it's the beginning.'

Even so, my hands were shaking when I put my key in the lock. The house was quiet at first and I exhaled slowly. Then, from the lounge, came a shout.

'Oh here she is,' called Dad. 'Here she bloody is, Lady Muck.'

'Yes, it's me,' I said. 'Just going upstairs to get something.'

I started to creep up to my room, but Dad called again.

'I didn't make the final of the Business Awards,' he called. His words were slurred. 'Found out at lunchtime.'

I closed my eyes briefly. Dad was still grumbling.

'What do they know anyway,' he was muttering. 'Bunch of bloody twits.'

'Dad?' I said, one foot still on the bottom step. 'Who looked after the shop all afternoon?'

'I shut it,' he said. 'What do you care?'

So he'd been in the pub since lunchtime? Oh, I'd made a big mistake here. Big mistake.

'And then I went to the Three Tuns,' he said. 'And do you know who I saw in there?'

Oh god, who had he seen?

'I saw your Billy.'

I clung on to the banister, feeling weak with fright.

214

'I'm going to bed,' I said desperately, even though it wasn't even seven o'clock.

'Nancy!' Dad roared. 'Get in here.'

I slunk round the corner of the door into the room, trembling. I hated that I was so scared of him.

Dad looked at me and the scornful smile he wore on his face dropped.

'What,' he began. 'What have you done to yourself?'

'Dad,' I said.

'You look like a slut,' he said brutally. 'Like a silly slut.'

I hung my head.

'Billy told me all about your lies,' Dad carried on. 'Working in insurance, are you? Really?'

'No,' I said. 'I work on a magazine.'

'A magazine,' Dad said. 'With a load of women's libbers and poofs no doubt. Spreading shit.'

'It's a good job,' I said.

'You had a job,' Dad said.

'I don't want to work in the shop.'

Dad scowled.

'I don't care what you want,' he said. 'We've got a shop and you'll work in it.'

'Dennis doesn't,' I said.

Dad dismissed Dennis with a wave of his hand.

'Too good for us, are you?' he said. 'Too good for the shop and too good for poor Billy?'

'You said Billy's uncle was a twit,' I said.

'Well maybe that's all you deserve,' Dad said. 'What are you going to do now? If you think I'm going to be supporting you, you've got another think coming ...'

'Good,' I said. 'I'm not staying. I'm moving out.'

'Moving out,' said Dad in a silly voice. 'Oh listen to her, she's moving out.'

'I've got money, and I'll get a flat with a friend.'

215

'You bloody won't,' Dad said. 'Bringing shame on our family like that.'

'She's a woman,' I said. 'I'm getting a flat with my friend Suze.'

'Billy said you've got a boyfriend,' Dad said. 'With long hair.'

'He's called George,' I said. 'He's very nice.'

'Bollocks,' said Dad. 'I know what goes on. He's probably on drugs. And you're a slut. I never thought a daughter of mine would dump a nice lad like Billy and take up with a long-haired poofter.'

That was as nonsensical as it was insulting but it was useless trying to argue with Dad when he was in this mood. I turned to go, but that annoyed him.

'Where do you think you're going?' he said.

'I'm going to do some work,' I said. 'I've got a job interview on Monday morning.'

Dad stood up and stared at me.

'What sort of interview?'

I stood my ground, though I was quaking in my sensible shoes.

'There's a new magazine launching in Britain,' I said, trying to keep calm and hoping we could discuss this like adults instead of shouting. 'It's called Mode. It's aimed at young women like me and my boss thinks I'll be perfect for it. I've done a lot of work to prepare for it and I really think I stand a good chance.'

'Done a lot of work, have you?' Dad said. 'Show me.'

I didn't want to. I didn't want him to see the features we'd written on marriage or sex or the Stones.

'I don't have it,' I lied.

Dad's eyes flickered to my bag, which I was still gripping tightly.

'In there, is it?' he said.

'I don't have it,' I said again.

'Give it to me.'

I shook my head but Dad grabbed the bag anyway. He pulled

out our dummy magazine and started leafing through it, his face getting redder and redder with rage.

'This is disgraceful,' he said. 'Disgusting.'

Furious even at the thought of his meaty fingers on my hard work, I lost my temper.

'Oh don't give me that shit,' I said. 'What about those bloody magazines you sell? The ones on the top shelf? The ones that Mr Forester comes in for every Monday? I know what's in those, and it's not fairy stories. Now give me back my work.'

I went to grab the magazine but Dad swiped at me and caught me across the cheekbone with the back of his hand.

I stumbled against the coffee table and sat down with a thump onto the floor.

'Want it back?' said Dad. He drained his glass and dangled the magazine in front of me. I didn't move, scared he would hit me again. My heart was pounding and there was a rushing noise in my ears.

Feeling dizzy I watched in horror as slowly Dad began ripping up my magazine. First he pulled off the cover, featuring one of George's pictures and our carefully etched lines. He pulled it off, then he tore it in half, once, twice, three times. And he scattered the pieces on the floor.

He did the same thing to every single page. I sat on the floor and sobbed as he tore up those pieces of paper that amounted to hours and hours of hard work. The falling scraps of magazine looked a bit like confetti, which was ironic considering it was me calling off my wedding that had started all this.

When he'd finished, Dad threw the final torn scraps in my direction and glanced at me with disgust.

'I'm ashamed of you,' he hissed. 'You're a disgrace.'

Then he stepped over me and left the room. A minute or so later I heard the front door bang shut and his footsteps on the path as he headed for the pub.

'Oh no,' I said. 'Oh no.'

Still crying, I scrabbled round on the floor, gathering up all the pieces of paper but it was no use. The bits were tiny and there was absolutely no chance of me being able to piece it all together. The magazine was completely ruined and our interview was two days away. What on earth were we going to do?

Chapter 39

2016

Sometimes I wondered how anyone did anything before the internet. I supposed back in the day I'd have had to go to the library or some dusty council office and look stuff up in books of birth certificates. But obviously I started my search for Nancy Harrison on trusty Google.

There wasn't much. In fact, there was hardly anything, but I supposed that wasn't surprising if she died when she was in her early twenties.

All I found to begin with were various obituaries of a head-teacher from Yorkshire called Dennis Harrison. He'd died a few months ago and his obituary had been in all the broadsheet newspapers.

I clicked on the first link and scanned it. He'd been a maverick headteacher at one of the country's top public schools, introducing all sorts of new teaching methods and causing quite a stir. Yawn. I wasn't interested in that … and then halfway down, the obit started to talk about his early life.

'Dennis was born in 1941 in South London to mother Mary and father Frank,' it read. 'He grew up helping in his parents' newsagents with his sister Nancy. Dennis was estranged from his father. After his sister's death in 1966, after his mother's death several years before, he and his father remained at odds. Dennis considered his in-laws his family ...'

I felt sorry for Dennis, losing his mum and sister in the space of a few years and not speaking to his dad. And I felt sorry for Nancy, being reduced to a passing comment in her brother's obituary. Was that all her life amounted to?

I printed out one of the obituaries and carried on my search, this time checking the images that came up.

Among reams of photos from yearbooks from the class of 1966 at various American high schools, I saw the same black and white image appear several times. I clicked on it – which took me to a Rolling Stones fan site – and studied it closely.

The photograph showed the band, who were very young, sitting in a booth in an amazing sixties nightclub with a black and white checked dancefloor. They weren't posing – it was a candid shot. Mick Jagger was sitting on the left hand side of the booth, closest to the camera, while the others – I struggled to think of their names, though I knew Bill Wyman and I thought the one with fair hair had died young – all laughed together. One of them was drinking a pint. Mick Jagger, whose long legs were stretched out under the table, was talking earnestly to a young woman who sat opposite him. She had a notebook in front of her and she was wearing an amazing dogtooth checked mini dress. Her head rested on her left hand and her long dark straight hair had swung forward, hiding her face as she wrote. Was this Nancy Harrison?

I scrolled down the page and found the picture caption.

'At the party for the launch of their 1966 LP Aftermath, the boys were in demand,' the caption read. 'They were interviewed by newspapers but always said they enjoyed speaking to writers from magazines more. At this party they spoke to writers Suze Williams (Viva) and Nancy Harrison (Mode) about their views on Harold Wilson and who they thought would win the upcoming

World Cup. Brian tipped West Germany to take the prize – something he later denied ...' The copyright said George Mann.

I stared at the photo. Was that Suze or Nancy, then? It was impossible to tell – though I thought it had to be Nancy purely because Suze had short hair in the photos from the first issue of Mode.

I remembered seeing an interview with the Stones in one of the other issues of Mode that Emily had found. Now I leafed through them to find it. It was in the third issue of the magazine – a double-page spread with a fabulous photo of the band all standing in a row, legs wide, shot from low down, making them look like they owned the world. The byline on the interview was Nancy Harrison – who must have been dead by then. How sad and brilliant that the magazine had carried on printing her work even after she'd died. I turned the page round to read the photo credit and once more it said copyright George Mann.

I printed the photo out, and turned to Google once more, typing in *George Mann photographer*.

This time I had loads of hits. Hundreds in fact. He was still alive, living and working in Paris as far as I could tell. He was a fashion photographer and shot portraits too.

I found his website, which was all in French, and called up the page that had his contact information on it. There was a phone number. Did I dare call him and ask about Nancy Harrison? He must have known her ...

Vanessa made me jump as she came into my office with a page proof for me to read.

'Sorry,' she said. 'You were away with the fairies there. Working on the relaunch issue?'

I looked up from my screen.

'Sort of,' I admitted. 'Trying to find out what happened to Nancy Harrison.'

'Have you replied to Suze?' Vanessa asked, coming round my side of the desk so she could peer at my screen.

221

'Not yet,' I said. 'I wanted to find out if she was a murder suspect before I committed.'

Vanessa giggled – it was a strange sound.

'What have you found?'

I showed her the obituary for Nancy's brother and the Rolling Stones picture.

'So I've found this George,' I said. 'But he lives in Paris and his website's all in French. I was going to phone him, but I'm nervous. I can't really speak French, apart from ordering a drink.'

'I speak French,' Vanessa said, to my surprise.

'You do?'

'My degree's in French,' she said. 'I lived in Paris for a year too.'

Well if that wasn't a lesson in learning more about your staff I didn't know what was.

'Do you want me to phone him?' she said.

'Yes please,' I said. 'I'll talk to George – presumably he's English – but I was worried about speaking to an assistant.'

Vanessa gave a very Gallic shrug and picked up my phone.

She dialled the number and waited.

'*Bonjour…*' she said, and she was off, gabbling away. I picked out a few words – Mode, mostly. And Nancy Harrison. Then she paused, nodding, and grinned at me. '*Merci*,' she said.

She looked at me.

'He's coming to the phone,' she said. She handed it to me just as a voice said: '*Bonjour*?'

'Oh,' I said. '*Bonjour*. Is that George?'

'Speaking,' he said – oh the relief of him talking in English. 'My assistant tells me you want to know about Nancy Harrison?'

'I do,' I said. I explained who I was, and that we were recreating the first issue of Mode. Then I fibbed a bit and said we were doing a 'where are they now' piece about everyone who was involved in that first magazine.

'I know Nancy died,' I said. 'But I don't know anything else. I saw your name on lots of photos from the time and I thought you might have been friends with her.'

There was silence on the other end of the line, for so long that I thought we'd been cut off. But then George spoke.

'We were friends,' he said. 'More than friends, in fact. She was my girlfriend. At least, I hoped she was going to be. It was fairly complicated because she was engaged to someone else when we met.'

'Messy,' I said.

George chuckled.

'Not as far as Nancy was concerned,' he said. 'She was very single-minded. She knew what she wanted and how to get it.'

'What happened?' I asked. 'Were you there when she died?'

'No,' George said slowly. 'And I have always been sorry about that. I was in Paris actually, on a job.'

'Go on.'

'I was away and Nancy was dealing with lots of things. She and Suze – do you know about Suze?'

'I've met her,' I admitted.

'Really?' George sounded astonished. 'She keeps herself very much to herself these days.'

'I had to sweet-talk my way in,' I told him and he chuckled again. I did the same, warming to this kind-sounding man.

'So Nancy had been fibbing to her father – pretending she had a respectable job when really she was working on a magazine and spending all her time with Suze and me, at various shindigs.'

I stifled a giggle at the old-fashioned word.

'But her ex-fiancé spilled the beans. He told her dad what she'd been up to – out of spite as far as I could tell. She turned up on my doorstep battered and bruised after her dad took out his anger on her.'

I gasped.

'Did he kill her? Her dad?'

'Oh goodness me, no,' said George. 'At least not directly. She took an overdose. Accidentally, I've always assumed. And she died.'

'Oh,' I said. 'How sad.'

'I was heartbroken,' he said. 'My boss told me and I made the decision to stay in Paris with him. I couldn't handle London without Nancy. I felt responsible, you see. I knew what her father had done to her. But I'd believed her when she'd said she was all right and I went off to Paris that morning without a care in the world.'

'Did you ask Suze what happened?'

'I tried,' he said. 'But I didn't know where she was for ages, and then when I found out she was working for Mode, I did write, but she didn't reply. I always assumed it was painful for her, too. She was the one who had a Valium habit, you see? It must have been her pills Nancy took.'

I wasn't sure what to say. It seemed a sad, insignificant end for someone who had a bright future, though it did explain why Suze was reluctant to talk about her friend.

'I've got lots of photographs,' George was saying. 'Reams of the bloody things. I spent a lot of time with Nancy and Suze back then, so they were often in my photos. Would you like me to email you a selection?'

'Oh I'd love that,' I said. I gave him my email address and thanked him profusely for all his help, then hung up.

'So Suze isn't a murderer?' Vanessa said.

'Not a murderer,' I said. 'Just someone who feels guilty about a friendship that went wrong.'

'Email her then,' Vanessa said. 'Email her and tell her we need her help.'

So I did.

Chapter 40

1966

I went to George, of course. I knew Suze would still be working at Bruno's and I didn't want to be alone. I wanted to feel George's arms round me, to feel his lips on mine. Dad made me think I was worthless, like I was – at best – an irritation to be swiped away like an annoying fly. At his worst, like today, he made me feel uncertain and unsafe. George, though. George made me feel like I meant something.

I rang the bell to his tiny flat above the studio and leaned against the doorframe, weak from fatigue, hunger and emotion. My lip had swelled up where Dad had hit me, and my cheekbone was tender.

George's footsteps came bounding down the stairs and he flung open the door.

'Nancy ...' his voice trailed off as he saw my bruises. 'Oh, Nancy. What happened?'

'Dad,' I said. I tried to stand up straight but I stumbled a bit and George caught me.

'Woah,' he said. 'Can you manage the stairs?'

'Slowly,' I said, relieved he was here and with me. Carefully, we climbed the narrow steps, George leading the way and holding tight to my hand. Up in his flat, he steered me to the sofa and sat me down, then he bustled round like a mother hen, making me tea and toast and pouring me a brandy from a bottle Frank kept in the studio.

'I don't like brandy,' I said.

'Drink it,' he said, pushing the glass into my hand. 'It's good for shock.'

I looked at my hands, which were still shaking, and sipped obediently.

'I like your hair,' George said. He was sitting at the other end of the sofa, watching me closely.

I'd forgotten. I put my hand up to my head and touched my new style. It seemed like I'd had it done in a dream.

'I was so stupid,' I said, remembering how I'd thought Dad would be proud of me. How he'd give me his blessing. 'Dad was so angry and he knew about my job. Billy told him.'

A shadow crossed George's face.

'I thought you said Billy knew what your dad was like?'

I shrugged.

'I thought he did. But we never talked about it.'

'And he still told your dad?'

I tucked my legs under me.

'Maybe he didn't mean to,' I said, trying not to think too badly of Billy, who I'd almost loved, once.

George wrapped me in his arms and kissed my bruises gently.

'He's not important,' he said. 'I will be here for you. I'll make sure nothing happens to you ever again.'

I smiled at him.

'I'll look after you, too.'

We lay cuddled up together on the sofa for a long time, chatting about everything and nothing.

Much later, George went out and bought bread and cheese and we made sandwiches. I was still very sore and sad, but I was starting to feel better. I knew I'd have to write to Dennis and tell him what had happened and I knew that meant his already fragile relationship with Dad would finally fall apart, but we'd have each other. And I had George, and Suze. I was going to be all right.

It was properly dark in the flat now. George got up to put on the lights and chose a record to play. He paused before he came back to sit down.

'Nancy?' he said. 'I need to tell you something.'

I'd been lying on the couch, but now I sat up. His tone suggested he didn't just want to tell me he liked my hair, or he'd like me to stay the night.

'What?' I said. 'Are you married?' I giggled weakly.

George came and sat down and took my hands.

'Frank's moving to Paris for a year,' he said. 'Maybe two. Maybe forever.'

'Oh,' I said. 'Is it because Rosemary's leaving?' I'd always thought there was a spark between Rosemary and Frank, even though they were like chalk and cheese in appearance, with Rosemary's smart suits and Frank's shaggy beard.

George smiled briefly.

'I think he thought she might ask him to go to New York with her,' he said. 'But she didn't. His pride's a bit hurt.'

'Poor lovesick Frank,' I said.

George paused.

'Nance, Frank's asked me to go to Paris,' he said.

'For how long?'

He bit his lip.

'Forever.'

'What did you say?' I asked carefully.

'I said I'd think about it,' George said. 'But I've thought about it now and I've made my decision.'

I looked up at him, trying not to appear too desperate.

'And?'

'I'm going to stay here,' he said.

227

'Are you sure?' I said. 'There's lots of opportunities in Paris.'

George nodded.

'Just as many opportunities in London,' he said. 'Frank's always been more of a fashion photographer than me. I like snapping bands and actors – portraits.'

'So you're staying,' I said, throwing my arms round him. 'Oh thank god.'

George kissed me.

'I do need to go for a while, though,' he said. 'Frank's already out there and I need to help him set up his studio and tell him to his face that I'm not going. He's been really good to me over the years.'

'When?'

'Tomorrow,' George said, making a face. 'Sorry.'

'It's fine,' I said. 'I'll stay with Suze anyway. Oh, what will happen to this studio?'

George grinned.

'I'm hoping Frank will let me keep it on,' he said. 'I'll find an assistant and start up on my own.'

'You've got it all planned,' I said, feeling a glimmer of excitement. 'You go to Paris and tie up your loose ends, Suze and I will go to our Mode interviews ...'

My stomach plummeted to the floor.

'Oh.'

'What's the matter?'

I filled George in on what Dad had done to our dummy mag.

'When's the interview? Tuesday?'

I nodded.

'You've still got time.'

'Not much.' George looked stern.

'Nancy Harrison,' he said. 'You've survived your mum dying, your dad's violence, and living a double life for months and months. Suze has escaped from a mum who couldn't care less,

228

plus some very unsavoury characters in London and she's come out of it all with their flat and her head held high.'

'Riiight,' I said.

'You're not going to tell me you're going to let a tiny thing like your dad being an idiot stop you now, are you?'

'You think we can still do it?' I said.

'Of course you can.' He kissed my knuckles. 'You can do anything.'

'I should go and tell Suze,' I said, looking at my watch. 'She'll just be helping Bruno close up.'

'Stay here,' George said. 'Have some sleep, go to work in the morning and see Suze later. There's no rush.'

'There is a lot of rush,' I pointed out. But George kissed my neck and I decided he was probably right. I could stay a while longer …

The next morning I felt a bit like we were playing house as George made me a cup of tea in bed, helped me make sure all my bruises were hidden as best as they could be with make-up, and later kissed me goodbye when I left for work. I hoped one day we could make a home together, though right now I was more interested in moving in with Suze. I didn't want to split up with Billy just to tie myself down to someone else – much as I loved spending time with George I wasn't in a hurry to start washing his underwear or cooking his dinner.

That made me think of Dad. I thought he'd probably only notice I'd gone when he didn't have a meal on the table at teatime. I shuddered at the idea of how angry he'd be, then dismissed the thought. It wasn't my problem any more.

Except it was.

Chapter 41

I was finishing filing some back issues later that afternoon and thinking about going to see Suze after work when the phone on my desk rang.

'Home & Hearth,' I said into the receiver. 'Nancy Harrison speaking.'

'Nancy, thank god,' said a voice. My stomach lurched.

'Billy?' I said, alarmed. 'What? What do you want? Why are you phoning me at work?'

'It took me ages to find your number,' Billy said, his words tumbling over each other. 'I went to that other newsagents in the high street to find a copy of your magazine because I reckoned it would have the address in it, but I couldn't remember what it was called, just that it had Home in the title, so I had to search through a few different ones.'

I didn't care.

'What do you want?' I said again.

'I wanted to warn you,' Billy said. 'I think your dad's on the warpath.'

I'd been standing up when I answered the phone. Now I sat down heavily and leaned on my desk. Without thinking, I gently touched my swollen lip.

'It's too late, Billy,' I spat. 'I know you told him everything. And he made it quite clear how he felt when he belted me.'

'Today?' Billy said.

'No, not today, yesterday. Why are you phoning me, Billy?' I had no interest in talking to him. Not now. Not ever.

'He's coming now,' Billy said. His voice trembled a little bit. 'I think he's coming to find you.'

I let out a bark of laughter. Dad wouldn't get on a train and go into town. He hardly ever left Beckenham.

'I'm glad to hear you're so worried about me,' I said sarcastically. 'But I'm fine – now – no thanks to you. I'm at work and Dad's at the shop and I've got away.'

Billy let out a frustrated breath.

'Nancy,' he almost shouted. 'Would you bloody well listen to me.'

Startled, I shut up.

'I walked past the shop at lunch and it was closed,' he said. 'And I wondered why. So I went round to yours to see if everything was okay. And your neighbour – that nosy old bat – said she'd seen your dad waiting outside the Tuns for it to open earlier on. So I went down there and Mick behind the bar said he'd thrown your dad out for being rude – it was only just after lunch so he'd obviously had a skinful already ...'

'Get to the point, Bill,' I said, my heart beating faster.

'And Mick said your dad had asked someone what time the next train to Charing Cross was. So I ran to the station, thinking I might catch him, but the train was pulling out when I got there.'

I sighed heavily.

'Dad doesn't even know where I work, Billy,' I said. 'He won't come here.'

Billy paused for a minute.

'He does know,' he said. 'He knows the name of the magazine at any rate. I told him. And it's not like he's got to look hard to find your magazine and the address that's written inside.'

231

'Billy,' I said, bewildered by all this information he was giving me. 'Why did you tell him, Billy?'

'I'm so sorry,' he wailed. 'I was hurt and I just wanted to put you in your place, I suppose.'

I looked at my watch. It was almost five o'clock.

'This happened at lunchtime?' I said.

'Just after,' agreed Billy. 'I reckon it was about two o'clock when I saw the train leaving.'

So Dad would have been in town for well over two hours and he'd not shown up at my office. I breathed out slowly.

'He's not here,' I said. 'If he was going to come here, he'd be here by now.'

'You've not seen him?'

'No,' I said. 'Are you sure he was on that train?'

'Well, I didn't see him on it,' Billy said. 'I suppose he might have gone somewhere else.'

'Railway Tavern, probably,' I said, thinking of the pub that overlooked the station.

'Oh bloody hell,' said Billy. 'I bet he's in the pub right now, and I've just gone and got you all worried for nothing.'

'He's probably passed out in a corner,' I said.

'I'm really sorry Nance,' Billy said. 'Sorry for telling him and sorry that he hit you.'

'I'm sorry too,' I said. 'Sorry for lying.'

'I'm glad you're all right,' Billy said. 'Look after yourself.'

He hung up.

Shaking my head, I breathed a sigh of relief both that he'd been wrong and that we'd reached a sort of understanding. I'd probably never see him again, I thought. I wasn't even the tiniest bit sad about that.

I finished my filing, did a few other jobs, then I gathered everything I needed to have a go at rescuing our preparation for the Mode interview, and left work for the day.

As I reached the bottom of Berwick Street, approaching Suze's squat, I saw Dad. He was staggering along Peter Street, in the opposite direction from the squat. Instinctively I slunk behind the fruit stall at the end of the road, so he couldn't see me. He was dishevelled and wearing the same clothes as he'd worn yesterday. His face was ruddy and his knuckles bloody – I wondered if it was my blood. He looked like a tramp. As I watched him wind his way towards Wardour Street, I realised I felt nothing for him at all. Nothing but disdain and disgust. What a horrible, pathetic man he was. I wasn't scared of him any more. He wasn't dangerous and he could wander round Soho all he wanted, he wouldn't find me at Suze's – not with her big padlock and thick wooden panel on the door. But then I glanced over to the squat and gasped in surprise. The door was open.

Checking to make sure Dad was far enough away not to spot me, I ducked out from the safety of the fruit stall and ran for the squat, shutting and locking the door firmly behind me.

'Suze?' I called as I went up the stairs. 'Suze?'

I heard her footsteps above.

'Nancy,' she said, her voice quivery. 'Nancy? Did you lock the door?'

'Yes,' I said. 'Are you all right?'

I went into the living room. Suze was sitting on the couch, with her knees hunched up.

Her right eye was swollen shut and turning a livid purple. Her fingers on both hands were bruised and she had a large welt on her arm.

'What happened?' I said, horrified at the very sight of her.

She looked at me.

'Your dad happened.'

Sick with fear and guilt I dropped my bags and went to her.

'What did he do?' I said. 'What happened?'

'Have you got anything to drink?' Suze said.

I dug in the side pocket of my bag and found a small bottle

of gin I'd swiped from Dad's drinks cabinet before I left. I waved it at Suze.

'That's it,' she said, her teeth chattering – I wasn't sure if it was from fear or cold. 'Pour me some and I'll tell you the whole sorry story.'

Chapter 42

We drank our gin out of mugs because that's all we had. Suze cried. I cried. It was quite a messy business.

'He was in Broadwick Street when I left Bruno's after my lunchtime shift,' Suze explained. 'Obviously I had no idea who he was but I noticed him because he was kind of lurching about. When I walked past him, he started following me. Shouting stuff.'

'What sort of stuff?'

'Calling me Lady Bloody Muck, and asking why I was ignoring him when he was my father. I just thought he was crazy.'

'Sounds like my dad,' I said. I brushed back Suze's hair carefully and looked at her bashed face. 'Shall I put some ice on that?'

Suze shook her head, then winced.

'Don't have any,' she said.

'I'll go and get some from Bruno.'

She grabbed my hand.

'Don't,' she said. 'Don't go.'

She drained her gin and held out the mug for more.

'So he followed you?' I said, topping her up.

'He followed me down Berwick Street, but I just ignored him,' said Suze.

'Then as soon as I'd unlocked the door, he appeared.'

'You let him in?' I said, surprised.

Suze looked straight at me.

'He called me Nancy,' she said. 'He thought I was you.'

'Oh no,' I breathed.

'I'd just opened the door, and he said your name, and I turned round to look at him, thinking I could tell him I wasn't you,' Suze said. 'And he shoved me inside and followed me up the stairs. I couldn't get away.'

She started to cry again.

'He was shouting, and holding my shoulders and shaking me,' she said. 'I was so scared, Nance.'

'It's okay,' I said, feeling guilt weighing me down. 'It's not your fault.'

'And then, out of the corner of my eye, I saw our typewriters,' Suze carried on. 'And I thought about us getting jobs on Mode and finding a flat and I suddenly felt like I was stronger than I'd ever been before.'

A sudden memory of Dad ripping up our magazine floated into my head and I shuddered. How was I going to tell Suze all our plans were in tatters – literally.

'What did you do?'

'I kicked him,' Suze said, a small smile on her lips. 'I kicked him really hard in the shin.'

'And he stopped shouting?'

'Well,' Suze said. 'No.'

'He hit you?'

She nodded.

'He hit me. But I fought back. He didn't like it. He punched me, over and over, but I fought back and he gave up.'

Very gently I stroked her bruised fingers.

'You're so brave, Suze,' I said.

She smiled at me.

'It was all our plans that made me fight him,' she said. 'I had something to battle for.'

'Oh Suze,' I said, my voice wobbling. 'I think it's all gone wrong.'

For the first time, Suze looked at me properly.

'You've had your hair cut,' she said. 'No wonder your dad mixed us up.'

She took a gulp of gin and looked at me again.

'Did someone hit you?' she said, reaching out a hand to touch my cheek.

'Dad,' I said. 'Yesterday.'

Suze looked really tired.

'He doesn't like it when we argue, does he?'

I slopped more gin into each of our mugs and topped them up with lemonade. Then slowly, I told Suze what had happened yesterday when I went home – it seemed like a lifetime ago now.

'Do you think your dad will come back?'

'I don't know,' I admitted. 'I never thought he'd come here in the first place. He's really angry.'

'Are you scared of him?' Suze asked.

'I wasn't,' I said. 'But now I know what he's done to you, I'm terrified. I'm so sorry, Suze. So sorry.'

'We should swap names,' Suze said with a humourless laugh. 'You be Suze and I'll be Nancy and then if he tries to find you he'll find me instead.'

'That's not the answer,' I said, guilt making me snappy. 'The answer is getting on with our lives.'

'You're right,' Suze said.

'There's just one problem,' I said. 'Dad ripped up our magazine.'

'Can we stick it back together?'

I reached into my pocket and pulled out some of the tiny shreds.

'No,' I said. I opened my hand and the pieces scattered across the floor.

Suze stared at the bits in despair.

'So that's it,' she said. 'It's all gone? All our work?'

237

She started breathing heavily.

'That's it,' she said, panicking. 'It's gone. Our future. It's gone.'

She got up and started pacing across the floor.

'Without this, there's nothing to aim for,' she said frantically. 'We were stupid to try and escape, Nancy, so stupid.'

'Calm down,' I said, scared by her haunted look. 'Suze, calm down.'

Suze grabbed her bag and pulled out a brown bottle of pills.

'What's that?' I said. 'What are those pills?'

Suze poured a couple into her palm and swallowed them, washing them down with a swig of gin.

'It's just my Valium,' she said, staring at me defiantly.

I took the bottle. The name on the label read Edna Evans.

'Oh Suze, this isn't the way to cope. Where did you get it?'

Suze snatched it back.

'I told you, I know people. It helps me, Nancy. It keeps me calm.'

I rolled my eyes.

'Fine. But don't take any more,' I said. 'I need you to stay awake.'

'Why?'

'It's not over,' I said. 'The interview's not until tomorrow afternoon, right?'

Suze nodded, staring glumly into the bottom of her almost-empty mug.

'So we've got hours to make this work.'

'What do you mean?'

'I mean,' I said. 'We've got notes, yes? And loads of ideas?'

Suze nodded again.

'We don't need the magazine to show the people at Mode what we're capable of. We just need ourselves.'

'Re-do it, you mean?'

I shook my head.

'We don't have time to re-do it. But we can write a brilliant

238

presentation. Wow them with how excited we are, how talented, how innovative …'

Suze looked at me, a glimmer of a smile on her face.

'We've got copies of our articles,' she said.

'Exactly.'

'All right,' she said, chinking her mug against mine. 'Let's do it.'

Chapter 43

2016

Suze was eager as anything to help me with the relaunch of
Mode. I was absolutely thrilled – and more than a little relieved
– to have her on board. As soon as she got my email begging
for her help, she rang me and we chatted for ages about ideas
and cover lines and how to promote the new issue. She was so
full of energy, she was going to be a real asset. I wondered if I
could give her an honorary title, like consulting editor or something. I felt like she deserved to be rewarded for the help she
was giving me and I was fairly sure Lizzie wouldn't let me put
her on the payroll.

I didn't mention George, obviously. I didn't want her to think
I was digging into her past when it was clearly uncomfortable
for her. And I really didn't want to put her off helping us. I
knew we needed her much more than she needed us. No, I was
going to keep my conversation with George to myself. For now
at least.

Chatting to Suze, though, was a bright spot in a pretty gloomy
day. Later on that afternoon, as most of my team started leaving
for the day – they had things to do, unlike me – I sat at my desk,

staring at my budgets. They were small. Tiny, in fact. And I was expected to work miracles.

I spent about an hour moving money around, trying to trick the finance department into thinking I'd spent less than I had, then I gave up and opened my email instead.

I had one from Mum with the subject 'Exciting News'. I sighed and clicked on it to open it.

'Darling,' she wrote. 'I know how hard you're finding your new job …'

I rolled my eyes. Mum had barely asked me anything at all about work when we'd had lunch the other day.

'It sounds like rather a thankless task.'

That was true.

'I was talking to a friend, Bev, at work yesterday and mentioned you. I said you were stuck in this job and having trouble finding something else …'

What? I wasn't stuck, and I definitely wasn't even looking for something else.

'Bev agreed with me that creative jobs are simply never as engaging, as rewarding or as financially stable as other roles,' Mum wrote. 'And then this morning she came to find me and she mentioned she's launching a new journal for economists. She needs someone to edit it, darling, and of course she thought of you. She thinks you could do a really good job, and when I told her how savvy you are in terms of social media and whatnot, she was thrilled. She wants you to phone her and have a chat, but I said you'd bite her hand off for the opportunity. It's perfect for you, Fearne. It's creative but not frivolous and it could lead to you becoming the face of our research on television and radio – I know you enjoy that sort of thing. And, best of all, it's a well-paid job …'

And here she wrote a figure that was slightly less than half of what I was earning on Mode.

I felt sudden despair that whatever I did, however hard I

241

worked, however much money I earned, my mother would always wish I was the editor of some academic journal rather than an internationally-renowned fashion magazine. I wished so much that Mum would just be proud of me, but I was no longer sure that it would ever happen.

I clicked to reply to her message.

'Thanks for thinking of me,' I wrote. 'But I'm happy here for now. Fx'

I pressed send, and leaned back in my chair, marvelling that Mum could make me feel so shitty from fifty miles away in Oxford.

'No,' I said out loud.

I opened my email again and opened another reply to Mum.

'When I was a little girl,' I wrote, bashing the keys hard as I typed furiously. 'I used to make my own magazines, stapling bits of paper together, and drawing the covers. Do you remember? Probably not. I've got them all at home – I've saved them and I still look at them sometimes when I want to remember how far I've come. I have always wanted to be editor of a magazine. In fact, I've always wanted to be editor of THIS magazine. And now I've done it. It's not been easy to get here, and it's not easy now I'm here, but I've done it, Mum. Mode – that's the magazine I work on, in case you don't remember – is struggling, but I've come up with a plan to save it. And I'm going to do it. I'm going to save Mode.'

I paused in my typing. This was like therapy. I wasn't sure I should send it but it was definitely good for me to get it all out.

'I'm recreating the first issue of Mode,' I wrote. 'My team are all excited. I'm excited. I've tracked down someone who worked on that issue, and she's helping. It's going to be huge. We're planning to create a huge buzz. I'm even thinking we might change how magazines are sold forever – someone on my team has come up with some amazingly creative ways to

242

get young women to buy our mags. You're right, it's a struggle. It's the hardest job I've ever done, and it's emotional, and exhausting and some days I think I just want to give up, but I'm not going to. And do you know why? Because of you. Because you always told me that everything that's worth doing is hard. That the very fact that it's hard makes it mean something. That the reason I'm nervous about making it work is because I care. You told me that, Mum. You're the person who gave me my work ethic. It was you who told me if I worked hard I could achieve anything I wanted. And now it turns out that's not what you meant after all. You meant I could achieve anything I wanted, but you'd only be proud of me if I achieved what YOU wanted. And that's not fair, Mum. You moved the goalposts after I'd kicked the ball. Well, you know what? It doesn't matter any more. Because I'm proud of me. Bloody proud. And you can tell Bev I don't want her sodding job. I've got a job. And I love it.'

Worn out with the effort of putting so much emotion down in writing, I sat back in my chair and took a swig of – cold – coffee. Yuk.

I read through the email again. It said everything I'd ever wanted to say to Mum. But I knew if I sent it I might regret it. What should I do? I wished Jen was here so I could talk it through with her. Or Damo, even. I had no idea where he was – I'd barely seen him all day. I had no one to discuss it with, I realised. No one who'd care about my family problems.

Feeling really alone, I looked at my screen. Then I carefully dragged the email into my drafts folder and saved it. Never send anything written in anger, I thought. I'd keep the tirade to myself for now. But just writing it had made me feel better. And knowing I could decide to send it at any time made me feel better still.

'Final warning,' I said to Mum, even though she was miles away and probably wouldn't even have listened if she was in the same room as me. 'Final warning. If you put me down, or criticise my job once more, I'm sending the email.'

I stood up, feeling more in control.

'Final bloody warning.'

Then I switched off my computer and went home to my empty flat.

Chapter 44

1966

It was a long night. Suze and I trawled through our notes and rewrote our presentation about what we thought Mode should offer.

I sat at the desk and pounded away on my typewriter, while Suze paced the squat, checked that the copies we'd made of our articles were readable, and told me what to write.

It would have been hard enough to do all that anyway, but Suze was on a knife-edge emotionally. She kept drifting off, sometimes in the middle of a sentence – I imagined the Valium was to blame for that – or bursting into tears.

Each time she cried, I paused in my typing, and went to her. I sat with her and listened as she told me how Dad coming to the squat, along with that Vic showing up at Bruno's, had made her feel weak and vulnerable once more.

'You fought Dad off,' I said. 'You're not weak.'

'I'm always going to be looking over my shoulder for Vic or Walter,' she said. 'Always.'

'No,' I said firmly. 'No. They don't care about us. They'll move on, and Walter will forget you.'

Suze wiped her eyes with the back of her hand, smearing eyeliner across her cheek.

'Will you forget your dad?' she said. 'He'll always be there for you. What he did. How he smelled. How it felt.'

I pulled a tissue out of my sleeve and gently wiped her eyeliner away.

'We need to use it,' I said. 'Use that fear and the anger and the strength that you had when you fought him today, and that I had when I stood up to him yesterday, and we have to use it to make our lives better.'

Suze's face crumpled.

'I can't,' she said.

I took the mug of gin from her.

'No more,' I said. 'We need clear heads for this. And it's making you miserable.'

Suze protested, but I wouldn't budge.

'No more.'

We carried on working. Once, out of the corner of my eye, I thought I saw Suze swallow another Valium, but I wasn't sure and I didn't want to challenge her again.

Eventually, as the light in the room grew brighter, we finished.

It wasn't as good as our dummy magazine had been, but we had a presentation for Margi. We had an exciting vision for the magazine we wanted to read – the magazine we thought Mode should be. We had examples of our writing and proof that we had our fingers on the pulse of all the brilliant things that were happening in Britain right now. We had my Stones interview, and my personal pieces about why I didn't want to get married or have children. We had Suze's film previews and music reviews. We had lots and lots of ideas. And we had enthusiasm. If our enthusiasm was tinged with a hint of desperation then so be it. Sometimes it didn't hurt to show how badly you wanted something.

'This is good, Suze,' I said, gathering together the bundle of pages and slipping them all into a folder. 'It's really good. We've done the best we could do, under the circumstances.'

She nodded, but she didn't look very confident.

'I look terrible,' she said.

'We can have a go at hiding your eye with make-up,' I said. 'I've had a lot of practice. My bruises aren't nearly as bad as yours, so hopefully mine will be easier to cover, if I go heavy on the panstick.'

Suze nodded.

'What time is it?'

I looked at my watch.

'Just after four in the morning,' I said. 'I might try to get some sleep actually. You should too.'

I wasn't going to work the next day – I had the day off and so did Suze. Bruno was more excited about us going for jobs on Mode than we were. Our interview wasn't until three o'clock. We had plenty of time to catch up on some sleep before we had to start getting ready.'

But Suze shook her head.

'You go ahead,' she said. 'My head's buzzing and I can't sleep now. I'm going for a walk to clear my thoughts.'

'Do you want me to come with you?' I said, though my eyelids were drooping and I really didn't want to leave the squat.

'No,' Suze said. 'I won't be long. You get into bed and I'll try not to wake you when I come home.'

'Okay,' I said. 'But make sure you sleep, right?'

Suze nodded.

'I will.'

She grabbed her keys and headed downstairs while I stripped down to my underwear and snuggled down under the sheets. I remember thinking I might not be able to sleep because so much had happened that day, but I must have been asleep within seconds.

I woke to the noise of shouts from the market under Suze's window and for a second I wasn't sure where I was.

It was properly light in the room now – sun shining through the chiffon Suze had draped over her windows. I glanced at my watch. It was after ten o'clock. We really needed to start getting ready.

Suze was at the other end of the bed, top-and-tailing with me. Her head was turned to the wall, and she was fast asleep.

'Suze,' I said. She didn't stir.

I slid out of bed and pulled on the clothes I was wearing yesterday. I had an outfit for my interview hanging up at work, so I'd go and fetch it in a little while. In fact, I thought – glancing at Suze who was still out for the count – I'd go and get it now.

I grabbed Suze's keys from the side of the bed, and dashed off to the office to pick up my clothes. As I was leaving, my dress slung over my arm and the matching hat clutched in my hand, Rosemary appeared.

'So it's the big interview?' she said, with a smile. 'Are you prepared?'

I made a face.

'Everything's gone wrong,' I said, turning my head slightly so she wouldn't see my bruise. 'But I think we've got it back.'

'You're great,' she said. 'I'm off to a meeting now, but I'll give Margi a call later. Good luck.'

Thrilled to bits with the boost to my confidence that she'd given me, I sailed back to Suze's, locking the door behind me and running up the stairs. She was still in bed, covered with the blankets.

'Suze,' I said. 'Suze, I've got clothes and make-up. We need to get ready. Suze …'

I threw her keys onto the table and stopped short. Next to the keys was the brown medicine bottle. Its cap was off, and it was lying on its side. And it was empty. My stomach lurched. That bottle had been three-quarters full when I saw Suze take a Valium

248

last night. Maybe it was a different bottle? I picked it up and read the name Edna Evans on the label, realising in horror it was indeed the same one. Foolishly, I looked round the table and on the floor in case the pills had dropped out, but they were nowhere to be seen – Suze must have taken them all. And, by the look of the empty gin bottle – she'd washed them all down with booze.

Frantic, I threw the medicine bottle down and leapt onto the bed, shaking Suze violently.

'Suze,' I shouted, grabbing her shoulders. 'Suze, wake up.'

Next to me was a half-drunk glass of water. I picked it up and threw it in her face and to my absolute relief, she made a noise.

'Wake up, wake up, wake up,' I begged. 'Come on Suze, come on.'

I shook her again and she moaned softly.

'Did you take all these pills?' I said. 'Did you?'

She opened her eyes and stared right at me.

'Suze,' I said urgently. 'Did you take all the pills?'

Her eyes closed again and I started to sob. I picked up her keys and raced downstairs again, to the phone box on the corner of Peter Street. I phoned an ambulance and then, leaving the door open, I ran back to Suze and cradled her in my arms.

'Wake up, Suze,' I begged. 'Please wake up. I can't do this without you.'

Heavy footsteps on the stairs made me weak with relief that the ambulance men were here.

They marched into the room, filling it with their reassuring presence.

'She took Valium,' I babbled at them. 'And she drank gin. She's alive and she opened her eyes but just for a minute.'

'We'll take her to hospital,' one of the men said. 'Are you her sister?'

'No,' I said. 'She doesn't have any family. I'm her best friend.'

He looked round the squat, faint disgust showing on his face.

'Did a punter do this?'

I didn't understand.

'What do you mean?'

'A punter? Did he beat her up?'

'She's not a prostitute,' I said, angry at the idea. 'She's a writer.'

He gave me a look that suggested he didn't believe me, and even if he did, that wasn't much better.

'What's her name?'

As he spoke, his colleague lifted Suze up and put her on a stretcher. She looked so small and weak, with her bruised face, that I gasped.

'Her name,' the ambulance man said again.

'Nancy,' Suze said, ever so quietly. I rushed to her side. Her eyes were still closed.

'Did you hear that?' I said, weeping with relief. 'She spoke to me. She said Nancy.'

'Nancy?' the ambulance man said. 'Is her name Nancy?'

I opened my mouth to say no, but suddenly I remembered Suze saying we should swap places, and instead I found myself agreeing.

'Yes, she's Nancy,' I said. 'She's Nancy Harrison.'

Chapter 45

2016

Having Suze on board was amazing. She had more energy than the rest of us put together and she didn't seem to mind me bombarding her with questions almost every hour of the day and night.

Her support had really got my team excited about what we were doing. Riley was frantically planning the fashion pages and trawling all the vintage shops near the office for an outfit for Amy Lavender to wear on the cover. She'd been thrilled when we'd told her what we were planning and was completely throwing herself into the idea.

'Should I cut my hair off so I look like Twiggy?' she suggested when I rang her to make arrangements for the photoshoot.

'Absolutely bloody not,' shouted her agent, Babs, in the background.

I laughed.

'No, Pritti's got some wigs for you,' I said. 'And she's been speaking to some brilliant make-up artists about the perfect sixties look for you. We're going to have a lot of fun.'

Damo was busy designing pages. The original Mode only had

a few colour pictures inside – it was mostly black and white – so ours was going to look very different. But he was playing around with different fonts, experimenting with layouts and making all the dummy pages look amazing.

And Vanessa, well, she was unbelievable. She and Emily were running themselves ragged. Ness had commissioned some features from freelance writers, written a few herself, I'd written a couple too, and Emily was writing the rest. When she had any spare time – which was often long after everyone else had gone home – Ness would devote herself to her ideas about taking Mode to its readers. Luckily Lizzie had been bowled over by Vanessa's ideas. The two of them had put their heads together and somehow managed to arrange stands selling Mode in clothes shops, gyms and coffee bars. I hoped it was going to work. The rest of our plans were really coming together and that was the final bit.

Suze was adamant she didn't want to be featured in the mag, so we'd tweaked the day-in-the-life article a bit and instead of it being about Emily's life compared with Suze's in 1966, we'd done a generic 1966 woman and the same for 2016. Damo, who could draw beautifully when he wanted to, had drawn stylised cartoon figures to illustrate the piece. He'd based the 1966 woman on Suze or Nancy in the Rolling Stones picture. She had long straight dark hair and was wearing a black and white dress. Miss Millennial, as we were calling the modern woman, had long, wavy blonde hair. She was wearing skinny jeans and a flowery blouse. I loved it and I hoped Suze would, too.

Altogether, I was thrilled with the way things were working. I was happy, my team was happy and, most importantly, Lizzie was happy.

A week after I'd spoken to George Mann, I sauntered into work feeling content with my lot. The next issue of Mode had hit the shelves that weekend. It was the first of our 'weightier' themes and was called The Feminist Issue. We'd scrawled those words right across the cover and the model we'd used was a mouthy female comedian called Lou Little, whose hilarious – and fairly ranty – act had won almost as many awards as it had attracted critics. It had been a risk, there was no doubt, but I was hoping the sales would be up, even by a tiny amount. As long as we stopped that downward curve, I'd take it as a positive.

The magazine was on my desk. I avoided looking at it. I hated my first look at the new issue, positive I'd suddenly spot a gazillion mistakes on the cover. Instead I turned my attention to the new issue of Grace, which was also waiting for me. It was the first issue that Jen had worked on and I was interested to see what it would be like.

Still shrugging off my jacket, I picked up the magazine and stared in dismay.

Their cover star was Ali Gold, a singer who had been outspoken about the unequal treatment of men and women in the music industry. She was pictured staring straight at the camera, holding a board on which was scrawled the words *I am a feminist*.

I sat down in my chair so heavily it creaked.

'Shit,' I breathed. 'Shit. Shit. Shit.'

I had been worried Jen would take the broad ideas from Mode. That she would tell everyone on Grace that we were theming our issues, and they'd step up their game accordingly. What I hadn't considered for one moment – one ridiculously misguided moment I now realised – was that she'd just blatantly, out and out, boldly steal all our plans. That she'd take the fact that our next magazine was The Feminist Issue and simply nick it. And the truth was, with Grace's far better sales, it would look to everyone as though we were the ones who stole the idea.

I went through every emotion that day. I wrote and deleted two, or maybe three, furious emails to Jen. I picked up my phone to call her about ten times – though I knew she wouldn't answer even if I dialled her number. I went to the gym at lunchtime and did a kickboxing class, pretending my opponent's padded gloves were Jen's pretty face. But none of it made me feel better. I was angry, hurt, betrayed – and by the time I was ready to leave work that evening, I was just bloody sad.

As I hit the button for the lift, Damo grabbed my arm.

'No way,' he said.

I looked at him wearily.

'Don't start,' I said. 'I'm going home to cry. I don't want you to try and cheer me up. I want to wallow.'

'Sorry,' Damo said. 'I'm not going to let that happen. Let's go out.'

I shook my head.

'No.'

'Come on,' he pleaded. 'I know what you're like. You'll go home and feel all sorry for yourself and stew about what Jen's done. You'll get yourself in a tizz, you won't sleep properly and we'll all be sorry tomorrow when you're grumpy.'

I stared at him.

'So?' I said. 'I'm still going home.'

'Then I'm coming with you,' he said. 'I'll make us some dinner, we can have a glass of wine, we can talk about Jen if you want to, or we can just sit on the sofa and watch Netflix …'

I gave him a fierce look and he grinned.

'I mean actually watch Netflix,' he said. 'My days of "Netflix and chill" are over, baby. I'm a perfect gent. I'll go home whenever you tell me to.'

He put his arm round me and against my better judgement, I found myself relaxing against him. I had never been a woman who needed a man. I was independent and perfectly capable of doing everything myself. But right then I was tired, and sad, and stressed, and the idea of being looked after – even if it was just for one night – was really, really appealing.

'You can stay over,' I said. 'But you're sleeping on the floor.'

'Deal,' said Damo.

Chapter 46

It was bound to happen, right? Damo and me? It had probably been on the cards since he first walked into my office all those weeks ago – especially if what Madison had told me was true.

We had a lovely evening. He cooked pasta and made me have a bath while he got it all ready. I changed into my pyjamas and, with my face scrubbed clean of make-up and my damp hair piled into a top knot, I padded through into the living room to eat. Damo handed me a glass of wine, put the pasta on the table and pressed play on an eighties rom com he'd found on Netflix.

'This is the worst film I've ever seen,' he told me. 'But I know chicks like it.'

In silence, apart from slurping our pasta, we watched the first five minutes.

'Damo,' I said. 'Can you put Die Hard on?'

'I thought you'd never ask,' he said.

We didn't talk at all while the film was on, but afterwards – our tongues loosened by the wine – we sat close together on the sofa and discussed Jen and Suze and Vanessa and just about everything, apart from the way our relationship had ended.

Eventually, Damo yawned.

'I'm beat,' he said. 'Do you have a sleeping bag for me?'

Without stopping to wonder whether I was doing the right thing, I shook my head.

'I do,' I said. 'But I'd rather not get it out.'

'So where will I sleep?' Damo said, looking confused.

'With me,' I said. I leaned over and kissed him. He pulled away – for about ten seconds – and then he was kissing me back, his hands roaming over my back.

'This is a really bad idea,' he said into my neck.

'I know,' I said. 'We should stop.'

'Absolutely,' he said. 'You first.'

But we didn't, of course. And I didn't regret it for one minute. Until I woke up to John Humphrys' dulcet tones the next morning and stared at Damo, who was snoring gently next to me.

His tawny hair covered his face and he'd pushed the duvet down so I got the full glory of his buff torso. I sat up and rested my chin on my knees. What a bloody stupid idiot I was.

'Damo,' I said, pushing him a little bit harder than was necessary. 'Damo.'

He opened one eye.

'Morning, gorgeous,' he said.

'You have to go,' I hissed.

He pushed his hair out of his face and looked at me.

'What?' he said.

'You have to go.'

'Why?' he said. 'Have you got a husband I didn't know about?'

'No,' I said. 'But we can't go to work together.'

Damo sat up.

'Why the bloody hell not?' he said. 'No one would care. We've not done anything wrong.'

I closed my eyes.

'We've done everything wrong,' I said. 'We're supposed to be saving Mode, not getting our rocks off.'

'Our what now?' said Damo.

I glowered at him. This was no time for jokes.

'This is it,' I said. 'My dream job. The one I've been waiting for.'

I almost said it was the one I'd dumped him for, but I stopped myself. He knew though.

'The one you had your eye on when you left me?' he said.

There was no point in denying it.

'It's my dream job,' I said again.

'Oh and don't we know it,' Damo said. He got out of bed and started pulling on his clothes.

'I thought you might have learned something,' he said as he did up his jeans. 'I thought after what happened with Jen, you might have realised that some things are more important than work.'

I didn't speak, so Damo kept going.

'Friendship,' he said, as he poked his head through the neck of his t-shirt. 'That's more important than work.'

'Damo,' I began, but he hadn't finished.

'Suze won't talk about the sixties because she feels so bad about what happened to her friend,' he said. 'She could be massive off the back of this relaunch. You and her together would be on fire – you'd be on bloody Woman's Hour, and Newsnight, and Piers bloody Morgan.'

I winced. I'd thought the same thing.

'But she won't do it, because the memory of her friend is too much,' Damo ranted. 'You? You'd do it in a heartbeat.'

'That's not true,' I said. But it was true, really.

'You shat all over Jen and now she's done the same to you, and you still haven't learned your lesson,' he went on, shoving his feet into his shoes and running his fingers through his hair. 'I thought maybe we had something here. That you'd realised it's okay to have fun. That you can enjoy yourself and the world won't fall apart. That sometimes work has to come last. But no.'

I pulled the duvet further up my chest and hugged it.

'Work is really important to me,' I said weakly.

'You're trying to prove yourself to your parents,' Damo said, his face softening a bit. 'And there's no point. Nothing you do will ever be good enough for them, Fearne. Nothing. But that's okay. Because it's good enough for everyone else. You've done it. You're editor of Mode. And that's great. But you need to have a life as well.'

I nodded.

'You're right,' I said. 'I will never, ever meet Mum's expectations.'

'It's a waste of time even trying,' Damo said.

'I can't help it,' I whispered. 'It's not even about her any more. I just need to keep going. To keep striving. To be a success.'

'You already are,' he said.

I shook my head.

'It's not enough,' I said. 'It's never enough.'

Damo sat on the edge of the bed and pulled me close to him.

'It's enough for me,' he said. 'You're more than enough for me.'

I closed my eyes.

'You're a distraction,' I said. 'This was unprofessional and it could jeopardise the relaunch.'

'No it couldn't,' Damo said.

I nodded.

'I'm so close, Damo,' I said. 'I can't take my eye off the ball now.'

'Don't you dare,' he said. 'Don't you dare do this again.'

I pulled away from him.

'I'm sorry,' I said. 'You have to go.'

He stood up and picked up his jacket.

'Really?' he said.

I didn't say anything. He stayed for a minute, then he turned and left. I heard my front door slam and he was gone.

The last time I'd dumped Damo because work was more important, I'd known he was heading hundreds of miles away. This time, he was heading to my office – and I was about to follow. Somehow, I thought, it wasn't going to be easy to get over him.

I lay back on the bed and stared at the ceiling. I'd messed everything up. Again. And I wasn't sure that I could fix it.

I picked up my phone and opened my emails, scrolling through my drafts until I found the one I'd written to Mum. I opened it, and without reading it again, I pressed send.

Damo was right. Nothing I'd do would be good enough, but I wanted her to know what I was working hard for. What I'd fallen out with Jen over. What I'd hurt Damo – all over again – for. And I really hoped it was worth it.

Chapter 47

1966

I'm not sure why I told the ambulance men that Suze's name was Nancy. Just like I'm not sure why when they asked if I wanted to come with them to the hospital, I shook my head.

'Where are you taking her?' I said.

'UCH,' said one.

'I just need to tell some people what's happened,' I said, thinking of George – who was probably on his way to Paris by now – and Bruno, and Margi at Mode. 'I'll come later.'

The man looked at Suze's battered face and then back at me.

'Don't be too long, eh?' he said.

In a daze, I picked up my bag, and followed them down the stairs and watched them carry Suze into the back of the ambulance. Then I wandered off towards the office. Mode wasn't owned by the same company that owned Home & Hearth but their office wasn't ready yet so Rosemary had arranged for the interviews to be held in a meeting room on the top floor as a favour for Margi. I went into the building and pressed the button for the lift.

Gayle the receptionist, glanced at me.

'Margi just arrived,' she said.

Then she frowned, taking in my crumpled outfit.

'You're going for an interview, right?'

I should have said no. I should have asked her to phone up to the top floor and tell Margi that Suze had been taken ill and we wouldn't be able to interview today. But I didn't. Instead I smiled.

'Yes,' I said. 'I'm going for an interview. Just going up to change first.'

She gave me thumbs up.

'Good luck,' she said.

In the lift, I checked my watch. I was early to see Margi. I had time. Time to make this right and get my life – and Suze's life – back on track. We were down, that much was true, but we were not out. If anything, all our problems – Dad, Mum, Gordon and now Suze being poorly – just made me more determined to get this job and get things going.

'She's not poorly,' a little voice in my head whispered as I pressed the button for the Home & Hearth floor. 'She's taken too many pills. She could die.'

'She's going to be fine,' I said out loud. 'And I will get this job so she has something to look forward to.'

With a ping, the doors opened on my floor and I took a breath. Time to go to work.

It was quiet at Home & Hearth that afternoon, just as I'd hoped. Rosemary wasn't around – she must have been at her meeting – and there were just a few people on the subs desk. I dashed in, and headed for my rail in the fashion cupboard, finally thankful that I had so many spare clothes at work, given that my carefully selected interview outfit was now lying, discarded, on the floor of Suze's squat.

I picked a bright blue dress with buttons down the front and threw it on, straightening my skirt in the mirror. My new haircut was limp and flat, so I dug some dry shampoo out of the beauty cupboard and sprayed it on. Then I backcombed my hair at the roots to give it some height and pulled a wide hairband from the accessories drawer, knowing Lucy, the fashion editor, wouldn't mind if she even noticed. I put on some make-up, carefully hiding my bruise, and looked at my reflection. It wasn't as good as I'd planned, but it would do.

Then, I slunk out of the fashion cupboard and up the stairs to the meeting room. Sitting outside waiting to be called by Margi, I gave myself a talking to.

'This is the biggest moment of your life,' I said in my head. 'Do this, and everything else will fall into place.'

I checked my bundle of papers were in the bag, and tried not to panic. This was it.

A woman with artfully tousled Brigitte Bardot hair came out of the meeting room and smiled at me.

'Ah,' she said. 'I know who you are.'

I blinked at her.

'I've just been reading your Rolling Stones piece in Viva,' she said. 'I recognise you from the photos – I like your haircut. I'm pleased to meet you, Suze. I'm Margi.'

I stood up and shook her outstretched hand.

'Hello,' I said.

'Aren't there supposed to be two of you?' Margi said.

I stared at her, not sure what to say.

She looked expectantly at me and I pulled myself together.

'Sorry,' I said. 'It's been a long morning. My friend's ill, I'm afraid.'

Margi looked at the sheet of paper she held in her hand.

'Nancy?' she said. 'Nancy's ill?'

I took a breath. Now was absolutely the time to say that, no, she had it wrong. I was Nancy and Suze was ill. But once more, I didn't.

I nodded.

'That's right,' I said. 'She's really sorry, but she honestly couldn't have got here. She's going to get better soon though.'

Margi gave me an odd look, and for a minute I thought she was going to say something. Then she obviously changed her mind.

'Come on in,' she said. 'Let's have a chat.'

Once I was talking about my ideas for Mode, I felt better. Calmer. More in control. I talked Margi through all our features and she asked lots of questions about the Rolling Stones. I stumbled a bit when she asked about the marriage feature. Of course, I'd written it but she thought I was Suze. So I had to pretend it wasn't my writing, which got a bit tricky but I somehow got through it.

When it came to our ideas – and our presentation – I was on firmer ground. I was so excited about Mode and the chance of being involved in it from the beginning that I didn't have to pretend. I told Margi all about how we saw the magazine developing and I was pleased when she started to take notes.

'We made a dummy issue,' I told her. 'But my dad …'

I paused.

'He accidentally threw it away.'

Margi smiled.

'Bad luck,' she said.

'We worked all night to get ready,' I said, sounding slightly desperate.

'I can see that.'

Margi leafed through my presentation.

'Can I keep this?' she asked.

My heart leapt.

'Please do.'

'Suze, you've obviously worked very hard,' Margi said. 'I'd love to have you as part of my team at Mode.'

'Really?' I said, hardly able to believe that this terrible day had turned round.

'Really.'

'And my friend?' I said.

'If she's anything like you, then we need her too,' said Margi. She handed me a business card. 'Get her to phone me and we can arrange another time to meet.'

I wanted to throw my arms round her and tell her she'd just given two desperate girls a chance in life, but I didn't. I shook her hand and thanked her, and left the building in a calm manner that didn't reveal how excited I was inside.

I planned to go and see Suze in hospital, but I had a few things to do first.

Of course, I had to tell George everything that had happened but I had no idea how to make an international phone call or even where he'd be staying in Paris. Instead I wrote a note saying I'd be at Suze's and he had to come and find me SOON, and posted it through his letterbox.

It was all happening, I thought as I headed for the tube station. I was going to see Suze at hospital and tell her, yes, we were really doing this. She would be Nancy and I'd be Suze and we had jobs, and we'd get a flat, and we'd be safe. It was the beginning of our new lives, and I couldn't wait to get started.

Chapter 48

2016

For the first time in my whole life, I was late for work that morning. I slunk into the office, hoping to avoid Damo's accusatory stares, but when I dared lift my eyes to his desk, he wasn't there.

'Where's Damo?' I asked Emily.

'He's gone to the cover shoot,' she said.

'That's this afternoon.'

'He wanted to go early,' Emily said, frowning with the effort of remembering. 'Think he said he had something to do first. Or afterwards.' She gave me a dazzling smile. 'Something like that.'

He wanted to avoid me, more like. But relieved that I wouldn't have to face him – yet – I didn't mind. I was going to the cover shoot too. Like Suze had suggested, we were filming it for the website and I was interviewing Amy Lavender too. One of Emily's friends in digital was streaming parts of our chat live to our Facebook page. It was all terribly high-tech and made me feel a bit like my nanna when she tried to leave a message on my voicemail. But I was looking forward to it. Amy was always fun, disarmingly honest and absolutely gorgeous so I knew the pictures would look great. And there would be enough people around that – hopefully – things wouldn't be too awkward between Damo and me.

I spent the morning going through Lizzie and Vanessa's plans for the pop-up stalls selling Mode. The ideas were really good, the budgets all looked good to me, and I thought it wouldn't be long before lots of other magazines were doing a similar thing. I was very grateful I'd not mentioned Vanessa's ideas in detail to Jen, otherwise I was pretty sure Grace would be doing it already.

Just before lunch there was a knock on my office doorframe and Emily came in clutching a package.

'Just arrived by courier,' she said. 'It's from Paris.'

Vanessa had obviously filled her in on our chat with George Mann.

'Ooh it must be the photos,' I said, taking the parcel. 'I thought he was emailing them.'

I tore open the brown paper wrapping at one end, peered inside and pulled out a postcard with a beautiful black and white portrait of Jane Birkin on one side. I showed it to Emily and she nodded approvingly.

'Nice.'

I turned it over and read the message, which was written in a neat Sharpied handwriting.

'Dear Fearne,' it said. 'I sensed time was of the essence so rather than spend hours scanning in these prints and emailing them, I am sending them "snail mail" which ironically will end up being faster. Lots here of Nancy, a few of Nancy and me together, and a couple of Suze. I have the negs of course, so you're welcome to keep these. All I would like in return is a copy of your sixties-inspired magazine when it is printed. Those years were some of the happiest and the saddest in my life. Regards, George.'

'Oh he is adorable,' I said. 'What a sweetheart.'

While Emily read the message, I shook the photos out of the

266

package. There was a small bundle, fastened with an elastic band. I pulled it off and spread the photographs over my desk.

There were about twenty altogether, maybe a couple more, and they were all awesome.

'Oh blimey,' said Emily. 'What a treat.'

'Here's Suze, I think,' I said, pointing to one of the prints of a young woman with long dark hair and a heavy fringe.

'She's still got that dimple in her cheek.'

'She must have had all her hair cut off,' said Emily. 'Because she'd gone all Twiggy by the time Mode was launched.'

'So this must be George,' I said, looking at one picture of a handsome man with sideburns and hair that curled over his collar. Across the front of the print was scrawled 'self portrait 1965'.

'And that's Nancy, then,' said Emily, touching her fingertip to a photo of a very slim woman, hunched over a typewriter. She was turning to the camera and smiling, a cigarette in one hand. She had very short, Audrey Hepburn inspired brunette hair, an angular face with defined cheekbones, and dark, unreadable eyes.

'Isn't it sad that she was dead not long after that?' I said.

'Really sad,' said Emily. 'She was younger than me.'

I swept my gaze over all the photos. There were lots of Suze, on her own, with Nancy, and – I looked closer – with George. I picked up the photo of them together and showed it to Emily, eyebrow raised. In the picture, George and Suze stood with their arms round each other, he was bending his head towards hers and they were both laughing. Suze was wearing the black and white checked dress that I recognised from the Rolling Stones photo. It was a very intimate shot and they looked much more than friends.

'What's going on here, then?' I said. 'George said it was Nancy he was in love with, right?'

I turned the print round and looked at it again.

'Hold on,' said Emily. 'There's writing on the back.'

She was right.

'Me and Nancy,' it said, in the same handwriting that was on the postcard, though it was faded with age. 'April 1966.'

'It says Nancy,' I said in confusion. 'But this is Suze.'

I'd pinned the photo of the first Mode team on my noticeboard. Now I got it down and compared the two. She'd had her hair cut, that was true, but it was definitely the same woman in both pictures.

'I don't understand,' I said. 'How can George get them mixed up?'

Like she was performing a card trick, Emily turned over all the photos on my desk one by one. The ones with the thin, angular girl in them all said Suze, while the photos of the girl with the fringe said Nancy.

'This is so weird,' Emily said. 'It makes no sense.'

'George is in his early seventies,' I said. 'He is still working, he's got a great reputation, he was completely with-it when I spoke to him. As far as I'm concerned, there's no way he could have got this wrong. Anyway, by the look of it, he wrote these names on the photos a long time ago.'

'Maybe Nancy didn't die,' Emily said, thoughtfully. 'Maybe Suze died.'

'Suze didn't die,' I said. 'I've met her.'

'But what if you've met Nancy?' Emily said.

I stared at her.

'What if Suze is actually Nancy ... and that's why she won't do publicity and why she hides herself away in a cottage in a tiny village?'

'Why on earth would she do that?' I said. But already I knew that Emily was right. It was the only explanation for all the strange behaviour Suze – or was it Nancy? – had shown me.

'I've got no idea,' Emily said. 'Maybe she was scared of something or someone. Maybe she just fancied a change. But it must have been something pretty drastic to fake her own death.'

She picked up one of the photos of George.

'And to break his heart.'

I was stunned. When I'd started looking into Nancy Harrison's life, I'd never for one minute thought I'd stumble upon something like this.

Emily grinned at me.

'I know one thing, though,' she said. 'You're going to go and find out why she did it.'

Chapter 49

1966

She died. Suze died. She was dead by the time I got to the hospital, where I stood in the corridor in a daze as a stern-faced nurse told me I was too late.

'Her heart stopped,' she said, her face softening as she looked at me. 'She was very thin, and she'd taken a lot of pills and drunk a lot of alcohol.'

'I don't understand,' I said. 'You must have made a mistake.'

The nurse steered me into a room off the hospital reception. It had PVC chairs round the edge and dirty smudges on the walls where patients and relatives had rested their heads. I wondered how many other people had been given bad news in this horrible place.

'Are you her sister?' the nurse said. 'Are you Nancy's sister?'

'No,' I said. 'I'm …'

I paused, running my fingers through my hair.

'I'm her best friend. I'm Suze.'

'We need to tell her family,' said the nurse softly. 'Do you know how to get hold of them?'

I felt sick suddenly. Was I going to do this? Was I going to let her tell my dad that I was dead when I wasn't?

'She'd been badly hurt,' the nurse said. 'She was in a bad way. Do you know who did it? Should we call the police?'

Still dazed, I shook my head.

'No,' I said. Much as I wanted Dad to pay for what he'd done, I couldn't bear the thought of ever seeing him again. I wanted to start a new life without him – without all the baggage of my past – and if I told this nurse who'd hurt Suze, my plans would come crashing down.

I took a deep, shuddering breath. I had to do whatever I had to do to live the life I wanted to live. I had to cut all ties.

I looked at the nurse.

'I don't know who hurt Nancy,' I said. 'But I do know her dad's name and address.'

My hand didn't even shake as I wrote Dad's details on a piece of paper for the nurse.

'Will they need to identify her?' I said.

The nurse nodded and I winced inwardly.

'Her dad had cut her off,' I said. I lowered my voice, thinking of the assumptions the ambulance men had made. 'He didn't approve of her … lifestyle.'

The nurse looked confused for a second, then her expression cleared.

'Can I see her?' I asked. 'Her dad won't want to. But if I see her, then you can tell him it's all done.'

'I'm not really allowed …'

'Please,' I said, suddenly desperate to see Suze, to make sure this was all real and not just a bad dream.

The nurse dropped her shoulders.

'Okay,' she said. 'I'll get someone to take you down.'

I was shaking as I walked down the stairs towards the mortuary. I still felt like I was dreaming and I couldn't quite believe I was doing what I was doing.

I was shown into a bare room, with two tattered armchairs and a low coffee table with a box of tissues on it, and asked to wait.

271

Before I even had a chance to sit down, though, another nurse came in and asked me to follow her.

'Sorry about your sister,' she said.

I just nodded. The first nurse must have lied about my connection to Suze. Considering the scale of the lies I was telling, it seemed completely reasonable.

The nurse stopped by a door and paused, her fingers on the handle.

'I can come in with you, or I can leave you alone,' she said.

'Alone please.'

She nodded.

'I'll give you five minutes.'

She opened the door, I walked into the room, and she shut it behind me.

It was a small room with a hospital bed in the middle. Suze was lying on the bed, a sheet pulled up to her chin. She was so thin she barely made a bump and her pale face was almost the same colour as the pillow, though she had a blueish tinge around her lips. Her eyes were closed and one of her hands rested on top of the sheet.

I took a sharp breath. I think up until that point I'd thought this was all just a silly mistake. That it wouldn't be Suze, that she was actually upstairs on a ward, cross with me for not coming to tell her all about the interview at Mode. But I was the one who'd made mistakes. I'd been mistaken when I thought Suze was going to be okay, and I'd been mistaken when I thought the nurse had mixed her up with someone else.

Slowly I walked towards the bed.

'Suze,' I said, starting to cry. 'Suze, I'm so sorry.'

There was a chair next to the bed, and I pulled it closer, sat down and carefully took Suze's hand. It was frighteningly, shockingly cold and I almost dropped it again. But instead I squeezed it tighter.

'Your plan worked,' I said in a trembling voice. 'Your crazy

272

plan for us to swap names worked. I told everyone you're Nancy. And from now on, I'm Suze Williams. And we got the jobs, Suze. We got the jobs on Mode. Just like you said we would.'

I wiped my eyes.

'Suze,' I said. 'Your whole life, everyone let you down. Your mum, and horrible Walter, and all the people who could have been looking out for you. The people who you should have been able to rely on. They all let you down.'

My throat felt tight and it was hard to talk, but I knew I had to say what I wanted to say.

'And then, when you needed me most, I let you down too,' I said. 'I'm so sorry. I brought my dad into your life and he hurt you so badly. And I will feel guilty about that for the rest of my life.'

I looked at her hand, with its bitten fingernails, and at the bruises on her arm.

'I promise you I will make this work,' I said. 'I will work so hard to make a success of my life, because I'm not just living my life any more. I'm living yours too. And your life would have been wonderful, Suze. I know that. And my life is a little bit more wonderful because I met you.'

I sat there for a while, still holding her hand. It seemed wrong to leave her alone, but I knew I had to. When the nurse knocked softly on the door and asked if I'd finished, I stood up.

'I'm finished,' I said.

I followed her out of the room and back to the reception desk.

'Have you told her dad yet?' I asked.

The nurse shook her head.

'The local police will go round and break the news,' she said.

'Tell them he's a drunk,' I said coldly. 'And that he might be violent.'

A tear traced a slow path down my cheek.

'And can you tell her brother?' I added, pulling a scrap of paper towards me and scribbling down Dennis's name and the name of the school he worked at. 'Can you tell him she really loved him and that none of this is his fault?'

The nurse looked at me for a second too long, then she nodded again, and wrote down everything I'd said on a sheet of paper. Then she clipped it and Dennis's address to a file that had Nancy Harrison written on it in black marker pen.

'Can I take your details?' she said. 'I need your address in case we need to contact you.'

'I don't have one,' I said. 'I'm sorry.'

Then I turned away from her, ignoring her protests, and I walked out of the double doors, and into my new life.

Chapter 50

2016

I was upstairs working in my study when the doorbell rang. I had so few visitors that it made me jump. I pressed save on my computer keyboard and stood up so I could peer out of the tiny lopsided window.

Down below, I could see a bright blonde head and an enormous bag. It was Fearne. What was she doing here? We'd been in touch a lot over the last few days, but not in person – always on email or over the phone.

She rang the bell again and Cooper, my dog, bounded round the side of the house towards her. Traitorous beast that he was, letting her know I was in. He barked joyfully at her and Fearne bent down to pat him.

Realising she wouldn't give up, I sighed and went downstairs to open the door.

She didn't wait for me to invite her in – she simply brushed past me and went into the lounge. I made a face at Cooper, who was rolling in a patch of mud, shut him out in the garden and followed Fearne.

'Good morning,' I said pointedly.

'I've got something to show you,' she said. She was wearing very tight jeans and a white shirt and she looked fresh and young. But the expression on her face was a mixture of anger and – I thought – confusion.

She sat down on the sofa and pulled a large brown envelope out of her bag. She shook it from one end and tipped a pile of black and white photos onto the coffee table, spreading them out so I could see them.

'There,' she said.

My heart began to pound. I knew where this was heading. I'd been waiting for this moment for fifty years and the only surprise was that it hadn't happened sooner.

I walked over to where she sat and forced myself to look at the photographs. I gasped. There were faces I'd not seen for a long time.

'Oh,' I said. 'Oh my.'

I sat down on the sofa and waited for Fearne to speak but she didn't. She just carried on looking at me, as I looked at the pictures.

'Did you get these from George?' I asked, stroking his face in one of the photos.

She gave a brief nod.

'How is he?'

Fearne looked at me in disbelief and I realised she wasn't going to let me off the hook.

'I owe you an explanation,' I began.

She snorted.

'Actually,' she said, her voice icy cold, 'you don't. It's not me you need to explain things to, it's your family, and George, and Suze's family.'

I nodded.

'Let me start from the beginning,' I said.

It wasn't easy to talk about – I'd spent a long time trying to forget most of the details. But I found as soon as I started, everything came back to me. I told her about my mum, and how Dad had changed when she died. I told her about my brother and his offers of work in Leeds and she nodded in understanding, I hoped. And I told her what Dad had done to me, and then to Suze. And how I was strong and healthy, but Suze hadn't eaten properly for years, probably, and she'd drunk a lot, and taken too many pills, and her fragile body hadn't coped with Dad's fists.

Fearne dug around in her bag and found a packet of tissues. She pulled one out and blew her nose quietly.

'So what happened?' she said. 'You'd got away with it by 1979. You were riding high – editor of Mode. Why did you give it all up?'

'My brother happened,' I said.

'Dennis?'

I was impressed – she had done her homework.

'Yes, Dennis. He was a teacher and he was always ahead of the game. He was very creative and innovative and he began to make a name for himself in education. He wasn't a headmaster then, but he was attracting a lot of attention. He was invited to go on some politics show one day. A Sunday morning thing, you know what I mean?'

Fearne was listening intently. She nodded.

'I'd just taken over as editor of Mode,' I went on. 'And Margaret Thatcher had just been elected Prime Minister. We'd done a big piece on her – it was the first overtly political article we'd run and it was ...' I paused. 'Slightly negative.'

Fearne grinned for the first time since she'd arrived.

'Go on,' she said.

'I was invited on to this show to talk about what young women thought about politics and whether they were interested. And one of the other guests ...'

'Was Dennis,' Fearne finished.

I nodded.

'Yes,' I said, remembering my horror when I arrived at the television studios and found out I was expected to debate Margaret Thatcher with the brother I'd not seen for more than a decade. The brother who thought I was dead.

'What did you do?'

'I ran away,' I said. 'I was in the make-up chair when they told me who the other guests were. I was loving it. It was everything I'd ever wanted – a platform to put across young women's views, being taken seriously, a chance to talk about things that were important to me and other women like me. I have to admit, I'd mentally patted myself on the back a few times that day.'

Fearne gave me a small smile.

'You deserved to,' she said.

'Well, pride comes before a fall, doesn't it?' I said. 'And oh my goodness, I fell. The show runner read out the names and when I heard Dennis Harrison my heart stopped. I double-checked I'd not misheard and then asked what he did and where he came from. When she said he was a teacher from Yorkshire, I knew it had to be him. So I went to the loo, then I pretended to be ill. I handed in my notice at Mode a week later.'

Fearne was staring at me.

'Why didn't you just tell him?' she said. 'Why didn't you tell Dennis?'

'Well, for a start, five minutes before you're on live television is no time to announce that you're someone's dead sister,' I said. 'But mostly I was scared, Fearne. I knew my dad was still alive and I was bloody terrified that if I showed my face to Dennis my whole carefully crafted life would come tumbling down.

'I've thought a lot about Dennis over the years, hoping he was okay. Following his career …'

I swallowed a sob.

'And I know that he died.'

Fearne nodded, grim-faced.

'I thought about going to the funeral,' I said. 'But in the end

I just sent flowers. I wrote a message about happy childhood memories, but I didn't sign it.'

Fearne handed me a tissue and I wiped my eyes.

'What happened then?' she asked.

'I worked out my notice at Mode, then I went to India, hoping I would find an answer to my problems.'

'Did you?' Fearne said.

I shrugged.

'Not really,' I said. 'But while I was in India I wrote my first novel. It started off as a sort of musing on how I wished my life had turned out. But I discovered it was easier to write it if it wasn't about myself. I came home, found a publisher, and that was that.'

'But you were so young,' Fearne said.

I nodded.

'I published my first novel in 1982,' I said. 'I was thirty-eight.' I chuckled.

'Well actually I was only thirty-seven. Suze was thirty-eight. She was a year older than me.'

'Haven't you been lonely?' Fearne said. 'Hiding out here, all alone.'

'No,' I lied. 'Not at all. I've got Cooper and the people who live in the village are nice.'

'What about George?' asked Fearne. 'Did you miss George?'

What could I say? That I missed him every minute of every day – at first? That the pain of losing Suze, who was my best and only friend, almost destroyed me and that coupled with the pain of losing George made it difficult to get out of bed every day. That once I found out for sure that he'd moved to Paris, I'd thought many times of getting on a plane and simply turning up at his studio. But how would I begin to explain? What would I say?

Instead, I scratched my head.

'I missed him,' I said. 'And I missed Suze too. Dreadfully. So

I threw myself into work. I worked all the time. I ate, slept, breathed, lived Mode. And when I was made editor, I thought it would help.'

'But it didn't?' said Fearne.

'No,' I said. 'It didn't. I have been happy, by and large, but I've also been terribly, terribly lonely.'

Fearne patted me gently on the hand. And then, to my alarm, she burst into tears.

Chapter 51

There was something about Suze's house that made me cry, apparently. I'd cried more in her company than I'd done in the last three years.

Considering the horror of the story she'd just told me – which made my problems seem minuscule in comparison – she was very kind. She handed me some tissues, then she went and got me a glass of water from the kitchen.

'I've put the kettle on,' she said, when she came back. 'I think you could do with a cup of tea.'

I nodded, and blew my nose.

'I'm sorry,' I said. 'I'm not sure what came over me. Your story is so sad, and when you said about throwing yourself into work, it just really made me think ...'

I trailed off.

'Think?' prompted Suze – or was I supposed to call her Nancy now? I said as much. She grimaced.

'I'm not sure,' she said. 'It depends what happens next.'

I chewed my lip. I knew what I wanted her to do, but I wasn't sure what she'd think.

'So ... "think"...?' she said; obviously she'd had enough of talking about herself.

'It made me think of something Damo said to me yesterday,' I said.

I told her all about Damo and me, how we'd broken up when I'd dumped him for the sake of my career. How Madison had told me that his feelings for me had been rekindled when we started working together again. And how we'd spent the night together. She nodded as I spoke, taking it all in.

'So what did he say?' she asked.

I took a breath.

'He said that I was trying to meet unreachable expectations,' I said. 'That I would work and work and work and it would never be enough. That some things were more important than magazines, like friends and relationships and fun.'

I looked at her as she perched on the edge of her sofa cushion, looking like she might take to her heels and run away any minute.

'Please don't take this the wrong way,' I said. 'But I don't want my life to end up like yours.'

Suze looked at me, her eyes wide, then she chuckled.

'Oh god, of course not,' she said. 'It's been bloody awful.'

She took my hand.

'I think the one thing I've learned over the years is that a career is a wonderful thing. But it's just part of a life. And Damo is right, Fearne. Some things are more important.'

'Jen always said I'd walk over everyone to get to where I wanted to be,' I said, feeling a bit ashamed. 'She was right. I walked all over her. And when she did the same to me, I didn't like it.'

Suze nodded.

'It's not a nice feeling, knowing you're someone's Plan B,' she said. 'That you were just filling in the time until something better came along.'

'Oh god, that's exactly what I did,' I said, burying my head in my hands. 'We'd made all these plans – these brilliant, exciting plans – and I just dropped them like a hot potato as soon as Mode called.'

282

'And Jen did the same, when Grace showed an interest in her?' Suze said.

'Exactly,' I said. 'And it made me feel like shit.'

'Can you forgive her?'

I nodded, slowly.

'I think so,' I said. 'If she can forgive me.'

Suze smiled.

'So make amends,' she said.

'What about Damo?'

'Do you love him?'

'No,' I said. 'But I did once. I really loved him. And I think, if I let myself, I could love him again. But I've been so awful to him, I'm not sure he'd trust me ever again.'

'You're going to have to woo him,' Suze said with a smile.

'Woo him?'

'Oh don't pretend you don't understand,' she said, nudging me. 'You need to give him some old-fashioned romance. Show him you're serious about making it up to him. And you have to prove that you're willing to put your career in second place sometimes.'

'Sometimes,' I said.

I felt good, suddenly, like talking to Suze had made things much clearer.

'What about you?' I said. 'What are we going to do about your life?'

'It's a disaster,' Suze said, only half-joking. 'It's too late.'

I jumped to my feet.

'We can rescue this,' I said. 'As well as saving Mode, we can save ourselves.'

Suze groaned.

'Well, I think there's hope for you, my love, but I can't imagine there's much for me.'

I waved my hand to dismiss her concerns.

'You can get this back,' I said. 'When I was a little girl and I did something wrong, my mum always used to tell me that it wasn't the wrong deed that was the problem – it was the cover-up.'

Suze nodded.

'I'd agree with that,' she said. 'It's always the lies that bring down governments.'

'So tell everyone the truth,' I said. 'Tell your story.'

'No,' said Suze.

'Dennis is dead,' I said harshly. 'He's not going to be upset now.'

'He had a wife,' Suze said. 'And children. And grandchildren. It could affect them.'

'In a good way,' I said. 'Family is good. I bet they'd love to get to know you.'

Suze looked dubious, but she didn't disagree.

'And there's George,' I said.

'For heaven's sake,' she said. 'I've not seen George for fifty years. He's probably got a wife as well.'

'Oh he does,' I said, teasing. 'In fact he's got three.'

'Three?' shrieked Suze.

'The first one was English – an artist who he married in 1970,' I told her, quoting from George's website. 'They had a daughter and they divorced when she was five. He married a French model about ten minutes later, and split up almost before the ink was dry on the marriage certificate. Then he married another French woman. She was a politician. They had three children – two boys and a girl – and they were married until a few years ago when she was killed in a car accident. He's a granddad, your George, and he spends most of his time in his house in Toulouse, close to where three of his four children live. One of his daughters lives in London, actually. But I don't know what her name is.'

Suze looked slightly shell-shocked.

'Well thank goodness for that,' she said. 'Or you'd probably have dragged her down here too.'

I grinned.

'Journalist,' I said. 'Nosy.'

Suze nodded, as if she understood completely. Then she leaned into me, conspiratorially.

'I knew all that,' she said. 'I've got Wikipedia too, you know.'

I howled with laughter and so did Suze. And when we caught our breath, I saw my chance.

'So will you do it?' I asked her. 'Will you let me interview you?'

She gave me something of a resigned smile.

'Okay then,' she said. 'I'll do it.'

Chapter 52

2016

Three months later

'So you've got BBC Breakfast first thing tomorrow,' Emily told me. 'Then Woman's Hour at ten a.m., and Loose Women at lunchtime.'

I blinked at her.

'Riley's sorting you out some outfits, because you'll have to wear something different to each interview,' she carried on. 'And she's got some ideas for Suze too, when she arrives.'

'Nancy,' I said. 'We're supposed to call her Nancy, now.'

'Nancy,' she said.

She looked down at the list she held in her hand and carried on.

'Vanessa's off to Westfield today to launch the pop-up shops ...'

'Is she going on her own?' I said, worried she'd be overwhelmed.

Emily shook her head.

'No,' she said. 'She's got a whole team of interns going with her.'

'Good.'

I sat down at my desk and looked at the itinerary Emily handed me. It was crazy – packed with interviews for television and radio. It was a strange feeling being asked the questions instead of asking them myself.

Nancy's interview had been amazing. She'd been so honest with me – about her terrible upbringing, and the abuse she'd suffered at the hands of her dad. She had one photograph of her mum, which she even let us print in the magazine. She'd told me all about Suze – the real Suze – and how she'd also had an awful childhood. And she'd told me about the horrible day when Suze died and Nancy had made the drastic – but once she explained it properly, completely understandable – decision to pretend that the dying girl was Nancy and she was Suze.

We'd given the interview lots of space in the magazine, which was coming out tomorrow. We were expecting the first copies in the office later that afternoon. I was sick with nerves and I'd barely slept for a week. I was really, really proud of what we'd done but I still wasn't sure it was going to sell.

Last week we'd given the newspapers, TV and radio shows a shorter version of Nancy's interview – and they'd all grabbed the chance to feature her story. As I'd hoped they would. Considering she'd spent most of her life avoiding any sort of attention whatsoever, Nancy was already proving to be a natural at interviews. She looked amazing in photographs, and on camera, and her honest way of telling her story was winning her lots of fans. I wasn't quite as keen about spending so much time being interviewed, but Nancy was adamant that I had to accompany her to every appearance.

'It's good for Mode,' she said. And I couldn't really argue.

Lizzie was over the moon with the interest we were generating and she was confident it would all turn into massive sales when the magazine hit the shelves, tomorrow. Urgh. I couldn't think about it. It was all so bloody nerve-racking. And we were halfway through our next issue which we had to make sure was just as good – if not better. I wasn't sure I could take the pressure of being Mode's editor … ah, who was I kidding? I was loving every minute.

'So do you have everything you need?' Emily said.

'Yes, I think so,' I said. 'Maybe another coffee?' I added hopefully.

She grinned at me.

'I'll get you one.'

She turned to go, then turned back straight away.

'Someone's here,' she hissed, making a face.

'Who?' I said, peering past her to see who'd come out of the lift.

It was Jen. Walking through the Mode office, keeping close to the wall and staring at her feet as though she hoped no one would see her.

'Shall I tell her to come into your office?' Emily said.

I thought for a minute, then nodded.

'I suppose so,' I said.

Emily scurried off, and I sat at my desk trying to do calm breathing. And failing.

'Hi,' said Jen.

'Hi.'

I nodded to the chair on the other side of my desk.

'Shut the door,' I said. 'We don't want the whole office trying to earwig on our conversation.'

Jen nodded.

She came in and sat down. She looked – I had to admit – pretty amazing. Her hair was the same as it had always been, shoulder-length, bleached blonde, but it looked like it had been cut and coloured by someone who really knew what they were doing. She was just wearing cropped black trousers, and a plain fitted t-shirt, but they both looked expensive and she had a new handbag.

'Freebies,' she said, seeing me looking. 'People give you stuff when you're an editor.'

'What do you want, Jen?' I said, a bit more surly than I intended to be.

Jen paused.

'I want to say sorry,' she said. 'I was hurt and upset but I should have told you Grace had approached me about the job. I did it all the wrong way and I'm really sorry.'

'You took all our ideas and you stole them,' I said. 'I was really proud of our feminism issue and it sank like a bloody stone because you did one too.'

Jen looked at her feet.

'I know,' she said. 'It wasn't deliberate, you know. The bigwigs at Grace were pressurising me to come up with some brilliant ideas, I was terrified I was going to let them down, and I just started blurting stuff out.'

'That doesn't make it okay,' I said.

'I know.'

We sat in awkward silence for a few seconds, then she spoke again.

'I'm not the only person in the wrong, though,' she said.

I winced. She was absolutely right, but I hated apologising. I took a deep breath and wondered where Emily was with my coffee.

'I treated you really badly,' I admitted. 'I only thought about Mode and I didn't think about your feelings, or the plans we'd made for The Hive.'

Jen looked at me expectantly.

'I'm sorry,' I said. 'I know you wouldn't have gone to Grace the way you did if I hadn't dumped you for Mode.'

She grinned and I let out my breath in relief.

'I suppose I should thank you, really,' she said. 'I bloody love it.'

I laughed.

'Isn't it amazing?' I said. 'All those years of being told what to do and now we're the ones making decisions.'

'It's completely terrifying,' Jen said. 'But it's exactly like I always hoped it would be. Sometimes, if I see someone reading Grace on the tube, or on the bus, I want to go and tap them on the shoulder and tell them it's my magazine.'

'Have you ever done it?' I asked, amused that she felt the same way I did about Mode.

'No,' she snorted. 'But I might one day.'

She looked at me in fake sympathy.

'It might happen to you, you know,' she said. 'If you ever see anyone reading Mode that is. How are those sales going?'

'Oi,' I said. 'Our sales have not been good, but you wait – I've got a packed promotion schedule tomorrow. I'm even going on Loose Women.'

'Oh really?' said Jen. 'Is that a challenge?'

I laughed again.

'I think it might be,' I said. 'We're not colleagues any more. We're rivals.'

'Rivals,' agreed Jen cheerfully. Then she looked at me, serious again.

'And friends?'

I paused.

'And friends,' I said.

'Oh thank god for that,' she said, collapsing back into her chair. 'I miss you.'

'I miss you too,' I said.

We grinned at each other for a minute.

'I did wonder,' I began.

Jen looked interested.

'Yes?'

'I did wonder if we could carry on,' I said. 'With The Hive.'

Jen's grin became wider.

'Really?' she said. 'How would we do that? With all the other stuff we've got going on?'

'No idea,' I said. 'But I reckon it's worth a try. Are you in?'

'Hell yes,' said Jen. 'On one condition.'

I raised my eyebrows, questioning.

'You tell me what's going on with Damo.'

Really?' she said. 'How would we do that? With all the other
authors we got going on—
No idea,' I said. 'But I reckon it's worth a try. Are you in?'
Hell, yes,' said Jan. 'I'm one of a kind—
I raised my eyebrows, questioning.
You tell me what's going on with Damo.

Chapter 53

Nothing was going on with Damo. Nothing at all. In fact, since
we'd spent the night together, he'd barely spoken to me.

He spoke up in meetings, came up with some great ideas,
spent hours over layouts and got the whole design team really
excited about how they were going to make Mode look beautiful.
I heard his voice and his laughter drifting into my office when I
was at my desk and away from him, but when I was around, he
sat hunched over his keyboard, headphones on, gaze fixed on his
screen.

I was devastated. Romance aside, I'd got used to chatting
through things with Damo, to heading out for a drink with him
after a tough day, or just enjoying some easy banter with him in
the office. Now all that had gone and I missed it desperately.

'I'm not sure I can save this one,' I told Nancy on the phone.
'He's so angry with me, and there's nothing I can say to make it
better.'

'Then you have to show him,' she said. 'You may be a writer,
but sometimes words aren't enough. Old-fashioned romance,
remember?'

I mulled over her words for a couple of days, pondering some
big gestures to show Damo how I felt.

Should I hire a boat to trail a flag along the Thames, proclaiming how sorry I was? Or project love messages on to the Houses of Parliament? Should I take out an ad in Mode? That was one I did genuinely consider, actually. But I soon dismissed it – I wasn't convinced anyone ever read our classified section, let alone the people who worked on the mag.

I was at a loss. I said as much to Jen, now.

'Nancy said I had to use good old-fashioned romance,' I said gloomily. 'But I've been racking my brains and I can't think of anything.'

'There are agencies,' Jen said. 'Romance agencies. They plan proposals and stuff.'

I was horrified.

'I don't want to plan a proposal,' I said. 'And if I did, I wouldn't want someone else to do it for me.'

Jen made a face.

'Just an idea,' she said. 'What about personalised cupcakes?'

'Naff.'

'An ad at Piccadilly Circus? Something on the side of a bus? Or on the escalators at Oxford Circus tube?'

I rolled my eyes.

'I don't have a million pounds to spare,' I said. 'Just no, no, no.'

We sat together, heads in hands, for a few minutes.

'Madison said I call and he comes running,' I said, thinking aloud.

'Who's Madison?'

'Damo's flatmate. She's like an Aussie goddess,' I said. 'She told me all about what he thought of Fearne, before I told her I was Fearne.'

'Ouch,' said Jen with a grin.

'Yeah, it wasn't nice to hear,' I admitted. 'She was pretty annoyed with me.'

'So she said you call and he runs?' Jen said.

I nodded.

'So I'm thinking, what about if I run when he calls?'

'What, like a marathon?' Jen looked confused and I laughed.

'No,' I said. 'Just to show that work isn't always my priority.'

'Riiight.'

'Nancy said words aren't enough and I thought she meant for me to do something big. But what if it's actually something small I need to do?'

'Like a date?' Jen said.

'Exactly.'

I paused.

'If I can get him to talk to me.'

Jen smiled.

'I'll send him in on my way out,' she said, picking up her bag. 'I'll tell him you've got some enormous layout emergency and you need his help.'

She leaned over my desk and gave me a hug.

'Masses of luck for tomorrow,' she said. 'It's going to be brilliant. But not too brilliant I hope.'

She winked at me.

'And good luck with Damo. I want a full report.'

Blowing a kiss over her shoulder, she headed out of my office.

I sat, drumming my fingers on the desk until Damo appeared in the doorway.

'Problem?' he said.

'Hmm,' I said, non-committal. 'Come in and shut the door.'

Damo looked slightly alarmed but he did as I asked.

'Sit down,' I said.

Obediently, he did as I said.

We looked at each other for a few seconds, until he said, 'So?'

'So,' I repeated. 'There is no problem. At least not with a layout.'

'Okay,' said Damo. 'So why am I here? I've got a lot to be getting on with.'

He fixed me with a stern glare.

'My contract's up in a couple of weeks,' he said. 'I should be doing a handover, but you've not recruited a replacement.'

'No,' I said. 'I've not. Because I was sort of hoping you'd stay.'

'Fearne,' he said. 'That's really not a good idea.'

I screwed my nose up.

'I know it doesn't seem like a good idea,' I said. 'But I want us to put all our problems behind us.'

Damo said nothing but I could see from his face that he thought that was unlikely at best.

'Okay,' I said. 'Here's the thing.'

I paused.

'The thing is ...'

Damo sighed, but it wasn't an exasperated sigh. It was more amused. Encouraged, I carried on.

'The thing is,' I said. 'I've been a bloody idiot.'

'Got that right,' Damo muttered.

'I was a bloody idiot in Sydney when I let you walk away from me,' I said, gabbling in my efforts to get the words out. 'And I was an idiot when I told you work was more important than you are.'

Damo made a face.

'You and me,' I continued. 'We're special. We just fit. You make me laugh, and you understand me more than anyone else I've ever met.'

Damo smiled.

'And it's not just one way,' I said. 'Who else do you know who'll listen to you talking about Iron Maiden album covers?'

Damo shrugged, as if to say I had a point, but he still didn't speak.

'What I'm trying to say is – I'm sorry,' I said. 'You're more important to me than any job.'

'You're saying all this, Fearne,' Damo said eventually. He scratched at a spot on the knee of his jeans. 'But I don't believe you.'

'Then let me prove it,' I said, urgently. 'Let's go out. On a date. Me and you.'

'A date?' said Damo. He gave me a small smile. 'What kind of date?'

'Oh I don't know,' I said. 'Drinks? Dinner, maybe, if it goes well?'

Damo nodded slowly.

'Okay,' he said. 'A date. Let's go on a date. When?'

I grinned.

'How about now?'

He looked astonished.

'Now?' he said. 'Now?'

'Why not?'

'Well, it's the middle of the day, for a start,' he said. 'And we've got work to do.'

'Meh,' I said.

He raised his eyebrow at me.

'And the new issues are due in this afternoon. Are you telling me you won't mind not being here when the relaunched Mode arrives on your desk? The issue we've sweated blood to get just right?'

I made a face.

'They'll still be here when we get back,' I said. 'Who cares if I'm here or not?'

I stood up, picked up my jacket and held out my hand.

'Shall we?'

He smiled at me.

'We'll be back by the time the issues arrive, right?' he said as we walked towards the door hand in hand and Emily pretended she wasn't watching.

'Totally,' I said.

296

Chapter 54

I lay on my sofa with my feet up, listening to Sounds of the Sixties. For years I'd avoided anything to do with the sixties. I turned over if a Stones track came on the radio, and any glimpse of the Beatles made me go cold.

But for the first time, I could remember the happy moments along with the sad. It had been painful reliving everything that had happened, and I was sure some of the interviews Fearne had lined up for me would be difficult. But it was the right thing to do. I couldn't change the past, but I could make sure it didn't limit my future.

'Baby, baby, baby, you're out of time,' I sang along with the radio, amazed that I remembered all the words.

Closing my eyes, I went through the itinerary for the next day in my head. BBC Breakfast, Woman's Hour, Loose Women ... We were going to be very busy. But I was looking forward to it, I thought, surprising myself.

My phone rang and Cooper went crazy, as he always did.

'Shh, Coop,' I said. I sat up and answered, expecting it to be Fearne.

'Hello?'

Cooper barked madly and I couldn't hear the person on the

other end of the line at first. I got up and shut him in the hall, then I tried again.

'Sorry, that was my dog,' I said.

'Hello?'

It was a voice I'd not heard for fifty years, but I recognised it straight away.

I sat down hurriedly as my legs turned to jelly beneath me.

'George,' I said. 'Oh, George.'

I could almost hear him smile.

'Hello, Nance,' he said.

Keep reading for an excerpt from *A Step in Time*...

Keep reading for an excerpt from *A Step in Time.*

Prologue

Afterwards I realised I was far, far drunker than I thought I was and that's probably why it all went so badly wrong. But at the time, I thought it was a great idea. Matty, my boyfriend, was out at the opening of a new club and I wanted to see him. So I left the hotel where I was oohing and ahhhing over a fancy brand of hairbrush, jumped in a cab and headed to the West End to catch up with my man.

I posed for the photographers outside the club, giving them a beaming smile and a cheeky look over my shoulder so they captured the back of my mini dress, and then I trip-trapped down the stairs in my super-high heels to find Matty.

At first, I couldn't see him. It was dark in the club and the flashing lights on the dance floor meant I took a while to get my bearings. But then I spotted his best mate, TJ, chatting to a girl I didn't recognise, and Matty's broad back in a tight white T-shirt, his head turned away from me, his tongue firmly stuck down another woman's throat and his hands all over her bum.

People talk about a red mist descending, don't they? I never knew what they meant until that moment. All I could think about was that some two-bit reality TV starlet was snogging my boyfriend. The man I loved. The man I intended to marry – just as soon as we agreed terms with *Yay!* magazine for the engagement photo shoot that would cover the cost of the huge rock I had my eye on.

Shrieking with rage, I launched myself at the girl. I took a fistful of her hair extensions in my hand and pulled her face away from Matty's.

'Get your lips off my man!' I screamed. And then – and believe me, I'm not proud of this – I pulled my arm back and punched her. Right in the nose. I honestly didn't know there would be so much blood.

Everything stopped. I couldn't even hear the music any more. It was like the whole room was suddenly in slow motion.

'AAAAAMMMMMYYY!' Matty was yelling. 'Whaaaat have you dooooonnnne?' He had blood all over his white T-shirt.

The girl he'd been kissing was squealing as TJ shoved napkins at her, and out of the corner of my eye I could see other clubbers filming the whole sorry escapade on their phones.

Sounds bad, doesn't it? Really bad. But that's not even all of it.

Realising I'd gone too far, I turned to leave. But like I said, I'd had quite a lot to drink at that hairbrush launch (honestly, it's the only way to get through things like that – the free booze) and I was wearing really high heels.

As I spun round, my foot caught on the edge of the dance floor and suddenly I was face down in a puddle of pina colada with my super-short dress up round my hips and my Hello Kitty knickers on display.

Lying there, my cheek stinging from the pineapple juice, I watched two men compare photos on their phones' screens and high-five each other. And then firm hands lifted me up.

'Out!' said one of the two bouncers who were either side of me. They were both twice as tall as me and seemingly three times as wide. They'd lifted me so high that my feet weren't even touching the floor.

'Don't worry, I'm going,' I muttered to the bouncer on my left. 'I just feel a bit ...'

And then I puked. All over his trousers.

Chapter One

'Get your lips off my man.' My boss, Tim, threw the paper down on his desk and glared at me. 'Amy's meltdown. Full story continues on pages three, five, seven and nine.'

I glanced down at the photo on the front of the paper and winced as I saw the now familiar shot of me face down on the dance floor, bum in the air, as a blood-splattered Matty gazed on in horror.

'Today's news, tomorrow's fish and chip paper,' I said hopefully.

Tim rolled his eyes and turned his computer screen round so I could see it.

'You are the only person who's ever made every single thumbnail on the *PostOnline*'s Sidebar of Shame,' he said. Sure enough, the column of pics down the side of his screen replayed each moment of that awful night in full technicolour glory. It was like a flipbook animation of the punch, the blood, the fall and the vomit.

'I'm sorry,' I whispered. 'I just really loved him, you know?'
Tim's face softened.

'I know you did, sweetheart.'

'So what happens now?' I asked, scared to hear the answer.

Tim was the producer of *Turpin Road*. It was the biggest soap in Britain and I was arguably its biggest star – at least I liked to think so. I played Betsy, a damaged but sparky barmaid at the Prince Albert pub. I'd been on the show for three years and I absolutely loved it. And Tim loved me. I'd had some brilliant storylines and I was tipped as the next big thing. At least I had been, until I punched a reality TV star called Kayleigh and showed my knickers to the world.

I gave Tim a sheepish grin.

'Suspension?' I suggested. 'I'll go to my mum's in Spain for a month, stay out of everyone's way, and when I get back all this will have blown over and the tabloids will have a new victim. Just write me out for a bit.'

I was wearing a scarf round my neck – I'd hidden my face with it when I'd come into the studios earlier to avoid the paps waiting at the gate. Now I wrapped it round my head like Dolly, the actress who played my on-screen granny, and picked up the phone on Tim's desk.

'Oh, hello, Betsy,' I said, in what I thought was a pretty good impression of Dolly's shrill cockney voice. 'Oh, your uncle's broken his leg, has he? Of course you should stay and look after him. About a month, you say? We'll miss you.'

I put the phone down again, pulled the scarf off my head and stared at Tim, waiting for the axe to fall.

I knew how these things worked. One of my co-stars had sent a photo of his willy to a fan via Snapchat, she'd screengrabbed it, shared it, and it was all over the internet about thirty seconds later. He'd been suspended for a while but he was back now and it was like nothing had happened. Tim adored me. The *Turpin Road* viewers adored Betsy. Surely my punishment would be similar?

Tim shook his head and my heart sank.

'Longer?' I whispered. 'Two months?'

'You assaulted her, Amy,' Tim said. 'You broke her nose.'

'She was kissing Matty,' I pointed out.

'You were given a caution. You were lucky not to be charged.'

'I wasn't charged because her nose was full of coke and she didn't want to make a fuss,' I said.

Tim shrugged.

'That's as may be,' he said. 'But she doesn't work for me and you do.'

He paused.

'At least, you did.'

I went cold. I buried my face in my scarf and looked up at Tim in horror.

'What are you saying?'

'Don't give me those puppy dog eyes Amy,' Tim said. 'You know what I'm saying.'

'I'm out?'

He nodded.

'My hands are tied, love,' he said. 'You punched someone, your pants are all over the *PostOnline* and there's bound to be more. They'll be after anything and everything. Ex-boyfriends, girls you fell out with at school, hairdressers you were rude to – it's all fair game now.'

I closed my eyes.

'Build them up, knock them down,' I said.

'Exactly,' Tim said.

'No,' I said. 'No. The viewers love Betsy. They love her and they love me.'

I jumped to my feet.

'Look,' I said, pointing to a framed photo of me gripping a gold statue that had pride of place on the office wall. 'Do you think the show would have won this BAFTA without Betsy's mental health problems?'

Tim shrugged.

I picked up a pile of magazines that were on his bookshelf and went through them one by one.

'Amy wins big,' I read, showing him a photo of me with an armload of statues at last year's soap awards.

'Steal Amy's summer style.' I opened *Hot* magazine at a fashion shoot I'd done and waved it at him.

'Amy bares all?' I fake-gasped, then giggled as I showed Tim the cover of *Cosmo* featuring a make-up-free me. 'I was in make-up for an hour before that shoot.'

'Don't,' Tim said. 'Don't do this.'

But I was on a roll. I picked up *Yay!*

'Amy and Matty: Our plans for the future,' I read. My voice shook as my bravado deserted me.

'I've lost him, Tim,' I said, hugging the magazine close. 'Don't make me lose this, too.'

'No one's bigger than the show,' Tim said sadly. 'But you'll be okay. You're very talented.'

'I can come back, right?' I said, still gripping my magazine. 'Betsy will come back?'

Tim looked down at his feet.

'We're killing you off,' he said.

I couldn't speak.

'It's going to be huge,' Tim carried on. 'The biggest whodunnit since 'who shot JR?'. People will be talking about it for years.'

I bit my lip. I didn't want him to see me cry.

'We're rewriting some stuff,' Tim said. 'And we'll film your last scenes this afternoon.'

I felt sick. This afternoon? How could my entire life change so fast? But I pasted on a smile, took a deep breath and stood up, throwing *Yay!* down on the desk.

'Okay then,' I said briskly. 'Let me have the script A-sap, yes? Thanks for everything.'

I air-kissed him on both cheeks and legged it out of his office, down the corridor and into the safety of my dressing room. And then I started to cry.

Chapter Two

I never let myself cry for too long because I hated when my face got all puffy and my eyes swelled up. So after about ten minutes sobbing into the cushions on my dressing room sofa, I forced myself to get up and face the rest of the day. At *Turpin Road* we shared our dressing rooms, though I'd heard that on other soaps they got their own. I shared with two other actresses, which I quite liked, actually. They were nice enough and generally I enjoyed having someone to hang out with. Not today, though. Today I was relieved that they weren't around and I had the place to myself so I could wallow in gloom alone.

I knew that I'd be called on set soon, so I dragged myself into the shower, trying to think about anything and everything apart from the fact that in the space of twenty-four hours I'd gone from being TV's hottest star to a jobless, homeless, boyfriendless nobody. I stifled another sob as I shampooed my hair. Crying wouldn't solve anything.

By the time I got out of the shower, I had thirteen missed calls – mostly from my agent, Babs, who'd been phoning me non-stop since the story went viral this morning – and a script pushed under my dressing room door. That was it then, the end of Betsy. I picked up the envelope – it was very thin, so obviously the script wasn't very long. Poor Betsy. I took a deep breath before I opened the flap and scanned the text.

Interior: The Prince Albert
Betsy is clearing empty glasses after closing time. A noise makes her jump and turn.
BETSY: You! What are you doing here?
A hand reaches out and whacks Betsy on the head. She falls, motionless, to the ground.

Disgusted, I threw the papers to the floor. I'd given this show three years of my life, and this was how they repaid me? I was their biggest asset. In my head I heard Tim's voice in my head saying: 'No one is bigger than *Turpin Road*, Amy.' I winced. What a way for him to prove his point.

Well, at least I didn't have any lines to learn really. I could just lie on the sofa and feel sorry for myself until I got called on set.

I slumped down and had had my eyes closed for about thirty seconds when my phone rang. Listlessly I looked at the screen. Babs. Again. I supposed I couldn't avoid her for ever, so I swiped the screen to answer.

'Hi Babs.'

'Bloody bollocking hell, Amy. What the flaming arse have you been doing?'

I held the phone away from my ear as she continued her foul-mouthed tirade. Babs swore like a trooper at the best of times, so when faced with a crisis – like now – she was really filthy. Eventually she calmed down a bit and I cautiously put the phone back to my ear. Her voice softened.

'How are you?' she said. 'Are you holding up?'

I felt close to tears again.

'Don't be nice,' I warned. 'I am barely holding it together and if you're nice I'll crumble.'

'Chin up,' Babs said in her no-nonsense Glasgow tone. 'I've got good news and bad news. Which do you want first?'

'Bad,' I said, bracing myself.

'The catalogue's pulled your fashion line,' she said. I groaned. That was the end of my wardrobe full of free clothes then.

'And the good news?'

'Hold on, I've not finished the bad news yet,' Babs said. 'Your nail varnishes are on hold but it's not looking good, and I've had a call asking you not to come to the premiere tonight.'

'I'd forgotten all about it,' I said. 'And all my clothes are at Matty's flat anyway.'

'Where are you staying?' Babs asked.

'Phil's,' I said, sitting up on the couch and picking up a cushion to hug. 'He's looking after me, like always.'

'Every girl needs a gay best friend, eh?' said Babs.

I laughed without any real humour.

'Yeah, well, it's not quite so fabulous when your gay best friend's boyfriend hates you,' I said. 'I can't stay there for long.'

'Where will you go?'

'Not sure,' I said. 'Maybe to my mum's for a while. Get some sun.' And a whole lot of grief, though – I was trying not to think about that. Another thought struck me.

'What's the good news?'

'What good news?'

'You said there was good news'

'Oh, yes,' Babs said. 'I just want you to know that this is not a disaster. I've got people out of worse scrapes than a small punch-up in a nightclub.'

I smiled despite myself.

'It wasn't really a small punch,' I said. 'More of a wallop.'

Babs made a dismissive sound.

'And my knickers are all over the internet,' I added, feeling another wave of self-pity.

'Ach,' said Babs. 'It's fine.'

310

'It's not fine,' I said. 'It's awful. I really just want to go away for a while. Disappear for, like, six months, longer even. I can get off the bloody media roller coaster and lick my wounds, then come back revitalised and ready for a new challenge.'

'Absolutely not.'

'Babs, I can't do this,' I wailed. 'There are paps everywhere. And Tim's right – they're going to dig up every tiny bit of dirt they can. This story will go on and on and on. Unless I disappear and give them nothing.'

'Oh, get over yourself,' Babs said. 'You're not bloody Greta Garbo. If you disappear now, everyone will forget you. Your career will be over.'

'Ouch,' I said. 'That's harsh.'

'It's true,' said Babs unsympathetically. 'But don't worry. I've got a plan.'

'You have?' I said, feeling marginally more cheerful.

'We need to make the most of this interest in you. Use it to our advantage and take control.'

'And how do we do that?'

'Oh, it's easy. We just need people to know how lovely you are,' she said blithely. 'Not Betsy – Amy. Your adoring public need to remember why they adored you in the first place.'

'Right,' I said, doubtfully. 'I'm not sure that's the most straight-forward idea you've ever had. How would we do it, anyway?'

'Reality TV, baby,' she said.

I took the phone from my ear and scowled at it.

'No,' I said. 'No.'

'Don't dismiss it, Amy,' Babs said. 'It can work wonders.'

'And it can destroy careers,' I said.

There was a pause.

'From where I'm standing, it looks like you don't have much of a career left to destroy,' Babs said. 'When you've hit rock bottom, Amy, the only way left is up.'

'I'm not doing *Big Brother*,' I said.

311

'Fine.'

'And only major channels.'

'Fine.'

'And I get to choose which show.'

There was silence.

'Babs, I get to choose.'

'Fine,' she said, grudgingly.

'And minimal publicity,' I said. 'I'll do what I have to do, but not too much. I've got to get away from all this.'

Babs made a huffing sound.

'You can't hide away,' she said.

I wished I could, but I knew she was right really. I bit my lip.

'I've got contacts everywhere – I'm sure we can get you into something,' Babs went on, oblivious to my misgivings 'Have a think and let me know what you want me to focus on. But do it soon. We need to strike while the iron's hot.'

'Okay,' I said, suddenly feeling very tired. 'I'll have a think.'

'Amy,' Babs said. 'It's going to be okay, you know.'

I tried to smile but it was more of a grimace.

'Yeah, we'll see,' I said. 'We'll see.'